HARVEST SONG

AN OTHERWORLD NOVEL

YASMINE GALENORN

NEW YORK TIMES BESTSELLING AUTHOR

A Nightqueen Enterprises LLC Publication

Published by Yasmine Galenorn
PO Box 2037, Kirkland WA 98083-2037
HARVEST SONG
An Otherworld Novel
Copyright © 2018 by Yasmine Galenorn
First Electronic Printing: 2018 Nightqueen Enterprises LLC
First Print Edition: 2018 Nightqueen Enterprises
Cover Art & Design: Earthly Charms
Editor: Elizabeth Flynn
Map Design: Yasmine Galenorn

ALL RIGHTS RESERVED No part of this book may be reproduced or distributed in any format, be it print or electronic or audio, without permission. Please prevent piracy by purchasing only authorized versions of this book.

This is a work of fiction. Any resemblance to actual persons, living or dead, businesses, or places is entirely coincidental and not to be construed as representative or an endorsement of any living/existing group, person, place, or business.

A Nightqueen Enterprises LLC Publication
Published in the United States of America

Acknowledgments

This is book twenty in the Otherworld Series, with one left to go. Delilah has come a long way from that timid, naïve young woman. She's come into her own, and now, she's about to take another jump.

I'm so grateful to my readers who've followed me this far. To those who have remained glued to the adventures of the sisters—thank you for the love you've given this world of mine, and for understanding my desire to offer you new worlds in which to explore.

Thanks also go to my husband, Samwise, who has been my biggest supporter as I've shifted my career to the indie side. And thanks to my friends who have cheered me on—especially Jo and Carol. Thank you to my assistants Jenn and Andria for all their help. And thank you to my fellow authors in my UF group, who have helped me learn what I needed to learn in order to take my career into my own hands.

A most reverent nod to my spiritual guardians—Mielikki, Tapio, Ukko, Rauni, and the Lady Brighid. They guide my life, and my heart.

And of course, love and scritches to my fuzzy brigade—Caly, Brighid, Morgana, and little boy Apple. I would be lost without my cats.

Bright Blessings, and I hope you enjoy Delilah's final book. For more information about all my work, please see my website at Galenorn.com and sign up for my newsletter.

Brightest Blessings,
~The Painted Panther~
~Yasmine Galenorn~

Map of the Otherworld

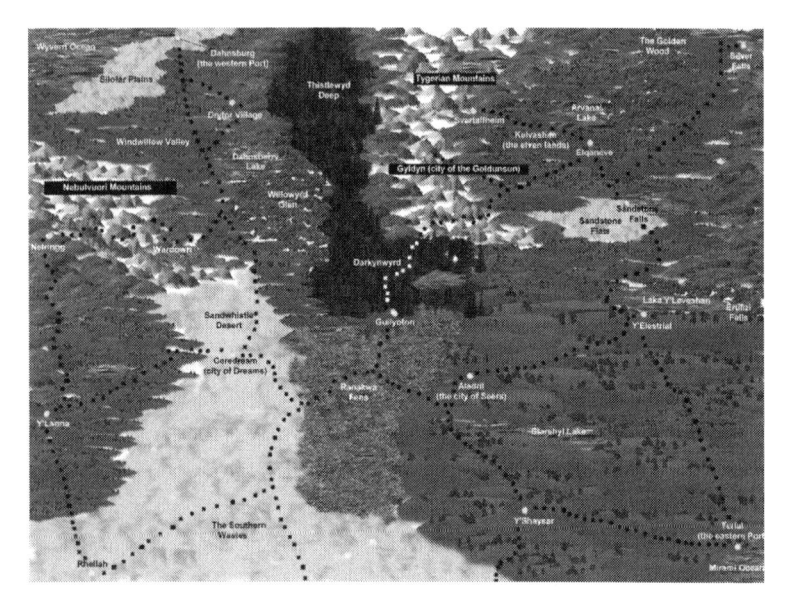

Welcome to the Otherworld

THE SILENCE THAT hit the room was about as loud as a semi crashing into a brick wall. Shade plastered a smile on his face and tugged at the collar of his shirt, but he had that terrified oh-shit-my-mother look in his eyes. Smoky was trying to keep a straight face, but his gaze met mine and he flashed me a look of sympathy. And everybody else? Well, they took a step back. Either they had already met Shade's mama, or they were as frightened of meeting a scary-assed dragon mother as I was.

I swept my gaze over the approaching woman.

She was tall, as were all dragons. Six feet in human form was considered short for dragons. Smoky's mother stood seven feet tall, but Shade's mother was even taller than that. I was six-one, and she towered over me. She had to be at least seven-four.

Her gown flowed, the color of smoke. The material shifted from iridescent gray to shimmering white to jet black, depending on how she moved. Her eyes were dark, arrestingly so, and she had rich, full lips and wide-set eyes and she moved as gracefully as a dancer. Her hair coiled down to her feet, continually moving like writhing snakes. All dragons had hair that moved on its own, but even Smoky's hair never seemed this active. Shade's was pretty docile in comparison, given he was only half dragon.

She stopped in front of me and I gulped, staring up at her. Shade's mother wasn't smiling, but that didn't necessarily mean anything. Dragons weren't given to excessive displays, in general.

I waited for her to speak, which was, I felt, the only polite thing to do. As I stood there, forcing a smile to my lips, I realized that I seldom thought of Shade in terms of his parents. Oh, we had talked about them when his sister had first visited to drop the bombshell on me that Shade's father was akin to an astral judge, jury, and executioner all rolled into one. But mostly, we left the subject alone.

"So you are the woman my son has chosen to take as a mate?"

Chapter 1

"YOU HAVE TO be *kidding* me." I stared at the dress that the sales associate was holding up.

A nightmare in tulle and ruching, the gown must have had twenty yards of billowing material draped in folds and layers with a train that spilled out, begging to trip me up. The color was a soft eggshell and the neckline had been contorted into a weird, asymmetrical shape.

"Did the designer drop acid or X or whatever the drug of the month is?" I asked. My question was met with an icy silence. "This is the third dress you've brought out that is light years away from what I asked. Have you heard a word I said?"

The woman's silence extended into a long, offended stare.

Camille snorted, and Menolly pressed her lips together, trying not to laugh. Iris glared at me, with an expression that I recognized as her *Will you behave* look.

I let out a long sigh. "Let me try this *again*. I don't want a *white* dress, or *any* shade of white, cream, ecru, eggshell, ivory, or any variant thereof. I'm *not* Cinderella. I don't want a ball gown, or a princess gown. I don't want a mermaid gown, or anything that looks like a cupcake. I asked you to show me something *streamlined*. Just a nice long dress that doesn't poof, fluff, or *spill* out. I want a pretty, simple gown in a lovely shade of *green,* or *something* that suits my coloring." I had explained this in detail to three different shopkeepers. Each time, we had gone through the same rigmarole, with the same result.

The sales associate let out a little huff. "I'm sorry, miss, but I don't think I can help you. We don't *sell* green wedding dresses. I suggest you might want to try a department store. Or look into buying a prom dress. Or you might find something appropriate at a *thrift* store." Her snotty tone ruffled my fur, but Camille grabbed my hand, squeezing tightly before I could respond.

"You're right," Camille said, brushing past the saleswoman. "And since you obviously *can't* satisfy our needs, then we'll find a store that will be happy to accept our money. If you'll excuse us, we'll be on our way," she said, her voice dripping with icicles. She motioned for us to follow her.

Grateful that it wasn't me on the other end of my sister the ice queen's shade, I grabbed my purse and slung it over my shoulder, following her out. We were almost to the car, Camille still fuming, when I happened to glance down the street.

There, a few doors down and still open, was a little vintage shop tucked between a tattoo parlor on one side and a used bookstore on the other. In the window, a mannequin was draped in a vision that took my breath away, a long gown in a rich green, no less.

"Wait!" I dashed toward the shop, the others following me.

The dress in the window was an elegant sleeveless A-line with a fitted bodice. The shoulders were beaded with delicate pearls, and a sheer chiffon overlay stretched across the upper chest. Gathered at the waist, the skirt flowed into soft layers to the floor, with flower appliqués spaced over the top layer that were the same dark silvery-green as the rest of the dress. It was everything I was looking for. Elegant simplicity, and as green as the forest. Praying to Bast that it fit me, I started toward the door before they could close, my sisters and Iris right on my heels.

"Pardon me, Your Majesty, Princess Menolly, Miss Iris, and Miss Delilah, but we have to check it out first." A man caught up to us, darting around us. One of Camille's bodyguards, he and the other four men who were tailing us did a good job of giving us the illusion of autonomy, but the fact was, anywhere Camille went, they were always in tow. She groaned, but waved them on.

Inside, the clerk looked worried as the guards entered, but after Jal, the head of Camille's personal retinue, spoke with her, she brightened up and beckoned for us to come inside.

The clerk was smiling as she saw us. She curtsied clumsily. "I'm honored to have you in my shop, Your Majesty. May I help you with something?"

Camille inclined her head, smiling. "Actually, my sister has a question." She motioned to me in what felt like a gesture that had been finely tuned for public use. I flashed her a bittersweet smile. Her life really *wasn't* her own, anymore.

I gestured to the mannequin in the window. "That dress—the green one. Do you think it would fit me?" I turned to Camille. "They always say you'll know the right dress when you see it. This is the right dress."

A soft smile played on her lips. "I know, Kitten. I can see it in your eyes."

The clerk peeled it off the mannequin. "You're in luck. I was going to change the window display tomorrow and this would have come down. Here we go." She glanced at the tag, then with a critical eye, scanned my figure. "I think it should fit you. Would you like to try it on?"

I nodded, surprised that I cared so much. Shade had been after me for the past two months to get it together and help him make some sort of plans for our wedding. I had told him whatever he wanted was fine with me, but he refused to let me off the hook. "You're not going to leave it all up to me," he had said. "I'm not taking the blame if you aren't happy with your wedding."

I wasn't the planning type. I would have been happy getting married in the living room with only my sisters, Iris, and Hanna there. But a month ago, something had happened that had thrown my laissez-faire attitude out the window. Now I was scrambling to make up for my procrastination.

A month ago, during August, I had traveled with Camille to Otherworld in order to find the last Keraastar Knight. Shortly before that, Greta had shown up. Greta was the leader of the Death Maidens, and she had trained me. This time, she had brought with her a message I hadn't expected.

SIX WEEKS BEFORE the trip to Otherworld:

I was sitting on the bed, clipping my toenails, when I felt a shift in the room. I slowly straightened up, glancing around. Shade was out. He was down at Iris's, helping Bruce to fix up their greenhouse.

I was feeling on edge. There had been too many unwanted surprises lately, so much so that I felt like I was constantly on high alert. Every noise, every nuance had become an instant alarm. Anything that shifted the energy had raised a red flag until we checked it out.

The constant vigilance was tiring, especially since Camille and Menolly had moved out right before the Summer Solstice. Everything about the past few months had felt off-kilter as I learned how to live in a house that had suddenly emptied out. Oh, Shade was still with me, yes, and Rozurial was still living out in the studio. Maggie and Hanna were with us. But the rooms seemed to echo with the absence of life.

Over in the corner, a figure began to form in a haze of mist. I reached for my dagger, but then relaxed when I recognized the familiar face.

The woman had long hair that waved past her shoulders, the coppery red strands the same color as Menolly's. On her forehead, she bore the same mark that I did—the silhouette of a black scythe, gleaming like obsidian. Her arms were a vision in vivid black and orange, covered with tattoos of autumn leaves and vines that twined their way up to her shoulders. Again, they were the same as the tattoos on my arms. The leaves burned with color, vibrant and alive. The woman wore a sheer robe the color of twilight over a long gown, and a wreath of autumn leaves wound around her head.

"Greta, I'm surprised to see you. Is anything wrong?"

It had been a while since I had talked to Greta. She was as corporeal as I was, yet she was long dead. She was my trainer, and had become a friend in the process. She lived in Haseofon—the home of the Autumn Lord's Death Maidens.

"I know. We've been giving you time to acclimate to your newest changes."

I had figured as much. Nine months ago, both Shade and I had faced turning points in our lives. A devil-wraith had siphoned off a number of Shade's abilities. He was half–shadow dragon, half-Stradolan—a shadow walker. The Stradolan were the descendants of the children of the Autumn Lord and Grandmother Coyote. As a race, they were elemental in nature, only taking physical form if they were half-breeds. And the only race they could interbreed with were the shadow dragons. The children were born sterile, but in physical form. The father was always Stradolan, the mother always shadow dragon.

When the devil-wraith attacked us in the middle of the night, it leeched away Shade's Stradolan powers. The loss had proved to be a major adjustment, and though he still struggled with it, he was doing better than I had expected.

As for me, in that same timeframe, I had found myself suddenly able to see ghosts. The spirits were everywhere, at times disorienting me to the point of nausea. Greta had told me that it was all part of my transition as I settled into my Death Maiden self, but the ability had manifested so swiftly that I had ended up spending two weeks in Haseofon, learning how to harness my control of it. While I couldn't exactly turn it off, I no longer felt like I was walking in two worlds at once.

"Then what's happened? What's wrong?" I realized as I spoke that, for the most part, I expected to hear bad news from any new messenger.

She held up her hand, smiling. "Nothing's wrong, but I bring you a message from the Autumn Lord."

I blinked. Usually, when Hi'ran wanted to talk to me, he came to me himself. Greta must have seen the look on my face, because she smiled again.

"This is his busy time of year, you know. He bade me bring you this." She held out her hand. In her palm, she was holding a carnelian heart.

I accepted it, turning it over in my fingers. The

stone was warm, pulsing with a spark that I recognized as Hi'ran's energy. I wrapped my fingers around it, closing my eyes. The energy reverberated through me, into my core, as I felt something deep inside me quiver and awaken. His voice reverberated throughout every cell of my body.

It's time, he said. *It's time to begin.*

I paused as the realization of what he was talking about swept over me. When I had first been claimed by the Autumn Lord, it was with the understanding that I, as his only living Death Maiden, would one day bear his child, by proxy. And now, Hi'ran was calling in my promise. Wide-eyed and a little frightened, I looked up at Greta. Her expression told me that she knew what I was thinking.

"But...how...? I'm on a birth control method that lasts several years at a time. I just renewed it a year ago when I was in Otherworld."

Greta smiled. "Do you think *Himself* wouldn't be able to negate that? He's one of the Harvestmen, an Elemental Lord of the Autumn. But I have answers to some questions he anticipated you might ask. You and Shade must go through two ceremonies. The first is a ceremony joining your hearts. The second, a darker ritual, will prepare the way for the Autumn Lord to mingle his essence with Shade's semen, which is sterile. This will quicken it, and allow him to impregnate you. I will be your priestess when it's time for the second ritual."

My stomach lurched as I realized this was *for real.* It had all seemed academic before, sometime far off in the future, like old age or retirement. Apparently, the future was closer than I had realized.

I bit my lip. "Well, we're planning to get married on the autumn equinox."

"That's perfect for the joining of hearts," she said. "You must both undergo a purification ceremony afterward, shortly before the second ritual. The wedding will seal your hearts together. The second ritual we will perform on Samhain, and then, well, nature will take its course."

I sucked in a deep breath and scooched back on the bed, crossing my legs. Her words reverberated through me. "Who should be our priestess for our wedding? Does it matter? I had my heart set on asking Camille to perform the ceremony."

Greta reached out to lay her hand on my shoulder. "You may ask your sister, if you wish. Whoever officiates at your heart-joining *should* be someone you trust and love." She settled down beside me on the bed. "You do realize what a great honor this is? I would love to be in your place, but I only came to him after I was dead. Delilah, the Autumn Lord would not have chosen you for this task if he didn't foresee you being happy in the role, happy with the outcome. He's a harsh taskmaster at times, but unlike some of the other Elemental Lords, and unlike many of the gods, he *does* care for those who live within the mortal realm. He may not always extend mercy, but he does have compassion. And he truly cares for those who bear his yoke."

I straightened my shoulders, nodding. "I know. I've thought about this a lot over the past four years since he claimed me. While I'm frightened, the truth is that I have always wanted children, and I've always known they'd be *different*, if only because of my *own* heritage."

"And Shade?" she asked, probing softly. "You love him?"

I ducked my head, blushing. "Shade? He's become my heart. He's my touchstone and rock, he's my anchor when I feel adrift. He's also taught me a lot about owning up to my responsibilities. He's the man I never realized I needed, until he showed up in my life."

As I spoke, the words resonated through me. I usually didn't wear my heart on my sleeve. Cats generally preferred to keep their emotions under control, expressed only to those who were closest to them. The concept of relationships had been foreign to me when I came over Earthside with my sisters. A relationship was an affair that *other* people entered, but one I didn't believe I would ever understand.

"What about Chase?" Greta knew all about my past.

"Chase? I love him like a brother. We were far too rocky together, and I couldn't be the woman he needed me to be. I don't have it in me to be the rescued princess."

"And Zachary?"

I had also touched hearts briefly with a werepuma named Zachary, but he had been too afraid, too unwilling to fight for what mattered. In the end, he had saved Chase's life at risk of his own, but now he roamed the hills of Otherworld, permanently in puma form.

I held an image of him in my mind, then let it go, watching it drift by. "He's a bittersweet memory."

"Then rest easy. Everything happens for a reason, even when it seems like pure chaos is raining down on your head." Greta stood, adjusting her robe. "I'll talk to you soon." And with that, she vanished before I could say good-bye.

THE DRESS FIT perfectly, looking like it was molded onto my body. I stared at myself in the mirror, trying to comprehend that, for once, I truly felt beautiful. I never felt ugly, but I seldom felt truly feminine, like the dress made me feel.

Iris let out a gasp. "Oh, Delilah. That's so perfect." The house sprite took a step back, shaking her head. "It won't need a single alteration. With a wreath of white roses, or perhaps lily of the valley, it would look exquisite."

"Kitten, you're so beautiful." Camille gave me a quick hug. "The dress was practically *made* for you." She worried her lip, a wistful look in her eye. "I wish Mother could see you now. The last of her little girls, getting married."

Menolly just stood back, leaning against the wall, watching me. After a moment, she gave me a thumbs-up. "You're all grown up, Kitten."

Those words meant more to me than what they said on the surface. I was second-born, but both Camille, the oldest, and Menolly, the youngest, had always treated me like the baby. I had been the naïve one, insecure and entirely too optimistic for my own good. I would never lose my playful side—at least I hoped never—but the past years had toughened me up enough to withstand the disappointments of life, and to cope with the struggles we went through. To have Menolly acknowledge that I had matured meant the world to me.

"What will you wear if I get this?" I asked. Menolly was my matron of honor, Camille was officiating, of course, and Nerissa and Iris were bridesmaids.

"I think if we wear a pale green, it would complement the rich tones of the dress." Nerissa and Iris immediately began discussing ideas for their gowns. Camille would wear her official robes as the Queen of Dusk and Twilight, naturally.

I paid for the dress, after finding a beaded vintage bag and a pair of opera-length gloves to pair it with, and we left the shop.

"We should stop somewhere for a drink," I said. "Want to stop at the Wayfarer?" It had been weeks since we had been out together, and I wanted the night to last.

"Lead on." Camille stared at the waiting limo, frowning. "I miss driving."

Ever since her coronation as the Fae Queen of Dusk and Twilight, she had been forced to make a number of radical changes in her life, not all of which had gone over well. For one thing, she wasn't allowed to drive anymore. She had a limo, and was always followed by a retinue of bodyguards. Lars, one of her guards, did the driving.

Tonight, they had brought a stretch limo so we could ride in style. Camille gave him the address of the Wayfarer.

On the way there, Menolly asked, "So are you still planning to hold the wedding at Birchwater Pond?"

"Yeah," I said. "We can't think of a more fitting place. And we're definitely honeymooning up at Silver Falls in Otherworld, though not right away. We want all of you to come. I know the danger of the sun, but we can rig up something to protect you, Menolly."

Menolly, a vampire, rubbed her forehead. "Roman won't be into camping, but he'll be at the wedding. I'll give it a try if we can figure out a way to protect me from the sunlight. Nerissa, are you up for a camping trip?"

Nerissa was Menolly's wife. They had both married Roman, the Prince of the Vampire Nation, when his mother, Blood Wyne, had ordered the match. It was a convoluted relationship. Menolly and Roman had chemistry, but Menolly and Nerissa had both chemistry *and* love.

"Of course. I love camping. It sounds wonderful, the idea of getting away from the city for a week or so. I'll be able to run free in my puma form without worry." Nerissa practically purred at the thought.

"Sounds good." I wasn't exactly disappointed that Roman most likely wouldn't be coming along on the camping trip. While he was trustworthy, he was entirely too formal for my tastes. "As I said, I'm not sure when we'll go. We want to see what happens with the war."

Camille frowned, staring out the window. "I just want it over with. I wish we would get some word from Trytian about how his father's army is doing."

Trytian, the son of a daemon general, was an unlikely ally of ours. Actually, the daemons themselves were our unlikely allies. Apparently the old "the enemy of my enemy is my friend" business had proved true. They were fighting against Shadow Wing in the Sub-Realms, trying to shave away the Demon Lord's advantages until we could figure out a way to kill him for good.

Iris let out a heavy sigh. "I know. Things feel like they're balancing on the edge of a razor. I've been uneasy lately." She paused, then added, "I might as well tell you this now. Bruce and I have been talking about moving out to Talamh Lonrach Oll."

I jerked around, my heart sinking. "*No!* You want to leave, too?" The thought of Iris, Bruce, and their babies leaving the land knotted my stomach. "Please, don't you go, too."

"We're just talking about it right now. But Delilah, there's so much uncertainty. We all know Shadow Wing is planning something, and my children need more protection than I can give them. Even the guards Camille sent over from Talamh Lonrach Oll to watch over the land are feeling it lately—they've doubled their rounds. I was talking to one of them yesterday. He said he feels like we're being watched by something that's biding its time. But they can't figure out what it is, and it's making everybody nervous."

I knew she was right, even though I didn't want

to admit it. Shade and I needed to scrounge up a powerful witch to ward the property, now that we were in charge. Camille was too busy with her own court, and we couldn't expect her to come out just to check the wards every week.

We reached the Wayfarer, where we crowded in. The place was jumping, and I watched Menolly as she gave a wistful look around the joint. She still owned the bar, though mostly just on paper. She stood at the counter, running her hand over the polished wood, talking to Derrick the bartender in low tones. She looked as uneasy as I felt.

"Are you all right?" I sat down beside her as Derrick moved off to take Iris, Nerissa, and Camille's orders.

She flashed me a quick shrug. "I suppose. I'm just thinking how much our lives have changed over this past year. We're all moving on, Kitten. We're growing up, changing our lives, changing our natures. Ever since Nerissa and I moved over to Roman's, those shifts have been hitting me right and left. The three of us have been together all of our lives. Now we're expanding out, and leaving that bond behind. I love my life, but... Growing up's a bitch." Her fangs descended just enough for me to see their pearly whites.

I was startled by her nostalgia. Normally, *I* was the one caught up in ruminating over the past, but during the past few months I had been too busy with the present to focus on what was slipping into the past. Once Camille and Menolly had moved out, I had turned my attention to my own life, and I had been mulling over what we needed to do in the looming battle against Shadow Wing. It was nearing end-game time, and the promise of that last clash loomed large in my thoughts.

"We aren't losing the bond we have. I'd say, rather, that our childhood, our time here, has become our foundation for our lives, rather than the entire building." I brushed one of her braids back from her face. Menolly was five-one, with a petite build and long burnished braids that fell to her lower back. She wore beads in them. She said when they clicked, it reminded her she was still alive. Well, *undead*. Like most vampires, she made little to no sound as she moved through her nights.

She glanced up at me. "Philosophical, much?"

"Not really. I'm not much of a philosophy type. But I think I'm beginning to understand what you and Camille have been trying to teach me over the past few years. I'm standing back, staring at life through the big picture, rather than a snapshot." I paused. I had hinted to Camille on our trip to Otherworld about what was imminent in my life, but I hadn't outright told her. Only Shade knew at this point.

"I need to talk to you and Camille. Nerissa and Iris, too."

"You want to talk in a private room?"

I shook my head. "No, I don't feel like being closed in. I want to go outside. It's a warm-enough night. I guess when we get back to the house will be soon enough for discussing deep secrets." I suddenly didn't feel like drinking anymore. I put down my glass and brushed my hair away from the back of my neck. I had cut it again, missing the ease of the short, spiky 'do I'd had for so long. My neck felt like something was tickling the base of it, making me edgy.

"Do you mind if we just go home?"

Frowning, Menolly shook her head. "Not at all. I'll gather the others." She paused. "Are you all right, Kitten?"

"Yeah, it's just...I feel like something's wrong." As she disappeared into the crowd, a cold chill swept over me and I wondered what change the wind was bringing with it this time.

ON THE WAY home, I glanced out the window, staring at the ghosts who walked the sides of the roads. They appeared to be from various times, long past, and yesterday. Normally, I shielded myself from them because the sights and sounds disturbed me. But tonight, for some reason, I decided to open up, to watch them wander past. Some were lost, not realizing they were dead. Others knew they were dead but still clung to the mortal realm, unwilling to leave. Some were cursed, trapped for one reason or another, while still others were mere fragments of memory, caught in a loop between the layers of time.

"Delilah? Delilah!" Camille finally broke through my thoughts.

"I'm sorry, I was off somewhere." I straightened up. "What did you want?"

"I wanted to know whether you have a guest list

yet. It's late, but we can still send out invitations if you want. I can lend you a secretary of sorts." She grinned. "There are perks to being a Fae Queen."

I laughed, then. "Taking advantage of your authority, are you? Thanks, but we're not inviting many people, and I can just call the ones we are. But if you could give me some help for the catering, I'd appreciate it, thanks. I don't want to put the pressure on Iris and Hanna, and I'm just not good at managing that sort of thing."

"Hey, while we're on the way home I want to ask your opinion about a situation that's been presented to me. I'd like your input on it, all of you." Menolly glanced at Nerissa, who nodded.

"Tell them," she said. "They'll tell you the same thing I did."

"What is it?" Iris asked.

Menolly brushed her braids back away from her face. "Okay, here's the thing. Erin's been promoted to head of security. I'm proud as hell of her. But..." She drifted off, looking uncomfortable.

"But what?" Camille asked. "I don't see the problem."

Menolly gave her a frustrated shrug. "Erin doesn't want the job. She's been offered another opportunity. *I* don't want her to accept it, but she wants to give it a try. I could stop her, order her not to go, but Nerissa and Roman both think I'd be making a mistake by doing so."

Even though Erin was by far older than we were—at least if you compared the human life cycle to the Fae life cycle—she was a baby by vampire standards. Menolly had sired her when Erin's life was on the line a few years back. It had taken everything Menolly had to do so—she had sworn never to sire anyone. But when she gave Erin the choice, Erin had opted for life as a vampire over death, so Menolly had reluctantly turned her. Now, she was essentially Erin's mother.

"What's the other opportunity?" I leaned forward. I couldn't imagine a job that had more prestige than being Roman's chief of security.

"Wade's offered her a chance to tour the country with him, setting up chapters of Vampires Anonymous all over the United States. Blood Wyne approves, and Roman's giving Erin free choice. Erin's waiting for *my* approval, and I know she wants to do it. I'm just…it's a scary world out there for vampires who are in the public eye." Menolly bit her lip, a worried look in her eye.

I began to understand her fear. "You're afraid she'll get staked at some hate-rally."

"Well, the hate groups are loud and violent. While the vampire rights bill is before Congress right now, even if it passes, we've got a long ways to go before society fully accepts us." She glanced at Nerissa. "Nerissa thinks I should let her do it."

"Of course I do." The Amazonian werepuma was one of the few women who could take on my sister and come out on top, in more ways than one. "Erin is spreading her wings. This is a great opportunity for her to grow into her new life. She's smart, and she's always been on the front lines. You know that. Hell, Erin is gay. She took on the haters when she was alive, and she can handle them as a vampire. This is a chance for her to champion yet another cause she's passionate about. And you know Wade thinks the world of her."

Menolly hung her head, lips pressed together. Wade had been a psychologist before someone turned him and his mother. He had decided to continue that career path, helping newly minted vamps adjust to their lives in death, and he had founded a self-help group for vampires to enable themselves to keep control over the predator within. Vampires Anonymous had caught the attention of Blood Wyne, the Queen of the Crimson Veil, and she had asked him to expand it nationwide.

I tried not to laugh. Menolly could be so fierce and deadly, and yet she was a yummy, gooey éclair inside when you poked certain areas.

"So let me get this straight. Erin has a chance to get in on the ground floor of something that can affect vampires' lives for the better, on a nationwide scale, no less. She can make an impact on society and the world, and you're dithering about whether to let her accept the job?" I leaned forward, tapping Menolly on the knee. "You know what you have to do."

After a moment, she let out a sputter. "I've grown used to having her around, all right? I'm just...I'm going to miss her, damn it." She sprawled back in her seat with a disgruntled grunt. "*I know, I know.* I have to let her do this. Grandmother Coyote told me years ago that Erin had a part to play in destiny, and I think this is it. So I guess I have to just bundle up my nerves and tell her to go with my blessing. But it's not easy."

"And you say you have no maternal instinct."

Iris laughed. "Remember, the nurturing instinct presents itself in many different ways."

Standing at three-foot-ten, the Talon-haltija was a Finnish house sprite. With ankle-length golden hair, she looked for all the world like she had just stepped out of a Swiss Miss cocoa commercial. In reality, Iris was a powerful priestess who could turn people inside out when she was angry enough. She had married Bruce, a leprechaun, and they had twins. The boy was named Ukkonen, and the girl was named Maria, after our mother. Other than Bruce's parents, we were the only real family Iris had.

"I guess that takes care of that issue. For the record, I agree with the others. You have to let Erin fly the nest." Camille glanced out the window. The limo rode so smoothly it was hard to believe we were moving. "So what do you think the guys are up to?"

"Drinking? Remember when they got bombed out of their minds the night we all went to the Demented Zombie for Iris's bachelorette party?" I snorted.

"Mostly, I remember Iris throwing up on the stripper when he shoved his junk in her face, and then you attacking him because he had fringe on his G-string." Menolly stared at me, a smirk spreading across her face.

"Don't remind me." I had a problem controlling my shapeshifting when it came to shiny things, birds, and ribbons. Tabby loved to play, and I couldn't repress my natural instincts very well.

"My guess is that Smoky and Shade are talking

over *serious dragon issues* while Roz and Vanzir are playing video games," Iris said. "Vanzir doesn't get to do much that he used to, now that Aeval has pinned him down as her baby-daddy."

As the limo silently glided up the long private road that led to the house, I grew nervous again. Something had set off my inner alarm and I couldn't seem to quiet them down. We broke through the heavily tree-lined driveway into the clearing that served as our motor court, and I stared at the house.

An odd light seemed to hover around the old three-story Victorian, the same rust color that the sunset took on certain evenings. At that moment, I noticed that the drive was filled with cars.

"What the hell?" I stiffened, every nerve in my body screaming *Danger!*

Camille let out a soft hush. "Come on. We'll find out what's wrong."

She pushed open the car door even as her guards sprang out behind us, pushing past her to head up the sidewalk to the porch stairs before she could take another step.

Leaving our packages in the car, we followed them. I knew in my gut that there was something going on inside, something that wasn't normal. Unable to quell my nerves, I rushed up the stairs, passing the guards as I slammed open the door. My thoughts were focused on Maggie, our baby calico gargoyle, and Shade.

I headed to the living room, where I saw the lights were off. My mood plunged even further.

Camille and Menolly were right behind me, with

Iris and Nerissa behind them. I fumbled for the light switch, afraid of what I might see. As I flipped it on, there was a sudden barrage of movement as a roomful of people jumped out from behind the furniture shouting, "Surprise!"

I blinked as I caught sight of a huge banner hanging against the back wall that read, "Happy Bridal Shower!"

"You guys, I can't believe you set this up!" I started to say, trying to calm my beating heart. But then a woman entered the room from the parlor, and my stomach knotted again. Shade's sister, Lash, was here. No wonder I had been on high alert.

Chapter 2

"OH, CRIPES. YOU scared the hell out of me!" I jumped as Shade appeared by my elbow. He slipped his arm around my waist even as Menolly laughed.

"Surprised?" He gave me a hug and a kiss.

"Truly."

"Really? Nobody said anything?"

"I'm floored. I had no clue." I still felt uneasy, but figured that I had picked up on the anticipation of the others and interpreted it as danger.

I glanced around. Everybody was here—Chase, Venus the Moon Child, Erin, Morio, Trillian, Roz, Vanzir, Marion Vespa, a couple other friends from the Supe Community Action Council—pretty much anybody who had become a close friend over the past years. The fact that they had all come out to celebrate my upcoming wedding both embarrassed me and yet warmed my heart.

As Lash stepped forward, I swallowed. Like her brother, she was half–shadow dragon, half-Stradolan. Her skin was the same rich brown skin as his, and her hair matched his—amber and honey. Where his eyes were dark brown, hers were the color of topaz. Lash was wearing a brilliant orange gown that set off her skin. She looked radiant, as though she were glowing from within. She might have been, for all that I knew.

"Delilah, well met, I hope? Happy...*bridal day*?" Her tone was more congenial than the last time we had met. She sounded more confused than anything else.

I instantly understood that she had no frame of reference for "bridal shower." "It's a local human tradition. Celebrating an upcoming wedding."

She grinned. "Good, then you can explain it to Mother."

I froze.

"*Mother*?" I had never met Shade's mother. His father had pretty much washed his hands of Shade. But apparently his mother was still in touch with him.

Lash flashed me a bone-chilling smile. "Yes, our mother decided it was time to meet the woman who will be her daughter-in-law."

And with that, the parlor door opened again and Shade's mother stepped through.

THE SILENCE THAT hit the room was about

as loud as a semi crashing into a brick wall. Shade plastered a smile on his face and tugged at the collar of his shirt, but he had that terrified *oh-shit-my-mother* look in his eyes. Smoky was trying to keep a straight face, but his gaze met mine and he flashed me a look of sympathy. And everybody else? Well, they took a step back. Either they had already met Shade's mama, or they were as frightened of meeting a scary-assed dragon mother as I was.

I swept my gaze over the approaching woman.

She was tall, as were all dragons. Six feet in human form was considered short for dragons. Smoky's mother stood seven feet tall, but Shade's mother was even taller than that. I was six-one, and she towered over me. She had to be at least seven-four.

Her gown flowed, the color of smoke. The material shifted from iridescent gray to shimmering white to jet black, depending on how she moved. Her eyes were dark, arrestingly so, and she had rich, full lips and wide-set eyes and she moved as gracefully as a dancer. Her hair coiled down to her feet, continually moving like writhing snakes. All dragons had hair that moved on its own, but even Smoky's hair never seemed *this* active. Shade's was pretty docile in comparison, given he was only half dragon.

She stopped in front of me and I gulped, staring up at her. Shade's mother wasn't smiling, but that didn't necessarily mean anything. Dragons weren't given to excessive displays, in general.

I waited for her to speak, which was, I felt, the

only polite thing to do. As I stood there, forcing a smile to my lips, I realized that I seldom thought of Shade in terms of his parents. Oh, we had talked about them when his sister had first visited to drop the bombshell on me that Shade's father was akin to an astral judge, jury, and executioner all rolled into one. But mostly, we left the subject alone.

"So you are the woman my son has chosen to take as a mate?" While she didn't sound aggressive, I still felt like a big juicy steak dangling in front of a hungry lion. She walked around me, slowly circling until I wanted to snap at her. I didn't like feeling on display. Finally, she came to a stop directly in front of me again. "Well? Nothing to say? Can you speak, girl?"

I jumped at the sudden question, then stammered, "I was waiting for someone to introduce us." I scrambled, trying to think of something to say that wouldn't set her off.

She gave me a long look, then turned to Shade. "Your betrothed makes an excellent point. I raised you to be a proper dragon and gentleman. Must I refresh your memory as to the etiquette of this situation? Please tell me that you haven't become brutish living with these creatures?"

I wasn't sure whether or not to be offended. But by the look on Shade's face and the sound of his mother's voice, I was sincerely grateful that I wasn't the one on the hot seat.

Shade shot me a dirty look, but obediently cast his eyes down as he turned to his mother.

"I'm sorry, Mother. I wasn't expecting you. You caught us by surprise. Seratha, please meet my fiancée, Delilah." He turned to me, motioning for me to step forward. "Delilah, I present my mother, Seratha."

Seratha slowly held out her hand to me. "Greetings. Now that my son has properly introduced us, I want to welcome you to the family. I realize you had no idea that Lash and I were going to be here, so I apologize for the intrusion. I know that among your kind—both human and Fae—'meeting the family' is considered an awkward situation. While I'm here, I must also inform you that Shade's father will not be in attendance, either now or at your wedding." A dark look crossed her face. "Do not expect his blessing, for it will never be forthcoming. I'm sure my son has explained the nuances of their relationship. Don't ever think to interfere, Delilah. There's absolutely nothing you can say that won't make it worse. As for me, I prefer to make up my own mind, without undo influence."

Her tone wasn't unfriendly, although she spoke in a far more formal manner than I was used to. But I appreciated her making the effort.

"I'm pleased to meet you. I realize that I may not be your first choice for a daughter-in-law, but I want to assure you that I love your son and I hope to make him happy." I paused, searching for something else to say.

Seratha frowned. "I do believe you in that." She frowned, then added, "Shade's devotion to the Autumn Lord was not something that his father and I would have chosen for him. But the Elemental Lords and the Hags of Fate will have their way. His father cannot accept the unchangeable, but

I choose to accept what is. I want a relationship with my son, and so I accept his choices. At least I'll have a grandchild, which is something I never expected to have, given the state of those born to Stradolan–shadow dragon unions. And that warms my heart, even if my grandchild stands to be the child of one of the Immortals."

That set the rest of the room to whispering. I blushed.

"Well, soon enough. I'm not pregnant *yet*." I had a sudden glimpse of what it was going to be like over the next year or so as I envisioned visits from Shade's mother to "help out."

Behind me, Vanzir let out a stifled laugh. I glanced over my shoulder, sticking out my tongue out at him.

"Mother, please. This is a delicate subject." Shade squirmed a little.

"What was Shade like as a little boy?" I asked impulsively.

Seratha laughed then, and her laughter lit up the room. "He was a willful little boy, that much I will tell you. I had to constantly be after him to mind his manners and not be disrespectful to his elders. He's lucky we did not live in the Dragon Reaches."

Shade shot another dirty look my way. "Quit asking her to tell tales on me." He glanced back at his mother. "I'm happy here. I don't think there's any place better for me. Especially since..." He trailed off, shaking his head. "Especially since I lost my Stradolan powers."

"Yes, about that." Seratha's focus narrowed and I had the feeling she forgot about everyone else in the room. She truly loved her son.

"I'm sorry we didn't offer you the support you needed. Your father's still angry, so it's probably best that you continue to keep your distance from home. It's not that I don't want you there, but...you know his temper. I promise I'll visit more often." She turned to me. "Take care of my son, Delilah. I'll be sending you a wedding gift soon. And let me know when I'm expecting a grandchild." She turned to her daughter. "Lash, I know you'd like to stay and talk to your brother, but we have business to attend to. Make your farewells."

As Lash quietly said good-bye to her brother, I breathed a sigh of relief. That had gone far better than I had any right to expect. A moment later, Seratha and Lash shimmered out of sight, disappearing as if they'd never been there.

Shade dropped into one of the chairs, leaning his head back. "I swear to you, I had no clue they were going to show up. Lash contacted me the other day and I told her what I was planning, but I never in the *world* expected for her and Mother to crash the party." He looked up at me. "I'm sorry, sweetheart. I had no intention of subjecting you to their scrutiny tonight."

I gave him a quick kiss on the forehead. "I'm just grateful that I passed muster." I glanced around at everybody else. "All right, then. Let's get this party started. Camille, Menolly, did you know about this?"

They nodded, grinning.

Iris piped up. "Of course we knew about it. Do you think that the guys could pull this off on their own? Hanna and I worked for several days on the food. We cooked it all at my house so that you wouldn't see it."

I perked up at that. "There's food? Cake? Please tell me there's cake!"

Hanna laughed. "Of course there's cake. This party's for you, so it's jampacked full of sugary sweets. And Cheetos."

After that, we got into full swing, trooping into the kitchen to the big buffet that was spread across the dining room table. It felt like old times, with all of us gathered together. As they brought out presents, it dawned on me that I was getting married in less than two weeks. There was still a part of me that wanted to run away, not because I didn't love Shade but because everything was moving so fast that it made my head spin. I was a cat. I didn't like change, even when I knew it was for the best.

As the evening wore away, people made their farewells until it was just our core group left. Camille and her husbands, with her guards keeping watch outside. Nerissa and Menolly, and Vanzir and Roz stayed. Bruce left for home to take over care of the twins. His mother was still visiting from the summer. The Duchess had arrived in early June to help Iris while Bruce taught a course in Ireland for two months. She had stuck around after he returned in August. As much as the leprechaun might put on airs, she was always available to help out when needed. It occurred to me that, even though she was looking forward to a grandchild, Seratha wouldn't be quite the same type of doting grandmother. I doubted we could call on her to dash over from the Netherworld to babysit on date night.

We were sitting around the living room, finishing off the last of the chocolate cake. I was poring over the loot that people had given us—mostly personal things, since we already had a house full of stuff—when Shade pointed at my laptop.

"I have a present for you. You'll find it in your email." He looked like the cat that not only ate the canary, but spit out the feathers.

I frowned. "Email?" Opening my laptop, I brought up my email program and waited while it loaded. Sure enough, there was an email from Shade. I opened it, and inside was a link. Clicking on the link, I was surprised to see a registration form pop up. "What's this—?" I started to say, but then froze as I read the text printed on it.

"You *didn't*!"

"I *did*. And I'll even go with you, I love you *that* much." He snorted. "And you have to know that I love you, if I'm willing to do this."

"What is it?" Camille asked.

I turned the laptop around so she could see the screen. On it was the form indicating that I was the proud bearer of two tickets to the *Jerry Springer* show, a special edition that would be taped in Seattle come January.

"I can't believe this!" I clapped, blushing. I had been infatuated with Jerry Springer ever since I first came Earthside. I couldn't explain it—there was no rhyme or reason to it, but something about the man fascinated me.

Camille burst out laughing. "*Best. Fiancé. Evah*!

You win the prize, Shade."

I threw my arms around him. "I love you, even though you did sic your mother on me."

"She was more on my case than yours," he said, laughing.

An hour later, as we were winding up the evening, Roz and Vanzir disappeared with Iris. Vanzir had promised Camille he would gather some flower starts from Iris's greenhouse for her. Hanna and Nerissa were in the kitchen washing up, while Camille played with Maggie, our baby calico gargoyle. I was in the living room, along with Menolly, Smoky, Trillian, Morio, and Shade, when a massive thump sounded from the front porch. It sounded like a large rock hitting the porch.

"What the—?" I started, but Shade motioned for me to sit down.

"I'll check," he said.

As he headed for the front door, I froze. The feeling I had earlier—that something was wrong—suddenly swept back full force. I had ascribed it to Lash and Seratha showing up, but now it was back. A wave of panic swept over me.

"Wait!" I jumped up, calling to him. But I was too late.

As Shade opened the door, a wall of flame drove itself through the opening, hitting him square on. He shouted, stumbling back as the door slammed open. There, standing in the doorway, was a burly man carrying a massive iron sword, followed by at least two demons. He took one look at Shade, who had dropped to the ground to roll out the flames, and plunged his sword deep into Shade's side.

A MOMENT LATER, I realized that the scream ringing in my ears was my own. By then, Smoky had shoved me out of the way as he, Morio, and Trillian raced past. Menolly followed them.

I was getting my bearings as Smoky took on the man with the sword. From where I stood, it looked like Trillian, Morio, and Menolly were engaging the demons, but they were blocking the door, and I couldn't get through to Shade. Cursing, I headed for the front window, shoving the sill up and busting out the screen so I could scramble onto the porch. It was then that I saw two more demons waiting behind the others. One of them turned on me, charging my way.

The demons weren't simple Tregarts, nor bloatworgles, nor any other type I was used to. These were midnight horror-movie types, bipedal with ruddy orange skin and curling horns rising off their heads. Their long claws glistened in the glow of the soft white faerie lights that Iris had strung around the porch, and their eyes glimmered with a dangerous light.

I didn't have my dagger with me, so I did the next best thing and landed a strong kick to the demon's stomach. My foot landed hard against him and for a moment, I could have sworn my leg had shattered. Groaning, I staggered back, grateful as I realized that nothing was actually broken. He dove for me, and I grabbed the porch railing and vaulted over it, dropping into the grass below, wincing as my sore leg hit the ground.

I raced toward the back of the house, intent on getting to Shade via the back porch, but I froze when I saw a light from what looked like a portal in the trees nearby.

The demon lunged at me and I took off again, heading for the back porch. At that moment, the porch door slammed open and Camille came racing down the steps, Maggie in her arms. Hanna was right behind her. My sister thrust Maggie at Hanna, who instantly took her.

"Take Maggie to Iris's! Tell them what's happening!" Camille shoved Hanna toward Iris's house, then turned back to me.

"Duck!" Camille shouted, holding out her hands.

I dove for cover as a blast of energy shot out from her fingertips, landing square on the demon. It knocked him back, dropping him to the ground, giving me time to make it over to her side. At that point, Morio joined her, and they grasped hands.

My sister's third husband was a youkai-kitsune, and he was proficient in death magic. They worked in tandem, and now they began moving toward the demon, driving a purple mist in front of them. The hesitation Camille had once possessed toward her magic had vanished. She and Morio forged powerful spells together, a deadly force.

Leaving them to take care of the demon, I headed up the stairs. Shouts echoed from inside, and I burst through the kitchen door, trying to take stock of the situation. Iris was standing on the table amidst the remains of the buffet, and one of the demons was splayed on the ground, inside out. The resulting mess had splattered over everything, and Iris had a crazed look on her face. Her brilliant blue eyes were lit up as a chilling power oozed from her.

Darting around the pile of demon guts, I searched anxiously for Shade. Sounds of fighting echoed from the living room, and Smoky bellowed something in his native language. Trillian suddenly appeared, blocking my way as he cast his gaze around the kitchen.

"Where is he? Where did he go?"

"Who? Where did who go?"

"The man who stabbed Shade," the Svartan growled. He stopped, suddenly, as the blood drained out of my face.

"Shade—where is he? Trillian? *Where's Shade?*"

Trillian clasped my shoulders, forcing me to focus on him. "Delilah, *did you see the man*? We have to stop him. We've killed one of the demons and Smoky's on the other, but the man got away." He didn't apologize, that wasn't his way. Instead, he gave me a slight shake, speaking firmly. "We need you strong and fighting. None of us will be okay if we don't stop him."

Suppressing my panic, I nodded. I knew the routine by now. No matter what, keep going. Deal with the aftermath after everything was done.

I forced myself to calm down. "Right. I didn't see where he went. Camille and Morio are out back, taking care of the last demon."

Trillian pushed past me, slipping out the back door. I heard a thud and made for the foyer, where

I saw Menolly, her eyes crimson and her fangs dripping with blood.

At that moment, I heard Camille's voice from out front. We raced through the door just in time to see the man who had stabbed Shade flicker out of sight, vanishing as Camille and Morio descended on him. He was there one moment, then *poof*—disappeared.

I staggered back, intent on searching for Shade, but something caught my attention. *Smell.* There was a smell I recognized.

"Crap, fire!" I hurried toward the kitchen, where Iris was frantically trying to quench a massive flame that licked through the door from the back porch. She had summoned an ice storm, aiming it toward the crackling flames that had overtaken the porch. They were licking at the walls of the kitchen.

I suddenly remembered the gas range as the fire blew through the door, knocking Iris back into the kitchen. She landed in the slimy remains of the demon, letting out a shout as I hurried to her side. The flames had caught hold of the curtains and were headed directly for the stove. I dragged the house sprite off the floor and headed toward the front door with her, even though she was struggling.

"I can put it out—"

"Stop fighting me. The gas—the fire's going to reach the gas!"

I shoved her through the door onto the front porch as a massive ice storm engulfed the entire house and yard. Smoky was standing to one side, focusing on the kitchen as he brought the storm to bear. Iris pushed out of my arms and joined him, adding her powers as the temperature around us plunged at least forty degrees and a blizzard obscured everything, blanketing the house.

Nerissa joined me, tugging on my arm.

"Shade! I found Shade," she said, and I realized she was carrying him over her shoulder. The werepuma, like most Weres, was incredibly strong. She was covered in blood and I suspected it wasn't her own. I helped her ease him down the steps and over to the car.

"I called Mallen. We're going to need him. And the fire department." She was panting, shivering in the icy chill of the sudden snowstorm.

We stretched out Shade on the hood of my Jeep. He was slick with blood, the scent cloying and metallic, and he wasn't moving. He didn't even moan.

"Shade! Shade!" I leaned down, pressing my ear to his chest. I could still detect a faint rise and fall. He was breathing, and his heart was still beating. But if he hadn't been part dragon, he'd have been a goner. The gash in his side was a good eight inches long.

Camille was by my side then, and she took one look at Shade and turned to hurry over to Iris and Smoky. She whispered something to Iris, who nodded. Smoky paused, then swept up Iris and in a blur, was gone.

Camille returned to my side. "It looks like the fire is out. Smoky's taken Iris to fetch the Duchess. She's skilled at healing." She glanced around. "The demons are dead but we have no clue who was with them, or where he went. He just—"

"Vanished," I said. "I saw." I stared at Shade, mute for a moment. Then, feeling as though I was running on autopilot, I turned back to her. "The gas? In the kitchen?"

"Morio managed to turn off the valve. Smoky and Iris extinguished the flames, but I don't think there's much left of the kitchen and back porch." She shook her head. "The guards are hunting for the man, though my personal guards refuse to let me out of their sight." She pointed to the men who were standing by the car, keeping a close watch on her.

"Shade's... Shade is..." I couldn't get the words out. He was hurt, I knew that much. "He won't wake up. He can't hear me. Camille, what if he dies?"

She brushed back his hair. "He's hurt, but the bleeding has slowed. Remember, he's part dragon and part Stradolan. He's got the blood of his ancestors in him. We'll get him through this. I promise you that."

At that moment, Vanzir jogged into the yard. Smoky appeared, stepping out of the Ionyc Seas, carrying Iris and the Duchess, who was holding a first-aid kit.

"Where's the dragon?" She went straight to the point.

Iris pointed toward Shade and I moved, giving the Duchess room to work. She lithely crawled up on the hood of my Jeep alongside Shade and began to examine him.

Vanzir was scanning the yard. "Roz is staying

with Bruce and the twins, along with Hanna and Maggie. What the fuck happened?" He froze when he saw Shade. "Crap."

"We're still sorting things out. A man and four demons showed up at the door and...then this," Camille said, pointing to the house where the smoke was still rising. "Iris and Smoky managed to extinguish the flames, but we have no idea who he was, or why they were here." She paused as a familiar truck came screeching up the driveway, an old beat-up pickup. "Just who we need. *Wilbur's* here."

Wilbur, our neighbor who resembled the scragglier members of ZZ Top, hopped out. He was managing his artificial leg fairly well now, and had only the smallest of limps as he hurried over to us. He was human and a powerful necromancer, but sleazy as hell, and he kept his brother's corpse around as a ghoul, out of survivor's guilt.

"What the hell?" He stared at the carnage. "That must have been some party."

"Demons."

Wilbur let out a grunt, then glanced at Shade. "Where are the medics?"

"Coming," Camille said.

"I'm going to take a look around." Wilbur headed off around back. "I'll let you know if I find anything."

Camille watched him go, then quietly said, "I have to admit, even though he's a pain at times, Wilbur's all right."

Menolly joined us at that moment. "Whoever the fuck was leading those demons, he's the one who set the porch on fire. I saw him before he ran around front."

"Who the hell was he? What did he want?" I reached for Shade's hand, unable to take my eyes off of him. I was trying to keep it together, but it wasn't easy.

"There could be any number of reasons. It's not like we don't have our share of enemies." Menolly suddenly took a big step back, her eyes widening as she glanced at Shade. "I'm on edge enough as it is. I'd better back off. Too much blood in the air."

I gave her an absent nod. "Go on." Menolly knew her limitations, and she always erred on the side of caution when family and friends were in the way. As she moved off, I leaned against the car, feeling bleak, hugging myself. "I wish Chase was still the head of the FH-CSI."

The Faerie-Human Crime Scene Investigations unit had been Chase's brainchild, but during Camille's coronation in June, he had been swept into the Keraastar Knights, and now his right-hand man had taken over. Yugi was good, but he wasn't Chase.

"Chase wouldn't be able to do anything." Camille shaded her eyes, staring at the house. "We were always the ones he called in for attacks like this." She sounded slightly defensive and I realized she might be thinking that I blamed her.

"I know that destiny played itself out. I know you weren't responsible for Chase's transformation. I just... Damn it. I thought I was acclimating to all of the changes. I felt like I was finally on board with the way our lives were turning. Now

I'm terrified again." I wanted nothing more than to turn into Tabby and leap into Camille's arms and huddle against her.

She took my hand, squeezing tight. "I know. I'm frightened too. Until we know who's behind this, we can't figure out how to proceed." She paused as Wilbur returned.

"All right, girls," he said, his tone devoid of his usual lecherous insinuations, "I found some things that might be helpful. For one thing, I discovered a weird energy signature over by two trees near the driveway." Wilbur was a necromancer who understood all about magic.

"A rogue portal? I saw it too," I said.

"I think it was temporary because it's not there now. The trees are fried—they look scorched. You might ask someone to check it out. Second, the demons? I recognize the type, even as splattered as you left them. I have to say, when you throw it down, you *throw it down*. Some of the sorcerers I've known over the years have attempted to summon them and I had the misfortune to witness what happened when one of the bastards was successful. I told him not to try it, but *oh no*, he didn't want to listen to *me*."

"What happened? And where did the demons come from?" I stiffened. I had the feeling we were about to hear something we really didn't want to hear.

"You already know what I'm about to say, Pussycat. These demons were from hell. The Sub-Realms, as you call them. And what happened? The demon appeared through the gate and promptly ripped off the sorcerer's head. Literally. Blood everywhere. It was a nasty business, and the only way that I escaped is that I happened to be near the door. Since there was a lock on the outside, I was able to lock the demon in and hightail it out of there before it could break through to attack me. I never went back. Grapevine has it the demon disappeared somewhere into the hills and for all I know, he's still out there. Meanwhile, Juan's head stayed separated from his body and that was the end of that."

"Lovely." I pressed my lips together for a moment, then asked, "So, the temporary portal. Did you sense any sort of sorcerer's energy off of it?" I glanced at Camille, not wanting to remind her that Shamas, our cousin, had studied with a rogue group of sorcerers before he first came Earthside. The fact that he had returned from the dead only a month ago, however, was something we couldn't overlook. I was fairly certain that he knew how to summon demons. I wasn't going to outright accuse him of doing this, but I didn't trust him.

Wilbur shook his head. "That's the odd thing. No, Pussycat, I didn't. I could feel the demonic energy thick around it, but nothing else." He stiffened. "Who's that?"

We turned to see another figure jogging from around back. He looked like a crazed Keanu Reeves, with longer dark hair and pale skin, and just enough mayhem in his eyes to make him feel dangerous.

"*Trytian*," Camille said, stiffening. "What's he doing here?"

Trytian was the son of the daemon general who was at war against Shadow Wing. He was always making a play for my sister, even though her husbands had threatened to gut him several times. If they weren't around, there was no way we'd trust him alone with her. But right now, we were on the same side, and we needed to work together.

"I just came through the portal," he said, sounding slightly winded. He glanced at Shade, then back at the house. "Fuck. I'm too late."

"What? Too late for what?" I froze.

Trytian let out a long breath, then shrugged. "I came to warn you. Shadow Wing found a way to transport Yerghan the Blade out of the Sub-Realms. He sent him here to kill you."

And with that, we knew who our enemy was.

Chapter 3

WE STARED AT him. Trytian wasn't smiling.

"Oh, crap. Are you for real?" I let out a slow breath.

Yerghan the Blade was a nightmare straight out of the pages of a history book. During the Scorching Wars in Otherworld, he had ridden at Telazhar's side as they razed city after city, creating the vast desert known as the Southern Wastes. By the time they were stopped, they had changed the face of our homeland forever. Both were sent to the Sub-Realms rather than executed, one of the biggest mistakes ever made. Back in June, we had gotten word that Yerghan had aligned himself with Shadow Wing.

"While Telazhar was still alive, Shadow Wing kept him and Yerghan apart. He was probably afraid they might pair up against him. But now that Telazhar is dead, Shadow Wing apparently no longer considers Yerghan much of a threat. Rumor has it that he promised Yerghan his freedom once he completes his mission over here. And that mission is to destroy the three of you." Trytian's expression was dark. "My father still considers us to be in your debt, and we still owe you a favor. So he bade me come warn you." He glanced around the yard. "Apparently, I arrived too late."

I glanced down at Shade, still holding onto his hand. He was breathing shallowly, but at least the bleeding had slowed. "Can you stay and help us find him? We killed the demons who came with him, but Yerghan got away." I nodded to the house. "If it hadn't been for Smoky and Iris, he would have destroyed the house."

For once, Trytian didn't joke around, or hit on Camille, or anything like that. He just stared somberly at the house, then looked at Shade. "Is he going to be all right?"

"I don't know. We're waiting for the medics to arrive. They're..." I paused as sirens wailed from down the drive. Within seconds, the FH-CSI medic unit appeared, followed by Yugi in a sleek, black Ford Taurus.

Trytian moved out of the way as Mallen leapt out of the medic unit, along with a med-tech I hadn't seen before. She was Svartan, unusual considering they didn't visit Earthside frequently. They hurried across the yard, carrying their gear. Mallen took one look at Shade and motioned to the other tech.

"We need to get him to the FH-CSI as soon as possible. Where's Smoky?" He looked around. "I want him to bring Shade via the Ionyc Seas." He looked closer at the wound. "I smell something odd. Who stabbed him? Do you have the weapon? I need to find out if it was poisoned."

"No, he got away. It was Yerghan the Blade," I added. Mallen would understand the reference. Anybody who grew up in Otherworld would.

Mallen stiffened. "*Yerghan the Blade?* He's still alive after all these thousands of years?"

"Yeah. Apparently he's been hunkering down in the Sub-Realms, and now he's here, Earthside, targeting us." I rubbed my forehead. I had a splitting headache.

Trytian joined us. "Speaking of Yerghan, I have another piece of information, one I almost forgot." He glanced at Mallen. "You *must* get Shade into treatment. Yerghan carries a soul-stealer blade."

And with that, my world crashed down as everything sped into fast-forward.

I had heard of soul-stealer blades, but had never seen one. Unlike sentient blades that could trap souls within themselves, or drain off life force, the soul-stealer blades were able to send a soul out of the body, deep into one of the outer realms, where it would wander forever unless brought back by an experienced shaman.

"Then Shade's not even in his body—" I started to say, but my mouth couldn't finish the sentence. Camille slipped over to my side and wrapped her arm around my shoulders as I stared down at Shade's unmoving form, realizing that he couldn't hear me, probably wasn't even aware of what was going on.

"We'll find him," she whispered. "We'll get him

back."

Mallen tapped Camille on the shoulder. "Get Smoky now, please."

"I'll be back in a minute," she said, taking off around the side of the house.

Mallen pulled out his cell phone and called the FH-CSI. "Get one of the psitechs to come in as soon as possible—emergency situation. Willow, if possible. She's the strongest of the lot." He paused, then added. "No, we're dealing with a soul-stealer blade." Holding the phone away from his mouth, he asked me, "What are Shade's heritages again?"

"Shadow dragon and Stradolan, but he's lost a lot of his Stradolan abilities."

He nodded, returning to his phone call. Meanwhile, while he was talking, his assistant was busy packing Shade's wounds with some sort of powder. It stanched the last of the bleeding. She gave Mallen a nod, stepping back. At that moment, Camille came running up with Smoky.

Mallen pocketed his phone. "No questions, now. I need you to take Shade to the FH-CSI, pronto. You'll have to take him through the Ionyc Seas. I'm afraid that the ride in the ambulance might make things worse than they already are." He motioned to me. "Delilah, come with us. And Vanzir, if he's around."

"I'll go through the Ionyc Seas with Smoky and Shade." I turned to Camille. "Tell Vanzir to meet us there?"

She gently pushed me toward Smoky. "I will. Don't worry about us. I'm going to call in some more of my guards from Talamh Lonrach Oll. Get moving."

Smoky said nothing, lifting Shade in his arms. I hooked my arm through the crook of his elbow, leaning close so that I would be within the protective bubble that surrounded him. Without a word, we shifted into the Ionyc Seas.

THE IONYC SEAS were made up of the current that flowed between the worlds. It both held together the different realms, yet kept them apart. The currents were almost alive, electric and flowing. Some creatures could travel through the Ionyc Seas without a problem—like dragons and other creatures of their kind. Humans and Fae could only pass through when protected by one of the creatures who could journey there naturally. If we stayed out on the Sea too long, even under the protection of a dragon, we would fall into a stupor and sleep in long cycles until we crossed off of the seas. I wasn't sure what would happen if we were somehow transported there without protection, but I had a feeling it wouldn't be good.

I leaned my head against Smoky's arm, taking the opportunity to close my eyes and try to rest. Although it would only take us seconds in the outer world, here it felt like we were traveling for a long, long time, and it gave me the time I needed to regroup. I pushed all thoughts out of my mind and dozed.

When we finally stepped off the Sea and into the

parking lot of the FH-CSI, I let out a long breath, relieved to be away from the house and all the chaos and mayhem. Smoky began to jog toward the building, and I followed him.

The FH-CSI stood on Thatcher Avenue, in the Belles-Faire district of Seattle. The building was at least four stories high, with three of them underground. There were rumors of yet another level below the surface, but no one had ever confirmed it. Combining a medic unit for Supes, an arsenal and a jail, a morgue and archives, as well as the headquarters for the investigations unit, it was an all-in-one building. Chase had been in charge of the FH-CSI until recently, when he became one of the Keraastar Knights, to our surprise.

As we hurried toward the front doors, they opened and two medics came out with a stretcher, rushing over to us. Smoky carefully laid Shade on the gurney and they took off at a run, rolling him toward the building. I began to follow, but Smoky caught my wrist.

"I need to go back and help at the house. I wish I could stay, but my duties are toward the family. Will you be all right here? Vanzir should be here any minute."

I wanted to say no, to beg him to stay just to have a familiar face around, but he was right. He needed to go home and help them find Yerghan.

"I'll be fine. I'll call you soon as I have news." As he turned to go, I followed the medics into the building, praying that we weren't too late.

I SUPPOSE THIS is a good time for introductions.

I'm Delilah D'Artigo. My sisters and I came Earthside some years back. We're half human, half Fae, and, at first, we worked for the Otherworld Intelligence Agency, which was originally the Y'Elestrial Intelligence Agency—that is, until the portals opened. We were sent over Earthside because our track record wasn't spectacular. Not only does our half-human side interfere with our abilities, but Camille ended up on the bad side of her boss. Lathe had decided that she owed him a blowjob. When she disagreed, he hit the final nail in our coffin.

Camille was born with magic in her blood. She pledged to the Moon Mother years ago. Over the past few years, she's been promoted in the Coterie of the Moon Mother, first to priestess, and then to High Priestess of the Earthside division. A few months ago, she ascended to the throne of Dusk and Twilight, joining Titania and Aeval as a Fae Queen out at Talamh Lonrach Oll—the Land of Shining Apples. Now she lives there, with her three husbands, Smoky, Morio, and Trillian. I miss having her at home, but destiny planned otherwise, and we've learned the hard way you can't fight fate.

Menolly, on the other hand, was a *jian-tu*, an acrobat of extraordinary talent, and she too was a spy for the OIA along with Camille and me. One day, she fell into a nest of vampires, an accident that forever changed her life. Tortured and turned, she was sent home to destroy us, but Camille managed to lock her in the safe room, and after a year in intensive therapy, Menolly returned to her duties.

Now, she's married to a werepuma. Nerissa is her heart-mate. And they're both married to Roman, Prince of the Crimson Veil, but that's more a marriage of convenience and politics. I think he's in love with Menolly, too, but he promised not to step between her and Nerissa and so far he's been good to his word. Once they married him, they moved out as well. So now, the house belongs to Shade and me.

And me? I'm Delilah D'Artigo. I'm a two-faced Were, with my cuddly tabby cat side, and my darker Panther side. I'm a Death Maiden, belonging to the Autumn Lord, and my destiny includes bearing his child.

None of us ever thought we were slated for great things when we were young. We thought we'd grow up, find careers, maybe marry.

We lost our mother—who was human—very young. Maria fell off of a horse and broke her neck. Our father foisted most of our care onto Camille's shoulders, who could barely take care of herself. He was always there in body, stern and unyielding, a proper soldier to the end, but emotionally, he lost his light when Mother died. He, too, became a victim of Shadow Wing's war. The truth is, our "family" is composed of those we have gathered around us. Because we've learned the hard way that if you don't look out for your own, nobody else will.

THE MEDICS MADE me wait in the reception room while they attended to Shade's wounds. Fifteen minutes later, Mallen came rushing through. He didn't bother to stop to talk to me, but rushed on past. His assistant watched him go, then sat down beside me.

"I'm Bethanie. Mallen is focused on helping your fiancé, and he asked me to talk to you for a moment." She reached out to take my hand. "The wound was severe but that's not the real danger. Mallen will be out to talk to you in a while, but first he has to diagnose how bad the damage is."

The doors opened and Vanzir rushed in, looking around. When he saw me, he hurried over to my side. "Mallen wanted me to help?"

"Are you Vanzir?"

Vanzir nodded.

"Please come with me." Bethanie stood. "The doctor's waiting for you. Delilah, it's best if you wait here for now. The procedures aren't pleasant and we need to be able to give our full focus to Shade." She gave me a look that said she wouldn't put up with any defiance, and led Vanzir into the back.

I fussed, pacing the room, wanting to go back anyway. Camille or Menolly probably would charge back there, but then again, they'd also be thrown out on their ear. It wouldn't do Shade any good if I interrupted their work. I pulled out my phone and texted Camille.

HOW? ARE THINGS GOING? DID YOU MANAGE TO FIND YERGHAN YET? I WAITED UNTIL SHE PINGED ME BACK.

NO. HE'S VANISHED. MY GUARDS HAVE ARRIVED AND THEY PERFORMED A RECONNAISSANCE OF THE LAND. THEY HAVEN'T FOUND ANY OTHER ROGUE PORTALS EXCEPT THE ONE AIMED TOWARD Y'ELESTRIAL. BUT WILBUR WAS RIGHT. THE REMAINS OF THE ONE HE FOUND HAS A RESIDUE ENERGY SIGNATURE POINTING TOWARD THE SUB-REALMS.

I thought for a moment. Shadow Wing might be a Demon Lord, but he wasn't a magician or sorcerer. Yerghan the Blade wasn't a sorcerer either. And if Shadow Wing had been draining his help right and left, how the hell had he managed to open a portal for Yerghan?

HOW IS SHADE DOING?

I stared at her text, not knowing what to answer. Finally, I texted: I DON'T KNOW. VANZIR IS IN THERE WITH THEM. I'M SCARED.

Another pause and then Camille answered.

I KNOW, KITTEN. I KNOW. NERISSA IS ON HER WAY TO SIT WITH YOU. I WISH MENOLLY AND I COULD COME, BUT WE'RE TRYING TO FIGURE OUT WHAT THE HELL TO DO ABOUT THE SITUATION. THE MEN ARE CLEANING UP THE BACK OF THE HOUSE. I'M AFRAID WE'RE GOING TO NEED TO BUILD A NEW KITCHEN AND BACK PORCH.

THAT'S THE LAST THING I'M WORRIED ABOUT, I texted back.

An hour later, just as I was about ready to go stomping back demanding answers, Mallen came into the waiting area and motioned for me to follow him.

"We stitched up the wound. He lost a lot of blood but given he's part shadow dragon, he'll survive. But I'm afraid that he was, indeed, attacked by a soul-stealer blade. And unfortunately, Willow, our psitech, hasn't been able to locate the direction in which his soul was sent. He's in a deep coma, and we can't bring him out of it until we retrieve his soul. And we can't retrieve his soul until we know where it is."

He led me back into a private room. Shade was lying on the bed, still as death, hooked up to several machines. I glanced at the monitors, not sure what all the graphs and charts meant. He was wearing no shirt, and had a wide bandage wrapped around his midriff. His arms were stretched out by his sides, and his eyes were closed. He looked to be in a deep sleep, and I wanted to run over and shake him, to wake him up.

The hospital room looked sparse, in that sterile way that all hospital rooms have. I noticed that there was no window, and the room felt warmer than usual.

"Can I hold his hand?" I looked at Mallen, unsure of what to do.

"It won't hurt him. You'll notice we raised the

temperature in the room. I want his muscles to stay warm and not freeze up. I also chose this room because there isn't an outside entrance. Given his attacker is still on the loose, I figured I'd make it harder for whoever it was to reach him." Mallen gave me a sympathetic look, and I wanted to hug him.

I was on the edge of breaking down. I had held it together during the attack, and while waiting out in the reception area, but seeing Shade laying there, so still, and knowing that his soul wasn't in his body was about to break me.

At that moment, Vanzir entered the room. He quietly came over, putting his hands on my shoulders. "There's one other thing Mallen says we can try," he said. "But you have to give the okay for it."

Mallen motioned for the nurse to leave the room. He closed the door behind her.

"Vanzir is correct. He's a dream-chaser demon, which means he can forcibly enter Shade's mind. He might be able to locate him, or at least get some idea of where he is."

"I thought you could only siphon off energy," I said, wiping my eyes.

Vanzir shook his head. "I can travel through a number of realms, remember? I was able to find Camille when Hyto captured her. While I wasn't on the physical realm, I was able to travel to her out on the astral."

I caught my breath, suddenly remembering. That had been a horrible time, a terrifying time. Smoky's father had kidnapped Camille and tortured her. Vanzir had been able to locate her, and had helped lead the rescue. I had forgotten that he had found her via the astral realm.

"That's right. I remember now. But can you do this the same way? Can you find Shade?"

He thought for a moment, then shook his head. "I don't think I can go about this exactly the same way, but I can use my abilities to enter Shade's mind, where I can try to locate a trace signature to follow. But I must have your permission before I do that. It's an extremely invasive procedure, and while I promise not to siphon any energy off of him, just the act of it could disrupt whatever is going on. I can't promise what the results will be. I can't even promise that it won't hurt him in some manner."

"Let me think. I need to think about this for a moment." I turned, walking out of the room. I needed to get away from the machinery and the smell of disinfectant and the silent hum that all hospitals had. The fact that this was a medic unit for Supes didn't change that.

I told the nurse at the reception desk that I'd be outside for a moment, in case Mallen needed me. As I headed out into the dark of night, I saw that the clouds had socked in. It was still relatively warm—in the low sixties—and a spatter of rain began to pelt down.

I turned my face up to the sky, looking for any signs of the moon, but she was in hiding, and the entire sky seemed faintly illuminated. I seldom prayed, although I was dedicated to the goddess Bast. I was no priestess, but merely a simple devotee. She had always been with me in my heart, and when I thought about it, I realize that my mother had introduced me to her early on. By the time Mother died, I had been added to the temple rolls as one of the members.

"Tell me what I should do," I whispered, not really expecting an answer. Where Camille was finely attuned to the Moon Mother and her ways, pledged heart and soul to the goddess, and where Menolly worshipped no gods, I was somewhere in the middle. I loved Bast, but I didn't expect anything from her. And I didn't feel that she expected much out of me, except to be the best I could.

If I let Vanzir enter Shade's mind, there was a chance it could hurt him. I understood this on a logical level. But my heart—my heart cried out, *Go! Find him!* If there was a chance that Vanzir could bring his soul back, surely it was worth the risk? The psitech hadn't been able to do anything. And then, as I turned to go back inside, I had a sudden flash—it was as though the image blasted itself into my brain.

Venus the Moon Child. He was a shaman, he had been the shaman for the Rainier Puma Pride until he became one of the Keraastar Knights. Venus was a crafty old shaman, and even though he was now one of the Keraastar Knights, surely he could figure out where Shade's soul was. I pulled out my phone, calling Camille.

"Camille, I need Venus at the hospital," I blurted out the moment she came on the line. "We have to have a shaman to find Shade, and the psitech can't do it. Mallen thought that perhaps Vanzir could manage it, but my gut tells me it wouldn't be safe.

But Venus—Venus knows how to perform these sorts of rituals."

"I'm not sure how carrying the spirit seal will have affected his abilities, but I'm more than willing to call him in on this. Come to think of it, he had the spirit seal inside his leg all along. So it must have been working on him even back then. I'll call you back as soon as I talk to him."

I paced, ignoring the rain that now skittered down around me. For once, I realized that Bast *had* answered, and I could feel her around me, trilling, almost like the feel of the soft purr that ran through me when I was in my tabby form. I would have to make some sort of offering to show my gratitude.

A moment later, Camille returned my call. "Venus is on his way to the FH-CSI. He'll be there as soon as he can. Keep us informed. We're doing research on Yerghan right now, trying to figure out where he might be hiding."

Relieved, and feeling like we might actually get some answers, I headed back inside. Mallen and Vanzir were waiting for me in Shade's room.

"I had an epiphany. I've called for Venus the Moon Child. I'm not sure if you know who he is," I said, turning to Mallen, "but he's the former shaman of the Rainier Puma Pride. He's one of Camille's Keraastar Knights now, but if anybody can figure out where Shade is, I'll bet you he'll be able to."

"That's brilliant," Vanzir said. "He'd stand a much better chance of finding Shade's soul than I would. I'll wait around till he gets here."

I shook my head. "No, you go home. Then, if you would, bring my Jeep here. I'll need a way home as soon as we know what we're dealing with."

Vanzir raised his eyebrows. "You trust me driving your Jeep?"

I gave him a faint laugh. "No, but life is a risk, now, isn't it?" I handed him my keys. "Just please, don't get any tickets."

Not only was Vanzir a dream-chaser demon, he was also a bit of a speed demon on the road. We kept warning him to rein it in, not only for the sake of his wallet, but for the sake of anybody else who might get in his way. He was doing better, but he still hadn't broken all of his bad habits. At times I regretted that we allowed him to drive, but once the genie was out of the bottle, it was impossible to put it back in.

Vanzir took off, and I turned back to Mallen.

"How often have you dealt with a case like this? Hell, I didn't even know that there were swords that could do this. We've dealt with a ghost trapped inside of a sword, but that's not quite the same thing."

"No, and usually those vessels are magically forged and cursed. An actual soul-stealer blade is also forged with magic, but it's not cursed. I don't know the exact process for making them, and they're seldom encountered now, thank the gods, but I do know that during the forging process, the ground bones of certain astral creatures are added to the metal, creating the force inside the sword that severs the soul from the body. It doesn't surprise me that Yerghan the Blade carries this kind of sword. Look at his name."

"Look at what he did," I said. "I remember my history lessons. His army was terrifying, and with Telazhar by his side, they threatened to turn Otherworld into a wasteland."

"I remember my history lessons, too," Mallen said. "I was born after the Scorching Wars, but not that long after. When I was growing up, Elqaneve was very insular. In fact, all of Kelvashan's borders were closed to strangers. The Elfin race were isolationists."

I stared at the elf, realizing just how old he had to be. He looked barely old enough to drive, and I had always thought of him as around our own age. I knew that he was far older than that, logically, but I just hadn't made the connection.

"What was it like back then?"

"Terrifying. I was born about a century after Telazhar and Yerghan the Blade were sent to the Sub-Realms. The Southern Wastes had originally been a paradise. Lush woodlands, swamps, even jungles. I never saw them, because I was born after the destruction, but my parents had visited and they used to tell me stories about how magical the land had been. But the destructive magic that Telazhar and his sorcerers had rained down throughout the entire area turned it into the wasteland that it is now. Their hellfire infused the very sands with rogue magic. To this day, that's a dangerous area through which to travel."

That much I knew. Traveling through the Southern Wastes was hazardous at best. Great sandstorms would rise up to sweep along the desert floor. Anyone caught within the gusting winds was likely to be afflicted by a magical hailstorm with any number of diseases or dangerous magic, including death spells.

"When did Elqaneve open its borders again?" At least the discussion was taking my mind off Shade.

"About two hundred years after that. Until then, the only ones allowed through our borders were a few dignitaries from Y'Elestrial and a few of the seers from Aladril. I remember the first time I was allowed to travel outside of our lands. I spent twenty years on a road trip, visiting every city that I could. It wasn't safe to go down south beyond Ceredream, since the magic in the sands was still too rife and there were too many rogue sorcerers still around. But I visited everyplace that I could. I ended up spending five years in Dahnsburg. Then I returned home to begin my training as a healer."

It occurred to me that there were so many people who had touched our lives that we knew so little about. I had no clue that Mallen had done any of this, or that he had grown up so close to the actual Scorching Wars. It made me want to sit down with everybody whom I had any acquaintance with, and ask them about their past.

"I'm part Fae, but I've only been alive for sixty-some years. Sometimes I feel so young compared to so many of the people I meet. Even Nerissa, Menolly's wife, is a lot older than we are. One day, I'd like to travel around Earthside, to see some of the places my mother went. She spent time in Madrid during World War II. That's where she met my father when he was on a secret mission over here, before the portals officially opened."

"You'll have plenty of time," Mallen said. "Don't rush the future. That's one thing I learned the hard way. Don't ever rush time. Let it play out on its own schedule, because sometimes when you rush it, you miss things and don't realize that you've lost them until they're gone. I lost the chance to watch my daughters grow, because I was too focused on my future and I ignored the present."

"That's right, you lost family in Elqaneve." I had forgotten, but now the conversation came flooding back. Mallen had lost his sister, his wife, and two daughters in the attack on Elqaneve. Our father had been killed during the battle, as well. Camille and I had lived through it.

"Yes. They were still so young, but I kept promising myself that I would go home and spend time with them later on, when it counted. I thought establishing myself over here was more important. Surely, they would be better off if I spent my time here while they were young, and then with them when they grew into young women. Only they never got that chance, and neither did I."

"Did the fires take them?" I closed my eyes, remembering the screaming of that night. The flames. The relentless lightning that destroyed the city.

He nodded. "Our house was one of the ones hit by the lightning. It caught fire, and my wife did her best to get everybody out. But when she realized that my daughters weren't in the courtyard, she ran back in. By then, the smoke was so thick that she couldn't see anything and she couldn't find them. She refused to leave. There was so much chaos and death that the neighbors couldn't spend time trying to convince her to flee. They had their own families to worry about. The next day, when they looked through the rubble, they found what was left of her body, and those of my daughters. The girls had been hiding in the closet, probably afraid of the thunder."

Mallen kept his reserve. Like most elves, he was able to assume an unreadable face when his emotions were high. But a single flicker of his eyes told me how much he was still hurting, and how much pain he had gone through.

"I'm so sorry."

"It's not something anyone could have prevented. No one anticipated what was about to happen. My loss was not the only loss that day. It's estimated that over one hundred thousand elves died during the fires, and another hundred thousand from the fighting. Kelvashan was decimated. The Elfin race was almost exterminated. Every single member of my race bears some sort of scar from the attack, whether it be on the body or in the heart. I doubt if we will ever fully heal."

"We lost our father. I think the hardest part was waiting to find out the truth."

"You and Camille were there that night, weren't you?"

I nodded. "I think we'll always have nightmares. Menolly managed to get away, back over here. Camille and I had to travel from Elqaneve to Y'Elestrial. We were there when the fires rained down. We were there in the palace when it was destroyed. We *do* understand what it was like that night."

Even now, when I closed my eyes, I could see the destruction and death raining down around us. I knew Camille still had nightmares as well. Once in a while we talked about it, and neither one of us cared much for the smell of roasting meat, given how many burned bodies we had encountered.

"We all bear scars of one sort or another." He let out a sigh. "Enough traveling down memory lane. The past is past and we're better off focusing the present."

A moment later, the door opened and the nurse popped her head in. "Venus the Moon Child here to see you."

I glanced at Shade, hoping to hell the old shaman would be able to locate my beloved's soul.

Chapter 4

VENUS THE MOON Child looked a lot more refined than he had when I first met him, but he was still the same old feral shaman at heart. His hair was plaited back in a long tawny braid, heavily interspersed with gray. He had shaved his beard, but his eyes were still luminous, and the brilliant fire opal he wore around his neck glowed with that same luminosity. He crackled with magic, the sparks practically flying off of him. He was wearing the colors of Camille's court—violet, black, and silver. The werepuma looked like he had just stepped out of the pages of some magical faerie tale.

"Delilah, I came as soon as I could. The guards are waiting in the reception area, although two of them insisted on following me to the room. They're right outside the door, and I need to let them know that everything's all right in here or they'll come bursting in to make sure nothing is wrong."

"Of course." I opened the door with him, allowing the guards to take a peek inside. "There are no windows, so nobody can come through except magically. If you want, you're welcome to stay inside with this."

One of the guards chose to do so, with an apologetic grin.

"We can't let anything happen to Venus, I'm sure you understand."

I nodded. The Keraastar Knights were integral to our future plans, and now that Camille had gathered them all together, we didn't dare chance losing any of them. Not again.

I motioned for the guard to stand in the corner, out of the way. Then Mallen and I explained to Venus exactly what it happened. His expression sobered when I told him about the soul-stealer blade.

"Well, that's not good. But you came to the right place. I've had experience in soul retrieval. I'm not certain if I can bring him back, but I should be able to find out where he is." He motioned for us to move away from the bed, then positioned himself beside Shade.

"Delilah, I need you to leave the room. Your energy is too frantic. It will interfere with my abilities to trace his whereabouts. Mallen, please monitor his condition. Even though what I'm about to do shouldn't jar the wound, it can affect his heart rate and pulse."

Once again, I left the room, wishing to hell that I could stay. This time, I refused to return to the waiting room. One of the guards brought me a chair and I sat down outside in the hallway, hugging myself as I strained to hear what was going on inside. I wanted to call Camille, but I wasn't sure what I could say.

Ten minutes passed, and another ten. I stood, pacing the length of the hall. I thought about peeking in, seeing if everything was all right, but the kind of work Venus was doing required absolute concentration, and anything I did to interrupt him would only disturb the process.

A few minutes later, I glanced over at the guard. "So are you a guard for the Keraastar Knights in general?"

He gave me a sympathetic look. "I really can't talk about my duties, Miss Delilah. I'm sorry. But if you want to talk about something else, to take your mind off of what's happening in there, I'd be happy to help."

Grateful that he understood, I asked him about Talamh Lonrach Oll.

"So my sister's gardens, how are they coming?"

It was a lame attempt at conversation, but at least it was something.

"The gardens are beautiful, miss. Her Majesty has a lovely eye for landscaping. We're increasing the apple orchards, and Her Majesty has also instructed the gardeners to plant a number of other fruit trees. She intends for the court of Dusk and Twilight to become an extremely fruitful place. And Their Majesties Titania and Aeval concur. It's hoped that by next harvest, Talamh Lonrach Oll will be selling fruit at the local farmers' markets."

That led us into a discussion about the seasons,

and how autumn was coming quickly. I didn't want to talk about the equinox, because that led me to thinking about Shade, but the guard seemed to be aware of my hesitation and he led the discussion to the fall cleanup, and how Talamh Lonrach Oll was expanding its borders once again. That was news to me, and it got me wondering just how big the sovereign Fae nation would become. Before I realized it, forty-five minutes had passed, and the door to Shade's room opened.

Mallen motioned for me to follow him inside. I thanked the guard, and he gave me a gentle salute. Venus was standing by Shade's side, looking grave. My heart began to plummet.

"Were you able to find anything? Were you able to find out where his soul went?"

"I know where to find him. But I can't retrieve his soul. You're going to have to do that."

I wasn't sure I had heard him correctly. "*Me*? I'm not a shaman."

"Delilah, Shade is lost in the Land of Wandering Souls."

The words reverberated through me, meaning nothing and yet, everything. Mallen led me over to a chair, and I sat down, clutching the arms.

"The Land of Wandering Souls? I've never heard of that before. Where is it? How do I get there?"

"That's a question for the Autumn Lord. The Land of Wandering Souls is found in the realm of eternal autumn. It's an elemental realm—a realm belonging to the season. The only ones who can travel there without help are those of that nature. The Harvestmen. I imagine the Death Maidens, too, given you're pledged to the Autumn Lord. But I can't find my way there."

I was silent for a moment, trying to digest what he had told me. "I have no clue what to do. I've never heard of the place, and Greta has never mentioned it. Neither has the Autumn Lord."

"I suggest you contact them as soon as possible. I don't know much about the realm myself, except that when a soul is out there too long, there's a chance it will be lost forever. The longer Shade's out there, the less chance of retrieving him." Venus gave me a little shrug. "I wish I had better news, sweetheart, but at least we know where he is. I'm not sure how the soul-stealer blade sent him there, but that doesn't really matter."

I could barely breathe, my chest felt so tight. I gripped the arms of the chair trying to brace myself as the impact of what he was saying hit home. His words kept ricocheting through me, and I was doing everything I could to prevent myself from turning into Tabby. I wanted to cry, but the tears wouldn't come. Numbly, I looked up at Venus after a moment.

"I'll have to contact Greta. How long do I have before he's lost for good?"

"I don't know. As I said, I know very little about this realm. I knew it existed, but I've never been there." He pressed his lips together then, reaching out to touch my shoulder. A wave of energy passed through me and I realized he was trying to calm my panic.

I closed my eyes, allowing him to work on me. He moved around behind me and placed both hands on my shoulders. The ripple of energy flowed through me like a soothing wave of heat, smoothing out the wrinkles and bumps and jolts. After a moment, I was breathing again, and I realized that my breath was matching his own—rhythmic and even.

I inhaled deeply, then let out the breath and stood, surprised by how steady I felt.

"Thank you, I needed that." Even as I spoke, I realized that I wasn't going to be able to contact Greta here in the FH-CSI. The energy was too sterile, and the closer I was in proximity to Shade, the more frazzled I felt.

"Is Vanzir back yet?"

Mallen popped outside to find out. I turned to Venus.

"I can't tell you how much I appreciate you doing this. At least we know where he is. There has to be a way to retrieve him." I felt weary, tired beyond words. "I'm so tired, Venus. Tonight was horrible." And then, a wave of tears rose up in my throat. "Shade threw me a bridal shower. I was shopping for my wedding dress and when I came home everybody was there, waiting to surprise me. And then, after people went home, we were just sitting around talking and having fun—and Yerghan attacked."

Venus worried his lip. After a moment, he said, "You know we're approaching the final battle. Shadow Wing grows desperate. When Menolly managed to wrest all the spirit seals away from him, it was a great blow. And now that all the Keraastar Knights are together, he feels the approach of the end. He no longer has a chance to use us, and he's losing what grip on sanity he had. I'm afraid that sending Yerghan after you was a desperate act on his part. The daemon army encroaches even as his own demons flee him."

"How do you know this?" I asked.

"The spirit seals. You have no idea how they've affected those of us who carry them. The Keraastar Knights are not simply integral to the downfall of Shadow Wing, but now that we're all gathered together, it increases our power to sense what is happening in this war. We don't talk about it much, but we're training with Camille to create a unified force. The Keraastar Knights, as a unit, are no longer individuals. We each have our own selves, our own pasts, but we're rapidly evolving into a hive mind."

I thought about what he said for a moment. If the Keraastar Knights could feel Shadow Wing's energy, then could he feel theirs? Could he feel Camille out there, wearing the Keraastar diamond? The thought chilled me.

"I have a question for you, and I'm not sure how you're going to feel about me asking. I know Camille would have said something if she was concerned, or at least I hope she would. Shamas—our cousin. What do you make of all of this?"

I still didn't trust Shamas. It wasn't that I thought he was out to muck things up, but the fact was, he had been dead and buried until we had gone to Otherworld to find the last Keraastar Knight. During the ritual Camille performed, Shamas had appeared to claim the last spirit seal.

His resurrection had thrown all of us for a loop, and while Camille and I had talked a little about it, she kept most of her feelings to herself. I didn't blame her. This was her burden to bear, and there were things that I would probably never know. But it still made me uneasy.

Venus shifted from one foot to the other, looking uncomfortable. "I'm not sure how much I should talk about this. I know she's your sister, but I am honor bound to Camille as the Queen of the Keraastar Knights. Just like I am honor bound to this seal I wear around my neck."

I stood there, unsure of what to say. At one point my sisters and I had been completely open; we hadn't had secrets and we had all worked toward the same goals. Now, Venus had just reinforced the fact that we were moving into different worlds.

"Don't worry about it. I'll ask her later. If she can tell me, she will." I held up my hand to forestall the apology I saw forming on his face.

At that moment, Mallen returned, Vanzir behind him.

"Sorry it took me so long, but Camille's guards thought they found somebody down at Birchwater Pond."

"Who was it?" I stiffened, part of me hoping that it was Yerghan the Blade and that they had managed to kill him, even though I knew that was a pipe dream.

"Martin. He came wandering over to look for Wilbur and somehow got himself on the path down to the pond. So how are things going?"

"I think I need to go home. I have to contact

Greta." I glanced back at Shade, then looked over at Mallen. "Take care of him for me, please? Call me if anything happens."

"Of course. And Delilah, whatever you need to do, do it quickly. We can keep his body alive, but after a while the comatose state takes its toll."

"Not only that, but if you take too long to find his soul, there won't be a way to bring him home," Venus interjected.

"Way to put the pressure on, guys," I muttered. And with that, Vanzir and I left for the house as the guards returned Venus to Talamh Lonrach Oll.

ON THE WAY home Vanzir kept quiet, refraining from asking me any questions.

I was grateful, since I didn't want to have to repeat myself several times over. By the time we pulled back into the driveway, the chaos appeared to have settled down, but I could see guards spread out everywhere. Camille had brought in an entire contingent from Talamh Lonrach Oll, and they were milling around. The lights were blazing in the living room. I was surprised that the electricity hadn't shorted out, given the fire in the kitchen.

"We still have electricity?"

"No, actually we don't. It seems Iris is a fiend for those battery-operated candles. She must have a hundred of them and so we brought them all up to the house. The electric company is coming out tomorrow, but for now, it's going to be a chilly night."

As we hustled into the house, I was overwhelmed with the smell of soot and charcoal. Someone had walled off the kitchen with a plastic tarp, and I didn't even want to look at the damage. As I entered the living room, everyone was gathered around, including Iris, Bruce, the Duchess, the twins, and Maggie.

"How is Shade?" Camille jumped up, a worried look on her face.

"I have a lot to tell you. But first, did you find any sign of Yerghan the Blade?" I glanced at Vanzir, adding, "Vanzir told me about the false alarm with Martin."

Wilbur, who was still there, let out a snort. Martin was sitting beside him, quietly content. The ghoul was an odd sort. I knew that Martin's spirit was actually hanging around, although the necromancer didn't seem to be able to pick up on him. I had a feeling that Wilbur's guilt over his brother's death was too strong to allow him to sense his spirit.

"No sign. Somehow he teleported out of the area, which tells me he has to have help over here. Either that or he's got himself some sort of handy-dandy mega-magic scrolls. One way or another, he vanished."

"You haven't heard the last of him," Trytian said. "Trust me, he'll be back. He wants his freedom, and if the only way he can obtain it is to kill the three of you, he'll be back to try again."

"But why would he bother? He's over here now. Shadow Wing can't follow him here. And he probably can't do anything about Yerghan if he just decided to take off and forget about us. I doubt if Yerghan's *rah-rah* in favor of Shadow Wing's growing insanity." Camille shook her head. "If I were Yerghan, I think I'd vanish into the crowd and try to make my way to Otherworld."

"You make a good point," Trytian said. "I suppose that might be what he's done, but if so, why bother making the attempt in the first place? I'll check through the grapevine. Chances are, Shadow Wing placed him under a geas of some sort. If that's the case, then Yerghan *has* to come through, or Shadow Wing may be able to yank him back into the Sub-Realms."

"You're probably right about that. Just because Shadow Wing is unstable doesn't mean he's stupid." Menolly let out a disgusted sound. "I hate these fucking demons. I just wish this were done with. Why don't we do what we had planned to do? Let's gate Shadow Wing over here and take him out?"

"If we're going to do that, then we have to plan it out step by step. We can't take any chances or go off half-cocked. We also need to find someone strong enough to gate him over here. That's going to be one hell of a sorcerer." Trillian shook his head. "We have to be smart about this. I know we all want the war over and done. And now that the Keraastar Knights are together, we actually have a chance. But we can't allow ourselves to screw up. If we were to gate Shadow Wing here and *not* be able to kill him, he'd have free rein. Do we really want that?"

"All right. It's settled. We start planning for this. But first, let me tell you about Shade. I asked Venus to examine him—we needed a shaman. Shade's trapped in the Land of Wandering Souls. It's a plane of existence in the realm of the Harvestmen. Venus can't travel there to bring him back, so I have to contact the Autumn Lord. Looks like I'm the one who has to find his soul."

"What happens if you don't—or rather, can't?" Iris asked.

"Then he'll be lost forever. To further complicate matters, the longer I wait, the more chance there is that I'll never be able to find him and bring him back to his body. So I have to move quickly." I slumped back in my chair, exhausted. "I can't believe that just a few hours ago I was out shopping for my wedding dress, and now I have to find my fiancé's soul. Can't anything in our lives ever be simple? Can't anything ever go right for a change?"

All of the adrenaline that had coursed through my body during the fight and at the hospital suddenly vanished, leaving a wave of grief in its wake. I felt like I was drowning, unable to surface, and suddenly I realized that I was sitting there in my tabby form. I hadn't even felt the transformation, I had been so numb.

I looked around, and spying Camille, leapt into her lap. I pressed myself against her heart, shivering. She wrapped her arms around me, holding me as she cooed to me. I couldn't stop shaking, and I let out a mew, aware that I should be trying to transform back, I should be trying to help Shade, but right now I felt frozen and numb and afraid.

"It's all right, Kitten. Everything's going to be okay. We'll make sure of it. We'll do everything we can to help. It's all right, just snuggle up against me right now." She looked over at Iris and said something that I couldn't catch.

I buried myself in her arms, taking a moment to breathe, to feel safe and secure. Camille had always protected me when we were little. She had stuck up for me when the other kids teased me. She had thrown punches when they tried to trigger me into turning into a cat and then chased me up a tree. She had beat the living crap out of several neighborhood boys when they pushed me into the water, knowing full well how phobic I was. And now, all I wanted was to curl up in her arms and feel safe.

She stood, carrying me, and headed into the parlor followed by Menolly, who brought two of the battery-operated candles. Iris followed behind, bringing Maggie. Camille settled down on the sofa, petting me gently, calming me down.

"It's all right, Kitten. It's all going to be okay. I promise you. We'll find Shade and bring him back into his body. Everything will be all right." Her voice was gentle, soothing, and I started to purr.

A moment later Iris began to sing softly, and the song turned into a second, and then a third.

Menolly was sitting on the floor playing with Maggie. She looked up at me as I cuddled in Camille's lap. "Would you like to play with Maggie? Maggie needs a hug."

Maggie let out a giggle and reached out her arms toward me. She wasn't allowed to play with me without supervision when I was in tabby form, given she was still too rough with other animals and children. I realized that I hadn't spent much time with her the past few days. Feeling slightly guilty, I stretched, gave Camille's hand a lick, and delicately stepped off of her lap. I jumped onto the floor, and in a moment, had turned back into myself.

Neither of my sisters said anything as I gathered Maggie in my arms. Iris held out a sack, and when I peeked inside, I saw a bag of Cheetos.

"Bless you." I settled myself on the other end of the sofa, crossing my legs so Maggie could sit in my lap. As I tore open the bag, stuffing a fistful of the orange puffs into my mouth, I realized that I was so tired I could barely keep my eyes open. But the confusion and fear had died down.

After finishing off half the bag, I set it on the floor, snuggling Maggie as she flapped her wings gently. Her fur was growing longer. Woodland calico gargoyles grew into being about as furry as a panda bear, and the swirls of color were growing more vivid and beautiful. She would be a toddler for decades to come, growing slowly over the years, and sometimes I wondered what it would be like for her living with me as the years progressed.

Maggie's native environment was the woodlands of Otherworld, but the little gargoyle was an orphan. She'd been raised in a food mill by harpies, rescued by Camille during a fight on the Space Needle. She had never known what it was like to be with her own kind except when she was very, very young. Her mother's spirit occasionally visited us, dropping in to check on her baby.

"Are you going to contact Greta tonight?"

I bowed my head, staring down at Maggie. "I should, but I'm *so* tired. I'm exhausted."

"Well, you're not staying here, that much I'll tell you. Not while Yerghan the Blade is still out there running around free. Everybody is coming back to my Barrow with me." Camille looked at Menolly. "Can you and Nerissa come, too? Will Roman mind? This matter concerns all of us."

Menolly gave her a shrug. "It doesn't matter what Roman says. Nerissa and I will come with you. Besides, he's really busy right now with some sort of political thing. We haven't been able to talk much the past few weeks. But is there a space for me to safely sleep, come the morning?"

"Oh, we'll make sure that you're safe. Plus, most of the Barrow is belowground, so you'll be safe from the sunlight. And my guards can be trusted to watch over you." Camille turned back to me. "So, do you need to contact Greta before we leave?"

I let out a breath. "I suppose I might as well try. Maggie should leave the room, though. I need as little distraction as possible."

As Menolly carried Maggie back out to the living room, Camille shifted so that I could lay down on the sofa and stretch out. Usually it was Greta who came to me, but I knew how to get to Haseofon without her. I had been a Death Maiden long enough to know exactly how to transfer myself over to the Autumn Lord's realm.

As I lowered myself into the trance that would allow me to move through dimensions into the realm of Haseofon, the room became very still. At first all I could hear was Camille's breathing and my own, and then finally, all I could hear was the beat of my heart, slow and rhythmic, calm and quiet.

I summoned up the image of the path in my mind, envisioning the jungle that I knew so well. Usually I traversed this route as Panther, but tonight I would make it in my two-legged form. All around me, the verdant greenery burgeoned out, a perpetual explosion of twisting vines and brilliant trees overshadowing me. The pungent scent of soil rose to meet my nostrils, and I shivered. While most jungles were hot, this one had a constant chill to it, like the edge of a cool autumn morning when the mist rolled down the mountain to cover the valley below.

Along the path, stones and twigs crunched under my feet as I hurried along, listening to the scuffling sounds in the undergrowth. Birds and animals abounded here, although I seldom saw them when I was Panther. Then, they hid from me, fearing for their lives. But today, I caught a glimpse of a fox beneath a low-hanging bush, and a brilliant bluebird flying overhead, and to my left, a skunk padded along through the undergrowth, followed by her babies, unconcerned with my presence.

The sky was covered by a layer of clouds, although here and there a shaft of sun pierced the blanket. I could sense the edge of rain hovering on the outskirts.

My nostrils twitched as the scent of a distant bonfire wafted past. It was late afternoon heading toward twilight as I wound along the path, through a small clearing. At the bottom of the ravine, far below me to my left, a stream cascaded along. The water raced over rocks, foaming white caps that roared, threatening to sweep away anything daring to cross its path. At the edge of the ravine, a log spanned across the water, held fast on either side by chains embedded deep in the ground. The first time I had come this way I had been afraid, terrified I might fall off, but over the months and years I had learned that I could easily dart across the trunk as long as I didn't look down. I set one foot on the trunk, and then the other. Summoning up my courage I scampered across, lightly jumping off the other side.

Still more forest awaited me, but here, the land was beginning to change. The jungle gave way to woodland, a brilliant array of maple and oak. These trees were always on the precipice of autumn, always prepared to drop their leaves at the first great windstorm of the season. But they never did. For this was the land of the Autumn Lord, this was the realm of the Harvestmen, and here this season ruled as king, holding sway over the land. No matter how hard the wind blew, the leaves never dropped, and new buds never appeared on the branches.

I shaded my eyes as a shaft of sunlight broke through the clouds, washing everything with a golden tinge. The beauty struck me dumb and I paused, just watching as the energy of the Autumn Lord's kingdom reverberated through my blood, through the beating of my heart, through the rhythm of my pulse.

In some ways I belonged here more than I belonged anywhere else. I was one of his chosen. I was a Death Maiden, and autumn was *my* season. Autumn burned in the core of my heart. I slowly let out my breath, reveling in the alertness of the land. It was awake and aware, a constant vision of the harvest, not yet claimed by the fallow slumber of winter, but long past the lazy days of summer. Autumn was the time of *action*, it was the time of busyness, a time of preparation.

As I stared into the distance, I saw the dark silhouette of rising towers against the glow of the sun. Then the clouds rushed in again, extinguishing the light, but I knew that I was close. I straightened and exited the valley, onto the path leading to the temple of Haseofon, where I prayed I would find my answers.

Chapter 5

HASEOFON.
Like some temple rising out of the ashes of Greek mythology, Haseofon was a vision in pillars and pavilions. Gray veins filtered through the polished white marble that composed the walls of Haseofon, and a wide flight of stairs led up to the main pavilion. The entrance, with its massive double doors, loomed well over ten feet tall. Along the sides of the building, light flickered through the stained glass panels of the keyhole windows.

As I jogged up the steps, I paused and focused on my apparel. I had learned how to change my clothing with just a moment's thought, at least while I was in the realm of Haseofon. Within seconds I was wearing a long flowing dress in pale sage green. It was a warm jersey, yet light and airy. As soon as I was properly clothed, I opened one of the great doors and entered the hall.

The ceiling, a great dome, arched over the entire expanse of the temple. Long draperies lined the walls in brilliant colors. Fuchsia and yellow, red, pink, ivory, all of the tapestries were embroidered with visions of trees and vines, of pastoral scenes, of the moon and stars.

At the back of the hall sat a raised dais. Pillows that reminded me of beanbag chairs lined the floor, and platters of roast beef and fragrant rice flavored with saffron, and great bowls of fruit covered the tables scattered around the room. To one side of the hall was a training section, complete with weapon racks covered with a variety of implements. Doors against the back of the room led to hallways where the Death Maidens slept.

I glanced around the room, looking to see who was here at the moment. The hall seemed relatively empty. In one corner I saw Mizuki, one of the other Death Maidens, playing her violin. I closed my eyes for a moment, listening to the wistful music as it transported me a million miles away.

"Delilah! I didn't expect to see you anytime soon." The voice was familiar, and as I swung around, a young woman who looked very much like me except for her long brown hair came running over.

"Arial, I wasn't sure if you'd be here or not." I accepted a hug from my twin sister, who had been here in Haseofon since she died at birth. It was a long story and convoluted, but the only time we had ever been able to see her otherwise was when she came in her spirit form—a leopard—to help us during battle.

"What are you doing here? Is everything okay?" Arial loved living in Haseofon, and she had never known anything else. She had lived here all of her existence. While she wasn't a Death Maiden, like I was, she served the Autumn Lord in different ways.

"I need to see Greta. I have to talk to her right away. It's important," I said, taking her hands. "It's about Shade. He's in danger."

She frowned, but gave me a quick nod and turned around. "Greta's out back, in the moonlight garden. Come, I'll take you to her."

Arial moved as though she were floating through the air. She was one of the most graceful creatures I had ever met. I wished Camille and Menolly could meet her, to talk to her like I could, but they weren't allowed into Haseofon. And Arial had never been able to leave the grounds of the temple without turning into her leopard self.

We headed through the maze leading toward the back of the temple, until we came to another set of double doors. They weren't as large as the front ones, but they were just as impressive. Arial pushed one of them open, holding it for me. I had done my share of walking around the temple grounds, but I seldom had time to explore the outer boundaries. I had never been to the moonlight garden.

We followed a small footpath winding through a looming forest of fir and oak and maple. The undergrowth was thick, although not as thick as our forests over Earthside, but there was the scent of faint decay, of trees winding down for the year. It was like that here all the time.

The path was lit with golden lanterns, sitting on rocks to each side, every few feet. The trail descended into the forest, weaving through and around the trees, and the chill evening air set me to shivering. I close my eyes, imagining a shawl around my shoulders, and it appeared, warming me just enough to take the edge off. Even though I wasn't here in body, my spirit felt the changes just as strongly as my skin would.

"How goes the war?" Arial said.

"I pray we're close to the end. We had a victory recently, a big one. I'm hoping it was enough to turn the tide." I paused, then said, "I truly wish you could come with me, in body as you are now."

"You know that's not possible. I can only remain in my human form while I am on the grounds of Haseofon. *Himself* did not have to grant me even that much, so I am grateful for what he's chosen to give me."

Sometimes I wondered if Arial blamed me. The deal my father had made had been that one of us should die, so that our mother and the other twin could survive childbirth. While logically I knew that if my father had not made the deal, all three of us would be dead instead of just my sister, I still had a streak of survivor's guilt.

"I know. I just wish… Well, you understand."

We were deep into the forest by now, and the trees loomed like giant sentinels, guarding our way. I felt conspicuous, and I realized that they were probably truly guardians, watching all who walked through the grounds of the temple. I wondered how far this realm actually extended. The Harvestmen all lived within in the Autumn Lands, not just the Autumn Lord. So it must be a vast plane.

"Where's the moonlight garden? We've gone quite a ways from the temple."

Arial laughed. "Don't be impatient. It just takes time to get there. It's a grove, not a kitchen garden."

But moments later, we entered a clearing. There I saw a circular garden, bounded by massive rosebushes and giant mums.

Rowan trees guarded the circle, which must have been a good acre in diameter. Curved stone benches lined the borders within the boundary of flowers and trees, and in the center stood a fountain that bubbled up with brilliant orange and yellow and red waters. They flowed in a continuous motion within the circular fountain, yet did not blend. In the center of the fountain stood a tall tree, carved in crystal, and through the trunk the water spiraled up, then sprayed out of the boughs and limbs. It was mesmerizing, and the sound, soothing.

The lip of the fountain was wide enough to sit on, and there, staring off into the forest, was Greta. She turned as we approached, a smile on her face. The fountain was lit up enough to illuminate all of us. I curtsied out of respect, and sat next to her. Arial wandered over to one of the rosebushes, cupping a blossom in her hand and bringing it up close to her nose so she could smell it.

"Well met, Delilah." Greta didn't seem surprised

to see me.

"Do you know what's happened?" It wouldn't surprise me at all if she knew. Greta seemed to know a great deal of things that went on in my life.

"Some, yes. I know some of it. *Himself* will be here in a moment. He told me that you were on the way, and that he would come to the garden when you arrived." She paused, looking wary. "Delilah, may I give you a piece of advice?"

I nodded. "Of course, I always value your advice. You're one of the best teachers I've ever had."

"Thank you," she said, nodding. "I wanted to tell you… Don't beg. When he gives you your options, accept them and follow directions. You will one day be the mother of his daughter. You must grow into the position. That means standing up for yourself, yet never throwing yourself on anyone's mercy, his included. He will appreciate it. And he will take it into account in the future. There is so much more at stake, even I can only see outskirts of what lies ahead, but what I can see transcends everything you think will be." She paused, looking like she was debating on whether to say something more. After a moment, she simply shook her head. "There is more, but it is not my place to say."

She cocked her head, listening for a moment.

I closed my eyes and I could hear what she heard.

A rustling in the leaves, of whisper on the wind. The slow scent of bonfire smoke wafted through the air, coiling around us like an elemental beckoning us to follow.

The smell of cinnamon and apples, of smoke

and soot and charcoal, of cold frosty nights, and the slow descent of the golden sun in afternoon.

The first apples beginning to fall from the trees, the shiver of leaves in the brisk chill night.

It stirred my blood with wondrous delight. I caught my breath, a ripple of hunger racing down my back. I wasn't sure what I was hungry for, but Panther raised her head, pacing within my heart.

Greta stood, dusting her hands on the skirt of her dress. "He's coming. I'll leave you now, to speak with him." She motioned to my sister. "Come, Arial, and walk with me back to Haseofon." She glanced at me. "We'll see you in a while, Delilah."

And with that, they left me alone in the garden.

I SAT STILL as night, still as a statue, shivering in the west wind that whistled past. I could hear his footsteps as he made his way toward me, striding across the land, a lacework of frost falling from his boots. With every step he left a trail of frozen gossamer webs across the grass. He was Lord of the Autumn, King of the Harvestmen, Lord of Fire and Flame, tempered with the chill of winter's first kiss.

As he entered the garden from the west, the wind whistled through his cape, sending it flowing behind him in a black trail. His hair draped over his shoulders, coiling black strands of jet, dark as coal, dark as night. Around his forehead a wreath of maple leaves illuminated his face, the leaves glowing with the burnished fires of the season. A pendant hung from a golden cord around his neck. The pendant was that of a skull, about the size of a small fist.

He held out his hand to me, a golden flame flickering from his palm. I took hold of his fingers, the fire crackling through my body, making me aware of every cell, of every nerve in my being. As he pulled me to him, I gasped, unable to breathe. He pressed his lips to mine, kissing me so deep that he sucked the breath out of my body.

I was floating in the middle of the sky with only the frosty stars to keep my company. And then, as I began to drift farther out, he breathed into my mouth, and my life force flowed back to fill my lungs and my blood, saturating me with both my own essence and his. The heat of his hands on my back burned through my dress, and everywhere he touched sang with its own orgasm, sending me into a climax the likes of which I had never felt.

I came hard, tears flowing down my face as I let out a scream, a pent-up ache mingling sadness and sorrow and worry and joy. As I shuddered, he held me tight, murmuring softly in my ear. I wasn't sure what he said, but his voice was comforting, soothing me back into my body, until finally he stepped back. He kept hold of my hands as he looked down at me.

"My Lord, I need your help."

"I know what has happened. Shade is part of me, he is my proxy. I'm all too aware of what happened." He motioned for me to sit on the bench, then took his place beside me. As he held my hand, tracing designs on my palm, I shivered. Being around the Autumn Lord's energy was taxing, even as much as it intoxicated me. He could never love me in physical form like this; his very presence would destroy my body—he burned so brightly with the fires of autumn. But on this realm, in spirit, he could take me and make me his own.

"What should I do? How can we return him to his body?"

"There is a way. What the old shaman told you is true. Shade is trapped in the Land of Wandering Souls. It exists within a realm closely connected to this, my realm. But *I* cannot return him to you. I am forbidden to enter. Even though technically, the dimension belongs to the Harvestmen, we cannot take action once someone has been sucked into it. But I *can* send you there. I can send you and your sisters there, and you can search for him. But it's a dangerous proposition."

My heart skittered in my chest. "We can go there? I thought my sisters couldn't come over here."

"They cannot enter Haseofon itself." He tipped my chin up. "But Delilah, if you stay too long, there's a chance you will be lost as well. You cannot go in body. I will have to send your souls there. And all who go must agree to it. I will not do it without permission."

"What exactly *is* the Land of Wandering Souls?"

"When a soul is separated from the body, but the body still lives, the soul often ends up lost. As you know, the Harvestmen are the reapers of souls. A few of the gods participate—Hel, Papa Legba, Kali, and others like them. But ultimately, we Harvestmen and our servants are responsible for the reaping of the souls. It's a complicated issue, with so many exceptions that I don't want to get into it."

"How does that play into Shade's situation?"

"At times, certain spells, or in Shade's case—magical weapons—can detach the soul from the body. If the body is not critically injured, it lives on, even though the soul can't find its way back to the host. The silver cord that connects it to the body has been severed, but the body still lives. In a number of cases, the soul ends up in the Land of Wandering Souls. And there it will stay, unless it's retrieved and returned to its body. Usually the victim is so confused that they don't know where they are, and that's one way they manage to lose themselves within the realm."

"So you're saying that Shade has no idea where he is?"

"Most likely. He may not even know that he's out of his body. Humans would call it something like a bad acid trip, but unfortunately there isn't an end to this. He'll stay there until his body dies or unless someone brings him back." Hi'ran's expression was grave. He was staring at the fountain in the center of the garden. "This was not meant to happen. If I could go get him, I would."

"Why can't you? You said the Harvestmen are not allowed into the Land of Wandering Souls."

"I claim the dead. Shade isn't dead. Whatever balance or order created our existence, it ensured that we would not be able to claim the souls of those who were still alive but separated from their body. I have a feeling the Hags of Fate may be responsible for the prohibition."

"But you can send us over there?" The thought of being detached from my body to enter a realm where souls were easily trapped wasn't all that appealing, but if it was the only way I could save Shade, I'd do it.

"Yes, I can send you. But you'll have to work fast once you cross over. The longer you stay there, the better the chance you'll have of being trapped. Think carefully as to whom you choose to take with you. They'll need to be strong-willed and have powerful egos, because one thing that I *do* know is that the Land of Wandering Souls is filled with the monsters created out of your own fear and imagination."

I caught my breath and let it out slowly. So it wasn't just a matter of wandering around until we bumped into Shade. "But if we're not in our bodies, how can they destroy us?" I already knew the answer, but I wanted to make sure.

"They can destroy your essence. They can destroy you as surely as you—a Death Maiden—destroy others. You'll feel like you're in your body, so I suggest you carry weaponry on your actual bodies when you enter the stasis. As long as you have it on your body when you transfer over, your soul will be able to utilize the essence of that tool."

I had fought enough creatures in enough battles to know that the mind was one of the most powerful weapons available. I wasn't about to dispute him or question him.

"How many can you transfer over with me? How many people can I take?"

"I suggest you travel with two or three others. No more. Otherwise, you risk losing them as well as Shade."

I didn't want to ask the next question, but I had to know. "What happens if we can't find Shade? What happens if I can't bring him back?"

"Then he will remain there, and I will find you a new mate."

I wanted to protest that I didn't want anybody else. Then I remembered what Greta had said. *No begging*. And I knew what Hi'ran's answer would be. He cared for me, and he might be bestowing a great honor on me, but when it came down to it, his will was my will.

After a moment, I said, "How do we get out of there once we find him? Because I *will* find him."

"I'll give you a token, a talisman. You will each have one. When you are ready to leave, you will activate them. Do not lose these charms, since they are the only way you'll be able to leave the realm. I'll give you one for Shade. But understand, this will not be easy. He may not even recognize you. You may have to remind him of who he is, and who you are. How you do that is up to you."

Hi'ran glanced at the sky. "I'm going to send you back now, to your body. Don't take too long to make a decision on who to take with you. The sooner you start, the better for Shade. Talk to Camille's healers. They will prepare you. When you are ready, touch the mark on your forehead and whisper my name. I'll come."

And with that, he leaned down and kissed my forehead on the mark that bound me to him. When I opened my eyes, I was back in the parlor, lying on the sofa.

RATHER THAN REPEAT myself twice, I motioned for Menolly, Camille, and Iris to follow me and went back into the living room, where I told everybody what the Autumn Lord had said.

"Have any of you ever heard of the Land of Wandering Souls?"

Most of them shook their heads, except for Morio.

"We have legends of it in Japan, although we have a different name for it. A dangerous journey, it is. Very few ever return from being lost there. When I first began learning death magic, my teacher told us about a spell designed to sever the soul from the body without killing the physical form. It was in preparation of creating a host for a walk-in."

Camille gave him a long look, but I had the feeling she knew what he was talking about.

"Have you ever performed that spell?" Iris asked, her voice wary.

Morio shifted his gaze away from her. "I know *how* perform it, but I never have. And I never will. To me it's one of the utmost violations—stealing someone's body while committing their soul to an eternity of confusion."

Unsettled that he actually had that much power and that I had never known about it, I framed my next question carefully. "Have you ever been party to retrieving a soul?"

He stared at me, his gaze direct. "No, but I've seen the ritual performed. And in case you were wondering, I've never *participated* in stealing somebody's body like that. As I said, I know how to perform the spell, but I've never taken part in any ritual. In fact, I was kicked out of one of my orders. My teacher cast me out because I refused to do so."

Menolly spoke for us all. "You can't leave the story hanging, not after telling us that much."

With a little shrug, Morio said, "As I grew up, I realized that I had a talent for minor death magic. You know, the kind you can learn without going into training for it. Grandmother Coyote decided that I should take up the specialty. She hooked me up with a teacher and I learned quickly, and was doing extremely well. But then, many years later, we came to the part in training where he taught me the spell to cleave a soul from its body. He wanted me to prove that I knew it, so he asked me to perform it with him. You have to understand, those who work in death magic work in shades of gray. Some veer into darker territories, and some try and stay on the lighter side, but all in all, death magic is a dark art. Isn't that so, Wilbur?"

Wilbur, who had stuck around, nodded. "No matter how you pretty it up, the discipline is a harsh one. Where you specialized in the more purely magical aspects, I chose the more practical ones." He looked at the rest of us. "Necromancers understand death magic just as much as Morio does, if not more so. But we put it to use in the physical realm, rather than using the energetic forms."

"Anyway," Morio continued, "I refused to take part. He had chosen one of the village girls for our practice victim. I knew that he was angry at her because she had refused his advances. When he wasn't watching, I freed her and told her to get the hell out of the village before he found out. I stalled as long as I could to give her time to get away. Finally I told him I wasn't going to perform the spell."

I was riveted. "What happened? Did she get away?"

Morio smiled. "Yes, she escaped. My teacher was so pissed that he beat me until I was black and blue. You have to understand, we were trained never to lash back at our teachers. So I let him beat me, because it was the appropriate thing to do. I had refused my training. After he finished, he headed back to his home to where he had locked up the girl, but she was long gone. I packed my things and ran away. My parents didn't live in the village, so I wasn't worried that he would try to take it out on my family. He'd have Grandmother Coyote breathing down his back if he did. But I made myself scarce. He didn't bother coming after me—I suppose he thought I wasn't worth the energy. For that, I'm grateful."

We were all staring at the youkai-kitsune.

"Well, that's more than I expected to hear." I thought for a moment, then asked, "I need a few volunteers to go with me. I don't feel like it's my place to request that any specific one of you go, because of the chance we might be lost there. But I need help. I don't think I can do this myself." I glanced over at Iris. "And *you* are not in the running. You don't get to volunteer. Your children need you."

She gave me a smile. "As much as I love you and Shade, I wasn't going to. My children come first. I'll fight in the demonic war, because their lives are at stake if Shadow Wing breaks through. But I'm afraid that their well-being and my ability to be here for them come before Shade."

I knew she was just being honest, but it still hurt to hear. But there was no way I could fault her for it.

"I'll join you," Morio said.

Camille started to volunteer, but Smoky shouted her down.

"You know very well that Aeval and Titania will never allow you to go. You cannot jeopardize yourself in that manner. I'm sorry. Camille, but your kingdom—and it is a kingdom—relies on you too heavily." He looked over to Morio. "Think twice about volunteering. You are her priest."

"I think it better if you stay home," Trillian said. "But I can go. Camille needs me the least—and I'm not asking people to contradict me. The fact is that Morio is her priest under the Moon Mother's watch. They work powerful magic together as a team. And Smoky, you big lizard, you can guard them better than I ever can. So I volunteer to go with Delilah in place of you, Camille."

Camille teared up, but merely fluttered her fingers to her lips. I could tell it wrenched her heart that she couldn't volunteer to help me. We stuck together, no matter what.

Menolly cleared her throat. "I'd go, except I'd be a liability during the daylight."

"I can go," Nerissa said. "People volunteered to save my life when I was trapped in the Sub-Realms. I'd like to pay it back in some way. I've been doing a lot of training, and I'm a pretty good fighter now. And I'm a werepuma."

A pained look crossed Menolly's face, but she merely said, "Bless you, love. I won't try to talk you out of it. You've trained under Venus, and that counts for a lot."

"I can take one other person with me. The Autumn Lord told me to bring no more than three others." It distressed me that neither of my sisters could go, but I knew that whatever help I had, it would only add to our chances to find Shade.

"I'll go," Rozurial said. "Vanzir's about to be a father—well, in a few months. I doubt if Aeval would take kindly to him going. But I'm happy to help. Shade's a good friend, and I don't like thinking about him being trapped there. Will that work, Delilah? Nerissa, Trillian, and me?"

I gratefully nodded. "I'm just so glad that I've got somebody going with me. To tell you the truth, I'm afraid. I don't go messing around in other realms much."

"Of course you do," Camille said. "You're a Death Maiden—you go off into the astral all the time."

I hadn't thought of it that way. It made the prospect of wandering off into a realm where souls got trapped a little less frightening.

"When you put it that way, it doesn't sound so bad. All right, we need to leave as soon as we can. Our bodies will stay in this realm, so I'd like to know we're being protected and watched over. The Autumn Lord told me that your healers can help, Camille."

"Of course," Camille said. "We're all going back to my Barrow anyway, and there, we can watch over you and make certain that you're all right. You'll all be safe." She looked at Wilbur, then her gaze flickered to Martin. "Did you want to come back with us?"

Wilbur let out a snort. "I can hear in your voice just how much you want me back there, sweet cheeks. But no, I appreciate the offer, but Martin and I will just head home and watch *Jeopardy*. I always DVR it just in case we miss it because Martin gets agitated if we don't watch."

At that, we all broke out into a laugh. Part of me wanted to tell Wilbur that the soul of his brother was watching over him, that he really didn't give a damn about *Jeopardy*. That it was just some routine function left behind in his body. But I decided not to bother. Martin the ghoul gave Wilbur a lot of comfort, and I didn't want to take that away from him.

We gathered our things, and Vanzir and Rozurial, along with several guards, escorted Iris to her house, where she and Bruce and the Duchess could gather everything that they and the twins would need for the next week or so. I hoped it wouldn't take that long to find Yerghan the Blade, but at least everyone would be safe out at Talamh Lonrach Oll.

"While you're off hunting for Shade, we'll continue our search for Yerghan. With luck, we'll be able to find and dispatch him sooner than later. At least he's not a sorcerer, and can't try to gate Shadow Wing over here." Camille rubbed her head. "I have a massive headache tonight."

"I'm sure the guys won't be happy to hear that," I said, joking.

She shot me a dirty look, but smiled. "Ha-ha, funny woman. Oh, tomorrow I'll send a contingent of workers out here to assess the damage and see what needs to be done to rebuild the house. Smoky and I can take care of the costs. There's no problem with that."

At that, I decided to take a look in the kitchen before we left. As I pushed aside the tarp covering the entrance to the kitchen, my heart fell. We had spent so many meals in here, so many nights gathered around the kitchen table planning how to find the daemon generals that Shadow Wing had sent against us. We had planned celebrations, eating dinner amidst a cacophony of laughter and conversation.

Now, the room was a skeleton of itself, filled with smoke and soot. The back porch and back wall had burned away, leaving only charcoal studs and piles of ashes in their wake. It tore my heart, and I began to cry as I realized that everything in this world that I held dear was breaking apart.

Shade was trapped in a distant realm, his body locked into a coma. The house that had become our sanctuary was now wounded, and regardless of how we built it up again, it would never be quite the same. I wrapped my arms around my stomach, weeping softly. A moment later, Menolly and Camille joined me.

As I stood there crying, Camille wrapped her arm around my shoulders.

"Sometimes I wish we had never come Earthside. Sometimes I wish we had stayed in Otherworld," I choked out, too exhausted to hide my feelings.

Menolly reached up, brushing my hair out of my eyes. "You don't really mean that. I know it feels like life would have been simpler, but you never would have met Shade. Camille would never have Smoky or Morio, and Trillian might not have come back in the picture. And I wouldn't have Nerissa."

"That's right," Camille said. "We would never have met Iris, or our cousins Daniel and Hester. So many wonderful things would never have happened. Maggie would be dead, for one thing. I know this is difficult, but don't wish away all the joy just because there are problems. I guarantee you, if we had stayed in Otherworld, we still would have faced danger. Telazhar would have still killed our father, and for all we know, we might have died in that storm."

I knew she was right. Everything she said was spot-on, but I couldn't stop crying.

"I think you need to sleep. Let's go back to the Barrow and you can rest. It's been a rough day and you need your strength." Camille turned me away from the kitchen. "This house will be as beautiful as it was, and it will be sturdier. The foundation is strong. It can withstand a little damage. And I'll come out to help with the warding. This will always be our safe haven, and we'll reclaim it from any damage done."

As we all shuffled out to the cars, the guards carrying Shade, I took one last look at the house over my shoulder. I knew I'd be returning, but it wouldn't be the same. Camille was right—we could strengthen it and make it stronger and more beautiful than before, but there was a little part of my heart that didn't want it to change. That didn't want anything to change. And yet, there was no way to hold back the future. It had already stepped in and taken over our lives. The floodgates were open, and there was no way to shut them.

Chapter 6

TALAMH LONRACH OLL was situated on thirty-five hundred acres, and the Triple Threat—as Camille had dubbed the three Fae queens before she took her place among them—were in the process of expanding the sovereign Fae nation again. They would be at their limit of five thousand acres then, and they were lobbying the government to increase that.

About half an hour from Seattle, to the northeast, the sovereign nation welcomed visitors of all backgrounds, but only Fae were allowed to live there unless they were connected to the community in some way. If someone married in from the outside, they were required to obtain a royal dispensation allowing them to move to the land, and that required background checks and a pledge to uphold Talamh Lonrach Oll above their former place of residence or affiliation.

The gardeners had worked overtime for several years now, using all of their magic to turn the woodland into a veritable fairyland. The trees had gone wild, shooting up faster than they had ever grown, and the foliage tumbled out in massive plumes and shoots and tendrils, creating a lush and opulent woodland. The plants of this land were awake, alert and ever watchful. They were used as guardians, working hand-in-hand with the Fae who made their homes here, and stray visitors did well not to disturb the plants or flowers, or try to harvest anything without permission.

The entrance to Talamh Lonrach Oll was guarded by a stone fence, with silver gates ten feet high that closed off the opening. Guards stood to either side when the gates were open, and at night, they guarded them from in front of the closed gates, when entrance was by permission only. There were ten guards, armed with bows, swords, and other weapons that we couldn't see. They were expert marksmen, and very few could stand up against them.

Camille's limousine entered first, the guards immediately forming straight lines, saluting as her car drove past. She must have told them we were with her, because they allowed the rest of us in without question.

We parked in the expansive parking lot as a string of carriages drove up, pulled by Friesians. The statuesque black horses were proud and haughty, with jeweled beads braided into their manes. The feathers on their hooves and heels were silky, combed and trimmed neatly, and they were the epitome of regal steeds. The carriages waited as we exited our cars, and the guards escorted us to them, where the footmen helped us in. They loaded Shade's body into a carriage of his own, where a healer waited to ride with him. Camille's carriage started off, and we followed.

As we clattered along the cobbled roadway, the foliage grew thick on either side, with ferns and huckleberry, brambles and blackberries, all spreading out. The berries were long gone, though, and the leaves were starting to shift color. Cedar, fir, and just about every other tree endemic to the Pacific Northwest lined the spacious paths. As we drew deeper into Talamh Lonrach Oll, I could feel the shift. For one thing, here in the sovereign Fae nation, electricity was off limits. Instead, they powered their nation via magic, and it made a drastic difference in the way the energy felt.

A hush fell around us. Oh, the hustle and bustle of a community was still intact, even during the night hours, but the feel was different without the buzz of power lines or the sounds of traffic. Everything felt a little more wild, a little less human, and as the eye catchers glittered to the sides of the road—shimmering orbs of light to guide the way—I realized that it felt like it did back in Otherworld.

We reached Camille's Barrow in about twenty minutes. The relatively slow pace of the horses combined with the cool night and the quiet serenity of Talamh Lonrach Oll served to calm my spirits, and by the time we pulled up in front of the palace, I realized I was breathing easier. I also realized I was absolutely exhausted. Camille was right. I didn't dare start the search for Shade tonight. I was too tired and I'd make mistakes that could be deadly.

Camille ordered the drivers to take us around through a back entrance, to avoid any crowds. As we wove through the labyrinth of the Barrow, Camille led us to a conference room. Servants were waiting, and they had assembled a light meal—a large terrine of a consommé, along with soft rolls fresh from the oven, and creamy golden cheese. They also brought fruit and pastries, none of it heavy, and we spent the next half hour eating and warming ourselves by the fireplace.

I was about to fall asleep in my chair when the door opened and Aeval and Titania entered, their expressions grave.

"The guards told us a little of what happened. Are you all right, Camille?"

Amongst the family, Aeval and Titania used casual names. They never required us to call them *Queen*, although in public we always did, to show our respect.

Camille nodded. "Yeah, luckily we didn't take heavy damage, except for Shade. And the house." She ran down what had happened, finishing with, "I want to send a group of contractors out there tomorrow to begin fixing the house, if you don't mind."

"Of course we don't mind," Aeval said. "This is your family, and therefore they're aligned with the court. If you weren't dedicated elsewhere, we would ask all of you to come live here." Her gaze fell on Maggie, who was snuggled in Hanna's arms.

It occurred to me that the Triple Threat had never really seen Maggie—we had kept her hidden from them for reasons that even we didn't understand. "Is that a woodland gargoyle?"

Camille shrugged. "I guess we've never told you about Maggie. I saved her life. She was doomed to be a harpy's lunch and I managed to snatch her away from the creature. We've been caring for her ever since. This was quite a while ago—at least four years."

Aeval glanced at Titania, who gave her a soft shake of the head. Turning back to Camille, Aeval asked, "Just how much do you know about woodland gargoyles?"

"Well, we found a book on their care and feeding. We don't know much except that it will be decades before she grows up, and we figured out what to feed her. Why?"

"It's just... They're extremely rare. It's a good thing you kept her under wraps and didn't tell anybody back in Otherworld because woodland gargoyles are prized for their pelts. I know it's barbaric, but you know how people can be. If I were you, I'd make sure that nobody in Otherworld ever knows you have her. What are you planning to do with her once Delilah and Shade marry?"

"Shade and I thought we would keep her with us. I don't know how viable that is, because I'm not sure yet what the Autumn Lord has in store for me."

"Well, she's always welcome here and shall always be protected. It would be dangerous for you to return her to the wild, in case you were thinking of that." Aeval glanced over at the food. "Is there anything else you need? I know that you can order it yourself, but you and your family must be exhausted."

Camille shook her head. "I think we're okay. I wanted to ask, although I already know the answer. If I wanted to go with Delilah into the Land of Wandering Souls—"

"No. Absolutely out of the question. Bluntly put, we will not allow you to go. You are the Queen of Dusk and Twilight, and while we accept your battle against the Demonkin and will help if we are able, this is not a journey that Titania and I can allow you to make. As the youngest Fae Queen here, you are subject to our decree, if only for your own safety."

Camille stared at Aeval, and I couldn't imagine what she was thinking. I knew my sister was used to taking orders from the Moon Mother, but that was her goddess. After a moment's silence, Camille stood.

"I gave my pledge to serve this Barrow as long as it did not interfere with the fight against Shadow Wing or with my pledge to the Moon Mother. I accept my duties." While she was calm and collected, she didn't look pleased.

Aeval gave her a gracious sweep of the head, then motioned to Titania. "Then we will take our leave. But anything that you or your family needs in the search for the soul of the shadow dragon, you have only to ask. We will do everything we can to help." And with that, she and Titania withdrew, followed by their guards.

"I begin to think that over the next thousand years I'm going to have days where it feels like I should never have accepted this crown." She turned to me. "If I *could* go with you..."

"I know you would. I knew back at the house that you wouldn't be allowed to go with me. We've already discussed this. Don't feel guilty about it. I have a feeling there will come a time when I have to do things that I don't want to do. And Menolly as well. This is what growing up means." I yawned, unable to help myself.

"I'll instruct the guards to take you to your rooms. You'll be safe—all of you. Sleep well, and we'll meet here for breakfast." Camille motioned to Jal, who quickly gathered several other guards to lead us to our chambers.

I wanted to sleep in the same room as Shade. I didn't want to sleep alone, and so the healers allowed me to stretch out on a bed next to his. They were monitoring him with some sort of equipment, although I knew it wasn't of human make, and I anxiously asked them how he was doing.

Perri, the head medic on the night shift, placed her hand on my shoulder. "He's functioning quite well, actually. We have the report of what happened from the FH-CSI. I wish there was a way we could help actually retrieve his soul, but we can provide backup. We're researching now what we can do to help you with the ritual you're performing tomorrow. We'll be watching over the four of you as you journey out to find him." She consulted a chart, looking slightly confused.

I nodded. "Just to clarify, his soul is trapped in

the Land of Wandering Souls. I'm a Death Maiden, and I'm going to journey there to find him. Three of my friends will be coming with me—a Svartan, a werepuma, and an incubus. I don't know if there's any special preparation you have to make given their species. Like my sister, I'm half human, half Fae. I am also a two-faced Were."

"I'm not certain, so I'll research it tonight. But this is all good information to have. It will allow us to know exactly how you're doing for your particular species. If I might ask, how did his soul get lost? I haven't had more than a chance to look over his chart yet." She motioned for me to sit on the bed, and handed me a nightgown. "I don't know if you came prepared for the night, but here's a bed gown in case you didn't bring anything of your own."

The gown was softer than my own, and felt warm and comfortable, so as I talked to Perri, I changed into it.

"He was stabbed by a soul-stealer sword." It was hard to keep the tears out of my throat, but I was so tired that I couldn't even cry at this point.

Perri must have noticed, because she handed me a small glass with a liquid in it that smelled like elderberry wine.

"This will calm your nerves and allow you to sleep deeply. It won't give you a hangover or cause any complications. We'll be guarding over you and your beloved during the night, so don't worry." She stood, closing the chart and hanging it at the bottom of Shade's bed. "I'll let you sleep now. We'll check in on both of you in a couple hours, but I don't expect anything to happen. Delilah," she added, pausing, "we love our Queen. We'll do everything we can for her, *and* her family. Please know that."

Reassured, I watched as she left the room, closing the door softly behind her. After I washed up in the bathroom and returned to my bed, I glanced over at Shade. He was so still that for a moment I was afraid he wasn't breathing. But then I saw the gentle rise and fall of his chest, and relief flooded through me. I kissed his lips. They were cool and unresponsive, but I could feel his breath as it slipped between them. I kissed his forehead.

"Tomorrow I'm coming to find you, my love. Please, hear me. Know that we're coming to find you, and bring you back home to your body. I love you. I've never loved *anyone* this way. You're my heart, Shade. Somehow, the Autumn Lord knew exactly who I needed in my life. Please come back."

Wiping my eyes, I crawled into the bed next to his, and pulled the covers up. I swallowed the drink the healer had given me, and within moments, I drifted off to sleep, my body relaxing as I fell into an uneasy haze of shadowy dreams, but nothing was clear, except the loss that I felt in my heart.

THE NEXT MORNING, I woke as she had promised, clearheaded and feeling rested. Perri told me that Shade was doing the same as he had been the night before, and she checked my vital signs before letting me head over to breakfast.

We all gathered in the conference room again, to a buffet of scrambled eggs, hard-boiled eggs, bacon, sliced ham, toast, pancakes, muffins and scones, fresh fruit and cheeses of all sorts, and plenty of coffee, which I had a feeling was a new addition to the meal offerings here.

Camille hadn't arrived yet, so I sat beside Menolly, who was drinking a bottle of flavored blood that Morio had made up for her.

"How are you doing this morning, Kitten?"

I shrugged. "Okay. Better than last night. Why aren't you in bed yet?"

"It's barely five in the morning. I'm surprised to see you so bright eyed this morning. I'll be heading off as soon as I'm done with breakfast here. I spent the night researching the Land of Wandering Souls, but there isn't much written about it. One thing I can tell you, though: Be careful about giving energy to your fears. It makes them real there."

I nodded, pouring maple syrup over my pancakes and bacon. "Yes, I know. The Autumn Lord warned me about that. I'm not sure how it all works, and the thought of leaving my body is a little frightening, but I'll do anything it takes to find Shade." I paused, then added, "Do you think Camille's happy?" I kept my voice low, not wanting the guards to hear me.

"I think she's as happy as can be," Menolly whispered back. "I think a lot of the stress will vanish once we take care of Shadow Wing. We're *all* tense. Hell, I'm not thrilled about having to live with

Roman, even though there's absolutely nothing wrong there. I'm just grateful that Nerissa is with me."

"Do you ever wish you hadn't met him?"

She thought for a moment, then shook her head. "No, not really. I mean, sometimes I fantasize about running away from it all. Grabbing Nerissa, and you and Shade, and Camille and her husbands and Maggie, and running back to Otherworld. But it's just a fantasy and I know it. These are just growing pains that we're all feeling. Every new situation requires some sort of adjustment. I just wish that the adjustments didn't all seem to show up at the same time."

I laughed, leaning my head against hers for a moment. "I fantasize about the same thing. I'm pretty sure Camille does, too. I think I've got it the easiest of all of you. I don't have to run a kingdom, I don't have to be the princess of vampires. I can go on my own way, as long as the Autumn Lord is happy with what I'm doing."

I paused, remembering that I had to fill her in on what had happened. "I need to tell you something before we head out to look for Shade today. Once he's back, after we get married, we'll be undergoing a ritual on Samhain. And then...it's time for me to get preggers with the Autumn Lord's child. He told me last month, before I went to Otherworld with Camille."

Menolly held my gaze for a long moment, a faint smile spreading over her face. "Well, *that's* going to be a change. I just hope we're done with Shadow Wing by then. I'd hate to see you pregnant and worrying about the war."

"Me too." I fell silent as Camille entered the room, followed by Smoky, Trillian, and Morio. It was hard to look anywhere else but at her, because she was in full regalia. She was wearing a princess ball gown that was a swirl of purple, blue, and black chiffon with an extremely low-cut sweetheart neckline. The skirt swept out like an old-fashioned hoop skirt, reminding me of galaxies sparkling against the night sky. The crown on her head was different than the one I was used to seeing—she always wore a simpler tiara when she came over to the house to visit since her coronation, but this one towered on her head, a sparkling jewel-encrusted headdress.

Menolly nudged me with her elbow. "That's a sight at five in the morning."

I gave her a shake of the head. "Good gods, if that's what she's required to wear most of the day out here no wonder she's so cranky. That crown alone looks like it weighs twenty pounds."

Camille gave me a long look. "You *do* know that I can hear you from over here?" But she laughed. "I'm dressed for court. I always hold open court after breakfast, and today is no exception."

"What's that mean?" I hadn't really thought about *what* she did out here.

"I make judgments, hand out punishments and give commendations, and basically do all the business that's expected of me." She paused, shifting her skirts as she sat down. "To be honest, there's a lot for me to do, and the formalities can be irritating, but they're a necessity. *This* is my job.

You think I'm cranky now, you should see me with some of the trivial crap in court."

As she took her place at the table, one of the servants took her order, then he consulted Smoky, Morio, and Trillian, and crossed to the buffet to fix their plates. The rest of us were expected to dish up our own.

"Perri instructed me to eat a hearty breakfast. You too, Trillian, Roz, and Nerissa. She said we'd need the fuel so that our bodies could sustain us as we travel through the Land of Wandering Souls." I wasn't complaining. Any instructions that led to a plateful of pancakes and bacon were good instructions. At least as far as I was concerned.

Nerissa delicately wiped her lips on a napkin. "When do we start? And is there anything else we need to bring?"

Perri had given me a set of instructions to pass around to the others. I handed them each a copy of the list. They weren't involved, and there weren't many, but they were explicit.

Eat a hearty breakfast. You will need to fuel. Don't drink alcohol, or take any medication other than anything you have been prescribed. Inform us if you are on any prescription medications. Wear warm, loose clothing. Don't wear anything binding, i.e.: bras, belts, shoes. Wear socks. Don't bring any electronics into the laboratory. Leave your cell phones in your rooms. Go to the bathroom before you come to the lab.

"Well, that's pretty forthright." Nerissa glanced

over the list. "Is there a safe place we can leave our jewelry? Like my wedding rings?" Nerissa wore two rings, one binding her to Menolly, the other to Roman.

Camille opened the tote she had carried in with her. A jarring juxtaposition in contrast with her outfit, it was covered with images of SpongeBob SquarePants.

I blinked, but said nothing.

"I'll keep them for you." Camille rummaged through the bag until she found a small coin purse. She handed it to Nerissa. "You can stow your rings in there, and anything else bigger can just go in my tote. This bag never leaves my side while I'm making my rounds. I'll entrust it to one of my guards when I'm done."

Nerissa placed her rings and a necklace in it. She handed it to me, and I added my ring that I wore that bound me to Shade, along with my earrings. Roz wasn't wearing much in terms of jewelry, and so he passed the coin purse along to Trillian, who added his wedding ring to Camille into the mix, along with a simple gold chain with a "T" on it. Camille fastened the purse and returned it to the bag, setting the tote on the ground beside her.

"Are you ready?" she asked. "I wish I could stay with you today. I'll come and visit as soon as I finish my duties for the morning. Did Perri say how long you'll be in...stasis, I suppose you'd call it?"

I shook my head. "She didn't say how long it would take. I don't even know if we can make an estimate. I suppose it depends on how long it takes to find Shade. I also have no clue if time runs differently in the Land of Wandering Souls. If the realm stands outside of time and space, we may be awake within minutes, even if it seems like it's been weeks to us. If not, then we might be out for several days or more."

There were so many variations that it seemed impossible to speculate. Even though Perri had reassured me that they would do everything they could to make certain we were comfortable and healthy during the time we were out in the Land of Wandering Souls, it was difficult not to worry. Mostly I worried that we might end up trapped.

Rozurial caught my attention. "Delilah, we're *going* to find him and return him to his body. Look at everything we've been through so far. Then just try to tell me that we can't manage this. You *know* we'll succeed."

"Thank you," I murmured, grateful for his reassurance.

Trillian popped the last bite of a muffin in his mouth. "With the connection you and Shade have, I imagine you'll know exactly what to do once we're there. I know the two of you aren't soul bound like Camille, Smoky, Morio, and I are, but you have your own bond through the Autumn Lord. Call on that. Use it for all you're worth."

His suggestion made sense, when I thought about it. While we hadn't been formally soul bound like Camille and her husbands, Shade and I were bound through the powers of an Elemental Lord. That had to count for something.

Feeling better, I finished my breakfast, adding one last waffle for the hell of it.

"I know Menolly's going to be sleeping throughout the day, and Camille has her work, but what will the rest of you do today?" I was still nervous, and small talk made me feel like things were back to normal.

"Well, while Camille is holding court, and Trillian is off with you, Morio and I thought we'd go out to the house and start looking at what it will take to rebuild it. Camille's going to send a team of construction workers with us, so hopefully, it won't take long before we have the house back in order for you." Smoky stood and stretched, his hair rising up behind him as it began to plait itself into one long, ankle-length braid.

Shade's hair moved too, but it was shorter, given he was only half dragon, and he never did much with it other than whisk it back into a ponytail. He and I really weren't into using it in sex play like Camille and Smoky did, especially after the one time I turned into Tabby and lunged for it, giving him a severe headache for a few hours, as well as a few scratches.

Vanzir flashed me a rueful grin. "Aeval has me taking parenting classes. I'm going to learn how to change diapers today." He rolled his eyes, but I detected a hint of pride in his voice.

Iris and Bruce were feeding the twins. "I'm going to be talking to some of the educators here, about school for the children."

Once again, my heart sank. "It's a long drive every day."

"As I mentioned, we're thinking of moving out here. For one thing, it's safer. For another, once the twins are old enough to go to school, it would give them the chance to study among other Fae." She gave me an apologetic shrug. "We love our house, and we'd like to keep it if you don't mind, but it would be so much easier if we were close enough for the children to walk to school every day, and then spend our weekends out on the land."

It occurred to me that I shouldn't be surprised. Everybody had been making plans to move on with their lives. It was the way of things. I gave her a nod. "That makes sense. And you, Hanna? What are you doing today?"

"I thought I might observe the pastry chef. These buns are delicious, and I wouldn't mind learning a few new recipes." She flashed me a smile, as if to say, *not all of us are running off*.

I was hoping I might see Chase, but he was apparently busy with the other Keraastar Knights. They had their own wing in the Barrow, and were under heavy guard, considering they bore all nine spirit seals within a relatively confined area.

Finally, we ran out of small talk. It was time to go. Part of me was impatient and wanted to get under way as soon as possible. And part of me was terrified. I wasn't sure if I was more afraid of the idea of getting stuck out in the Land of Wandering Souls, or of the possibility of not finding Shade. Silently, I gave Camille and Menolly a long hug. Nerissa did the same, kissing Menolly before she left. Trillian gave Camille a long kiss under the irritated eyes of the guards. PDAs weren't exactly acceptable behavior in the Barrows, but Camille didn't let that stop her.

Finally, we were ready. Waving to the others, we headed down the hall toward the laboratory, hopefully to find and rescue Shade.

Chapter 7

IN THE LABORATORY, we were each taken to a separate bed. We were dressed for traveling in warm, loose clothing. Perri had told us our clothes would translate to the appropriate gear once we made the shift over, including shoes instead of just socks, but it still seemed odd to see Nerissa with her hair pulled back beneath a brilliant blue bandana. She usually dressed for work—business casual—or for clubbing.

Shade was there, looking for all the world as though he were fast asleep.

Next to each of the beds, an IV stand stood, complete with bags full of pale pink liquid. I stared up at them, realizing that we were going to be jacked up to needles. I wasn't afraid of needles, but I hadn't expected this.

"Aren't you going to just keep an eye on us after I contact the Autumn Lord?" I glanced over at

Perri, who was consulting her notes.

She shook her head. "No. I found a recipe for a formula that will help the whole process. It's a mixture of magical herbs and compounds. We have to administer it through an IV drip because if we injected this much liquid into you at once, you'd bloat up like a balloon. It will work best if we introduce it into your system at a certain rate. Otherwise, the solution might propel you out farther than you really want to go. There are some realms that aren't safe to visit, out on the outer edges of the Ionyc Seas."

"Other than the herbs and compounds, what else is in here?" Nerissa poked at the bag, suspicious. "There's something about it that feels tingly when I get near it."

"This has some of the actual energy *from* the Ionyc Seas in it. We recently discovered a method to materialize it into the physical realm, then make a powder from it. This is going to be revolutionary for teleportation spells and the like." Perri sounded excited, her eyes were bright. I realized that a lot of the Fae and Elfin healers were actually scientists as well. It had never occurred to me before that they might actually try experiments to establish new procedures rather than simply relying on age-old remedies. I wasn't sure why it seemed like such a surprise, but it did.

"You guys really are cutting edge, aren't you?" The words slipped out before I realized that I had said them aloud. I blushed.

"Actually, we are. We've done a lot of consulting with the Elfin techno-mages, and have formed a new society—Healers for the Future." She motioned to a door against the back of the wall. "If you need to use the restroom, please do so now."

"What happens if we have to go to the bathroom while we're under?" Roz asked, only half joking.

"We'll take care of matters if you do. We have ways of tracking the bodily functions, so no worries there. If you need water, we'll hydrate you. If you need food, we'll add a nutritional formula to your IV drip. If your body temperature drops, we'll warm you up, and so on. You'll feel hunger and cold and heat while out on the other realm, but we'll be handling those issues for your bodies here. Any other questions before we begin?" She looked at each of us in turn.

"We have to carry our talismans on our body that the Autumn Lord gave me. That's a must." I held up the charm. I had given each of the others their talismans as soon as we entered the laboratory.

"That's fine. Just place them in your pocket. When you need them, you'll find them in your pockets out there and you'll be able to use them. But you need to remember where you put them—otherwise, you may think that you've lost them and we won't be able to help you." Perri motioned to each bed in turn, checking off our names. "Rozurial, please take the bed on the end. Nerissa, the next. Trillian, the third, and Delilah—you take the last."

"The Autumn Lord said he'll show up and help transport us once we're ready and I summon him," I said. "As soon as I'm in bed, I'll touch the tattoo on my forehead that links me to him, and he should arrive. I'm just warning you all in advance. You know who he is, so please don't antagonize him." On one level, I didn't think I had to ask. On the other hand, given Roz and Trillian's natures, it seemed reasonable to remind them.

"We've got your back," Trillian said. "I'll be on my best behavior."

"What about weapons? We're supposed to take them with us."

We had brought our daggers with us, although Roz wasn't allowed to bring his coat-slash-armory that he usually wore. Instead, he had chosen a sturdy short sword that looked so old that I wondered how long he had had it. He seldom fought with a blade, but it looked comfortable in his hand, and it made me wonder.

"I don't think I've seen that before." I settled on the bed Perri had assigned to me. The mattress was comfortable and firm but not so hard that it would give me bruises. I settled back against the headboard, holding my dagger on my lap.

Perri examined each of our weapons. "These will be fine. When you lie down, place them to your side on the bed, as though you could reach down and grasp it. We don't want your hands clasped around them because it will cause muscle cramps if you're in stasis too long."

As we stretched out, a twinge of fear raced through me. I wished my sisters could come along. We had faced so many dangers together, everything from demons to vampires to gods. Visiting other realms was always tricky, even without the possibility of finding yourself trapped. You never knew quite what to expect.

When we were all ready, Perri motioned to me.

"All right. You can summon him. We're ready, but we can't insert the IVs until he begins the ritual. We don't want to put you under before then."

With my left hand, I reached up and brushed the black crescent scythe on my forehead, closing my eyes as I called out for the Autumn Lord. A shiver ricocheted through me as I sensed he had heard me. And then we waited.

One beat... Two beats... Three...

A gust of wind raced through the laboratory, carrying with it the scent of crackling bonfires and ripe apples and yeasty cinnamon rolls on a cool, chill night. The walls of the room seemed to reverberate, like water in a glass that was trembling. A mist rose up, rolling along the floor of the room, and then the Autumn Lord stood there, his dark glory filling the room.

Trillian gasped, along with Rozurial. Nerissa sucked in a deep breath of air—so loud I could hear her from my bed. I started to sit up, but the tech standing next to my bed held me down.

"You are ready?" Hi'ran didn't address any of the others, but looked straight at me. His words echoed through the room.

"Yes, we're ready. They're going to inject us with a compound of herbs and potions to help us transfer over. Will that interfere with the ritual?"

Hi'ran shook his head, a faint smile on his face. "No, it will actually help. I'm glad they're keeping tabs on your bodies." He turned to Perri. "You may begin the injections. As soon as they're ready, I will shift the worlds so they move into the Land of Wandering Souls. I cannot bring them back, however." He looked at the others at that point. "You are all aware of this, are you not? You must give me your permission. I will not send you out there if you do not want to go." Hi'ran was deadly serious.

Nerissa was first to speak. "I'm still willing to go."

Trillian and Rozurial joined in, each pledging their own assent.

"Then close your eyes. I will open the gate. When you see the mist and hear me say 'Jump,' jump. I hope to see you back here, along with Shade. Good luck, and may the blessings of the gods go with you." He turned to me. "Delilah, remember: you are my only living Death Maiden. You are to be the mother of my child. Return to me."

As the healers began to insert our IVs, the Autumn Lord began to chant in a voice so low I couldn't catch the words. But the tone was resonant, hypnotic and mesmerizing. I closed my eyes and felt the twinge of the needle go into my arm. It hurt for a second, stinging as though I had been pricked by a bee. Then a delicious flow of warmth began to flood my body as a mist rose up in my mind. I no longer felt the bed beneath me but merely the floor beneath my feet, as mist roiled past. I turned and saw Nerissa, and Trillian, and Rozurial standing there.

The Autumn Lord's voice echoed throughout

whatever chamber we were in, the words so old, so ancient that they meant nothing and yet they meant everything. Like a trail of sparkles, they were magic incarnate, caught into sound bites, waves that rang through me with every word that he uttered. The next moment, he thundered, "Jump!"

And we jumped—all of us—as a door opened in the mist.

I TUMBLED TO the ground, shaking my head as I pushed myself to my hands and knees. I looked around, and saw the others beside me. A glance over my shoulder told me that the door no longer was there.

Panicked, I felt for my dagger and found it at my side, in its sheath where it should be. I touched my pocket and the talisman resonated from within, comforting, a promise to help me find my way home. As I stood up, I noticed the others were doing the same.

"Are we really here?" Nerissa glanced around, a look of bewilderment on her face. "I'd *swear* we were here in body."

"We are, for all intents and purposes." I glanced around, trying to get a sense of our whereabouts.

The landscape was oddly familiar, and yet different enough that it took on an alien feel. We were on a rocky hill, near a path that led down into a thickly wooded valley. I glanced back at the hill where the door should be. The mountain rose up behind me so far that I couldn't see the top. The precipice was cloaked in mist and clouds and it looked as though a storm was raging.

To the left of where we stood was another hill, much smaller with a rocky incline, up to what looked like a mesa. To our right was a dropoff into the valley, a steep slope of grassland leading down into the woodland below. A narrow path edged alongside the hill overlooking the valley, so steep that it made me dizzy. Straight ahead, the path wound around an outcropping on the mountain, looking as though it curved back some three or four hundred yards later.

I squinted into the distance. The sky was a silvery gray, but it seemed to be daylight. In fact, it reminded me of around 3:00 P.M. on a cloudy autumn afternoon in Seattle.

The mountain behind us loomed so large that there was no way around it. We stood at the beginning of the path. If we wanted to go in that direction, we would have to climb over the mountain itself.

Where we stood, the ground offered sparse vegetation, some straggling grasses and a few scrub brushes. But in the valley below, the grass was thick, looking almost like moss. From here it was almost impossible to tell whether the woodland was deciduous or coniferous. The soil itself was a deep ruddy red, the color of rust, although it seemed to fade into a russet brown below the grass in the valley.

In the valley, a river churned along. It looked as

though it wended through the woodland, and was so wide that I had my doubts whether we could cross on foot.

"Well, where do we go from here?" Trillian looked around, shading his eyes. "I'd rather not have to go over the mountain behind us if we can avoid it."

I realized they were waiting to take their cue from me.

I walked over to a large boulder and sat down, surprised that it felt so sturdy. I glanced around, wondering if Shade had been propelled into this realm through the same doorway we had been. Closing my eyes, I reached out, trying to get some sense of where he might be. I searched for his energy, reaching out for the familiar touch of his skin, scent of his body, feeling of safety when I was around him. Something inside stirred. Panther raised her head, wanting free. Nerissa jerked around, staring at me.

"Let her free. I can feel her from here. I think she knows what to do more than you do." Nerissa's voice was throaty, and I could feel her puma rising to meet my panther.

"You're right. I'll bet you can interpret for me when I'm in Panther form." I caught her gaze and she grinned.

"Big cats of the world, unite."

I stood back, summoning Panther as I let her off the leash. As I began to transform, my clothes morphed into the beautiful emerald collar I wore as Panther. My limbs welcomed the shift as they stretched and altered. It felt as though *here*, Panther belonged where I did not. A few moments later, I stood there on all fours, luxuriating in the feel of my skin and bones and muscle. Every sense seemed heightened, every noise louder.

I let out a low rumble as Nerissa stroked my back. I could sense the puma in her responding to me, and it took all the focus I had to bring myself back to my task at hand. I wanted nothing more than to encourage her to shift and then to run off and race through the mountains together, feeling the wind in our faces as we leapt from rock to rock.

"I know, I can feel it too—but I can't change right now. We're here to find Shade." Nerissa's voice was soft, soothing in a way that I didn't usually find people's voices, and she brought me back to why we were here.

I cast around, trying to pick up the scent. And there, faint but still detectable, I smelled a familiar odor. It was the smell Shade had when he was nervous. I sniffed again, inhaling deeply to fill my lungs with the scent. I could taste it on the back of my tongue, and I looked up at Nerissa, my mouth open with my tongue rolling out, as I let out a chuffing sound.

"Did you find something?" she asked.

I bobbed my head up and down, nosing at the ground where I could smell him. I slowly began to follow the odor, one step at a time, to make sure I didn't lose it. We were headed along the pathway that wound around the mountain. Part of me wanted to go lolling off into the grassland below because it looked softer and easier, but I forced myself to keep on track.

The path was about six feet wide before dropping off into the steep slope of grassland, and there were numerous stones and twigs along the compacted dirt trail. But it was relatively level, and if you watched your footing, it didn't seem all that dangerous. Nerissa was walking behind me, with Trillian and Roz behind her. A gust of wind railed against us, and I noticed it was blowing away the clouds, leaving a faint slick of pale blue sky in its wake.

We were about sixty yards along the trail when the scent suddenly vanished.

I stopped, looking back at Nerissa, who held up her hand to Roz and Trillian. While they waited, I took a few steps forward, but I couldn't pick it up anywhere. I cautiously approached the edge of the trail, glancing over into the grassland below. In my four-legged form, it didn't seem nearly so steep, and I sniffed at the edge of the grass, searching to see if I could pick it up again anywhere along the bluff. A moment later, I caught a faint whiff, this time about three yards down the slope. I looked back and let out another chuff.

Nerissa gave me a nod, and turned to the others. "I think she's picked up the scent again. It looks like we're going to have to go down into the valley. That's a steep decline, so be careful." She paused, then laughed. "I forgot, we aren't here in our actual bodies."

"We may not be here in body, but that doesn't mean we can't take damage." Trillian gave us a look that told us he was well aware of how dangerous this mission was. "Try to be careful. If you get hurt, it means that your body will take damage. In other words, if you stub your toe while we're here, chances are you're going to have a bruised toe when you get back to your body. And if you get attacked, you'll suffer damage in the outer world."

Roz let out a sound, but I wasn't sure what he had said and I didn't pay much attention. I was too busy searching again for Shade's scent in the grass. It was harder to track here on the slope, but I was relieved to get off that path. I wasn't sure why, but the trail had made me nervous, as though we were headed toward danger. There weren't any smells that seemed alien, and there was nothing I could see off the bat. But I had the feeling that danger lurked in those mountains.

The hill leading down to the woodland was extremely steep, but the grass was dry and it wasn't that difficult to keep our footing. Especially for me, given I was in my Panther shape. I reined myself in from running full tilt down the mountain, focusing on tracking the scent and following the trail. It was leading to the river, to the place just before it entered the forest, and I hoped to find some evidence that Shade had been there. His scent was clear in my mind, but there was part of me that wanted some tangible proof, some sign that I wasn't imagining things.

Overhead, a loud shriek cut through the air and I looked up to see a massive eagle passing by. At least I thought it was an eagle. It appeared to have a ten-foot wingspan, and for a moment I was afraid. Maybe it couldn't carry me off, but those talons could do some serious damage.

"Crap," Roz said. "That's one hell of a big eagle."

"There are some that big back over Earthside, and in Otherworld there are larger still. But you're right, it's impressive and it could be a deadly foe if it decides it's hungry." Trillian scanned the sky, watching as the eagle flew off to what I assumed was the east. I actually couldn't figure out what the directions were, so I arbitrarily decided north was behind us, up the mountain into the clouds. Which meant we were headed southwest into the valley.

"It's looking for something," Nerissa said. "I recognize the posture. It saw us, but we weren't its prey, so it left us alone." She shivered, and I could smell the faint aroma of fear wafting off of her. I could also smell Menolly mingled in with her scent, and if I had been in my two-legged form, I would have blushed as I realized they must have had sex that morning.

I picked up Shade's scent again, and once more, continued the descent into the valley. It was still faint, but at least it was present and by now I was convinced that I actually *did* smell him in the grass. I had some pretty vivid daydreams, but even *I* didn't have enough imagination to conjure up someone's perfume.

The descent was longer than it looked, and I estimated it took us about half an hour to reach the valley below. As I gazed back up the slope, it looked almost impossible to climb, and I was surprised that we had made it without incident. I had neither seen nor heard any other animals on the way down, except for the eagle. It almost felt like we were alone in the universe but I knew that couldn't be the case. My gut told me things would change once we reached the forest.

As we approached the river, I began to notice wildflowers dotting the lea. They looked like violets, except they were bright red, and other flowers that reminded me of lavender spiked up through the tall patches of grass. Though faintly blue, they didn't smell like lavender, but looked very much like the dusky plant. I was cautious to avoid pressing my nose against them. I knew very well that back Earthside, foxglove could cause heart palpitations if you inhaled much of the pollen. We had no clue what these flowers were, or what they could do, so it was best to be on the safe side.

The roar of the river grew louder as we approached the shore, and I saw now that it was even wider than I had thought. At least thirty yards wide, white caps flowed atop it, a vision of foam and froth. The current raged along, so swift that I could easily imagine being knocked off my paws if I stepped into it. I shuddered, watching the untamed rapids that roared by.

"I'm thirsty," Trillian said suddenly. He slowly approached the water, kneeling by the edge where it was spraying against the shore. He glanced back at us. "Do you think I should chance it?"

Nerissa shrugged. "I don't know, but we don't have another option, do we? I'm sure that they are going to hydrate our bodies, but... Will they know we're thirsty if we don't drink?"

"I'm going to take the risk." Trillian scooped up a handful of the water and slipped it. He shivered. "It's icy, but good. It tastes cleaner than any water

I've had in a long time."

I padded up beside him, lowering my head to lap at the waves that churned along. He was right. The water *was* clear, and tasted remarkably good as it rolled down my throat. Part of me wondered if we were seeing the river because they were giving us water back in the laboratory, but then I decided that no, this really was a different realm and we weren't creating it with our minds. If we could take damage here, we could drink the water.

We rested for a few minutes while I prowled around, searching for Shade's scent. Finally, I picked it up, heading directly toward the forest. I turned back to my companions and let out a low growl.

Nerissa stood, stretching. "Caught the scent again, did you?"

I gave her a bob of the head. Then I turned and slowly began to traverse toward the forest. Nerissa walked by my side, while Trillian and Roz followed behind us. We weren't far from the treeline when the river disappeared into the thick tangle.

I looked for a pathway in. Finally, Nerissa pointed to a trailhead that I had somehow missed. "There, that has to be the trail. Can you smell Shade? Did he take the path?"

I cast about, smelling for him. Finally, a few moments later, I moved onto the trail, following the faint odor. The others scrambled to keep up. As we entered the forest, the sunlight receded, kept at bay by the tangle of foliage twining in the canopy above.

The trail itself was spacious, wide and unmarred

by more than small patches of grass or a hand-sized pebble here and there. The trees looked familiar, a mix of deciduous and coniferous, but not quite any that I could identify immediately. One smelled like cedar, but didn't quite look like it. Another looked like a giant oak, but the leaves scattered below it on the ground were an odd shape, and I didn't get that sense of ancient foundation that oaks usually had. Again, everything felt familiar, yet *not quite the same.*

The sound of the river roared through the trees, and the undergrowth was thin enough that we could see the shimmer of the waves in the distance, about fifty yards away from the trail. I had hoped that the trail would be parallel to the river, right next to it, but instead, the swath of trees that created an island between the path and the water kept us just far enough away so we couldn't actively see what was going on. I wasn't sure why this bothered me so much, but it did, and I felt uneasy, like we were under observation of some sort.

Part of me wanted to change back into my two-legged form, but it would be harder to track Shade's scent that way. So I continued on in my panther form, snuffling at the ground, searching out the direction in which he had gone.

"This forest makes me uneasy," Roz said, voicing my own thoughts.

"I know. It doesn't seem like it should," Nerissa said. "But I'm finding myself uncomfortable as well. I feel like we're being watched. Delilah, can you sense anything?"

I paused, glancing up at her before closing my

eyes and trying to drift into the energy that surrounded me. First there was the energy of the trees, and they were watchful, but neutral. I didn't sense any danger from them as long as we kept to ourselves and didn't try to harm them. The water, though, felt mesmerizing, and I realized that the reason I wanted to walk beside it was because I was being urged to its side. Naiads, perhaps? Or undines? Or river sirens, maybe? Or perhaps even a kelpie, or a púca? Whatever it was, something was urging me toward the water.

I had to let them know, and this wasn't something that I could explain to Nerissa while she was in human form and I was Panther. I moved aside. As I transferred back into human shape, taking my time so it wouldn't hurt, I felt a dizzying sense of disorientation. The world looked far different than when I had been in panther shape.

As soon as I could talk, I nodded to the river. "The water—there's something enchanted about it. Or there's someone who's enchanting it. All I can tell you is that I'm feeling drawn to its side, and that's a scary thought, given all the creatures that can cast charms."

"Elder Fae, perhaps?" Trillian asked.

"I hadn't even thought of that. But can the Elder Fae enter this realm? Why would they even be here?" The idea of the Elder Fae making their home in the Land of Wandering Souls seemed almost ridiculous. Yet I couldn't think of a good reason why they wouldn't. Especially the ones who searched for human victims, or those who fed off of life energy.

"They probably can—the Elder Fae seem to be everywhere. What do you think it might be?" Trillian asked.

"I'm not sure. At first I thought maybe púca or a naiad, or even a kelpie. But now I'm not so sure." And then, before I could say another word, there was a rustle from a thick stand of brambles near us.

A large creature careened out, teeth gnashing, eyes bulging. It reminded me of Yannie Fin Diver—one of the Elder Fae I had fought with Camille—only this one was much, much bigger.

Chapter 8

"**FUCK!**" TRILLIAN UNSHEATHED blade, jumping back. He was closest to the creature and it almost sideswiped him as it lunged toward us.

I drew Lysanthra, grateful that we had brought our weapons.

Whatever it was we were facing, it was butt-ugly and massive. It stood at least eight feet tall, and while it was bipedal, it was by no means human in any shape, way, or form. Its thighs were tremendous and thick, as were its arms, but its torso was almost nonexistent.

It looked as though someone had taken a bodybuilder or power lifter and cut them off right under the boobs, piecing their top right onto their hips, just above the leg joints. Right then, I noticed that it was definitely male—the loincloth didn't cover up enough to hide his junk.

His body might be frightening, but his head was

worse. Bulbous and grotesque, his head contained a single eye in the center. His mouth was long and narrow, filled with teeth that resembled needle-shaped bones. He had no hair on his head, and he stank to high heaven.

His head was at least three times larger than it should be, and that one roving eye gazed down at us with a hungry, cunning look. The creature carried a massive club in one hand, and the other was dripping with blood, no doubt from his last victim.

"Watch out for that club, it's got spikes on it!" Roz jumped to the side as the creature took a swing at him. He pulled out his dagger, and with his other hand, he retrieved something else out of his pocket. At first I thought he had grabbed his talisman, but then I saw that it looked like a ping-pong ball or a golf ball. A bomb. Roz had brought some of his bombs!

The creature raised his club and swung it across in front of him, and we all jumped back to avoid being hit. The club reminded me very much of an Alley-Oop version of a caveman club.

"I think it's some sort of cyclops," Trillian said. "And they don't claim friendship with *anybody*. They're carnivorous as well—and I think, cannibalistic."

Wonderful. Not only did we have a big lug aiming for us, but he was looking for dinner. I stopped thinking and started running as he took off after me, flailing his club over his head.

"I'm not sure what to do with this thing!" In fact, the only thing I was sure of was that I didn't want to come in contact with that club when it came swinging for me.

I heard a thud, and then a grunt, but I didn't turn around to see what was going on. Instead, I headed for a tree that had limbs low enough and big enough for me to catch hold of. I swung myself up and began to climb as quickly as I could.

I scrambled up the tree, hurrying as fast as I could, until I finally reached a point where I felt safe to look back down. Sure enough, the cyclops was at the base of the tree, staring up at me with a disgusted look on his face. After a moment, he turned around and lumbered off toward the others.

I wasn't sure what I could do, so I kept my place in the treetop as I tried to think of what would be the best way to kill something this massive. I doubted if my dagger would do much damage unless I was able to pierce him directly in one of his vital organs, but given he didn't have a torso, I had no clue where his heart was, or anything else, for that matter. I supposed getting him in the eye would do, but that meant coming face-to-face with him, and I wanted to save that for a last resort.

As I watched from the treetop, I saw that Nerissa had the same idea. She had taken the opportunity when the cyclops was chasing me to find a tree of her own to scramble up into. At that moment, it occurred to me that, in my panther shape, I could probably tackle him better. I had more natural weapons in that form. I found a crotch in the tree I could nestle down in to change shape.

Trillian and Roz were trying to keep him occupied. Trillian had removed something from his pocket and he sent it sailing toward the back of the cyclops. I realized he had also brought shooting stars, and he was an exceptionally good aim. The star lodged itself directly in the nape of the cyclops's neck.

The creature let out a roar and swiped at the back of his neck, knocking the star out. A fountain of blood shot out. Roz kept his stars razor-sharp. He shouted for Trillian to get out of the way as he threw his bomb toward the creature. There was a loud explosion and my tree rocked slightly as the cyclops was knocked off his feet. He didn't look dead, but at least he was down.

By now I was in panther form and I leapt out of the tree, racing over to the side of the creature. Nerissa joined me, in puma form. By the time we reached the side of the cyclops, he was trying to push himself up, but he looked woozy, and blood dripped down from his eye.

Even though the thought made me queasy, I leapt for his face, snapping. I managed to catch hold of his nose and bit hard, pulling away. The tip of his nose came off in my mouth and I spat out the fleshy mass. Blood poured from his face and a jubilant triumph ran through me. I always enjoyed tearing into my prey when I was in panther form.

Nerissa took her turn, going for his face as well. She managed to catch hold of his cheek and ripped aside some of the flesh, exposing bone and muscle below.

The cyclops shrieked, pushing himself to his feet again. Apparently losing his nose and part of his cheek wasn't enough to do him in. He grabbed up his club, aiming for me as he swept it around. I jumped, leaping over it as it swept beneath my feet. My paws hit the ground again, but he was bringing it back around and this time the club made contact with my ribs, sending me skidding across the ground. I let out a loud roar as I rolled to a sitting position, trying to ascertain whether I was injured.

While the cyclops was focused on me, Nerissa leapt for him again, landing on his back as she bit into his neck and hung on. He dropped the club, flailing as he tried to dislodge her, but at that moment, Trillian and Roz came racing from behind, landing against him hard. Together, the three of them took him down. He toppled over face-first on the trail.

I painfully rolled to my feet. Nothing felt broken, although I was going to have some lovely bruises, so I jogged back over to their side. Trillian was in the process of slamming his blade down through the skull of the cyclops. Roz did the same.

Nerissa let go of the creature, ripping away another patch of flesh, this time exposing the back of his neck. The cyclops was bleeding like crazy, and this time he didn't stand up. He let out another grunt, and then, pinned to the ground by both of their swords, grew still.

Another moment passed and we realized we had managed to kill him.

Feeling slightly queasy, I padded to the side and took a bite of grass, then slowly began to shift back into my two-legged form. By the time I stumbled to my feet, Nerissa had transformed as well. We stood there staring at the body for a moment. Overhead, the sunlight began to wane, fading as sunset approached.

"Well, that was...exciting." I shivered, my muscles telling me they weren't all that thrilled. In fact, I hurt like a son of a bitch.

"Are you all right?" Trillian gave me a worried look. "I saw him hit you with that club and it looked like it bounced off your ribs pretty bad."

"If I hadn't been in panther form, I'd probably have broken ribs, but as it is, I'm just going to have some nasty bruises. I can also tell you this, though. Cyclops don't taste very good."

A nasty flavor, like raw liver, filled my mouth. I looked around for something to take away the musky flavor. One of the brambles looked a lot like a blackberry plant, and I decided to give it a chance. I swallowed three of the berries and nothing happened, so I ate a few more.

Meanwhile, Roz and Trillian were examining the dead cyclops. They rolled him over. He was really, truly dead. I grimaced when I saw that Trillian's sword had skewered the cyclops's eye from the back. Roz and Trillian wiped off their blades in the grass, looking as queasy as I felt.

"The Autumn Lord warned me that our worst fears could take form here, but I don't think I've ever thought about fighting a cyclops before." As I stared at the prone figure, I half expected him to vanish. But he stayed there, in a spreading pool of blood.

"I don't think that our fears are the *only* creatures that inhabit this world," Nerissa said, shivering. "Consider this. You said the Autumn Lord wasn't allowed to enter this realm, so the only thing he knows about it is from hearsay. The Elemental Lords may be immortal, but that doesn't make them omniscient."

She had a point. I cast my gaze around, scanning the forest around us.

"True. In that case, we need to be doubly on guard. Come to think of it, I'm not really afraid of eagles either, nor do I think about them that much. What about the rest of you?"

Roz shook his head. "No giant eagle or cyclops lurking in my anxiety closet. Well, at least not before we tackled this dude. Now, maybe just a little. I'd rather not fight another one. They're mean suckers."

The forest suddenly felt like it had grown denser somehow. As the sunlight began to recede, and early evening made itself known, an unease filtered through the air, making me twitchy. The sound of rustling in the undergrowth grew louder as the night creatures came out to play. The steady drone of mosquitoes and the sound of crickets announced sunset, and a dragonfly of sorts—although it was brilliant fuchsia rather than blue—darted past, hovered in front of me, and then vanished into the woods.

"Do you feel like something just opened up?" Nerissa asked. "It's almost as though the cyclops set off something. I felt like we were in a vacuum before he appeared, and now it feels like we're firmly ensconced here. Does that make any sense?"

"Perfect sense," Trillian said. "I'm feeling the

same thing. I don't know what happened, but I feel like now, we're actually here, and it's *not* a comforting thought."

"It's almost like someone held out a clapper board and yelled 'Action' and then everything started to happen." I realized I was holding my breath, and deliberately exhaled in a slow, easy manner to relax myself.

"Exactly. I suppose we should just get on with things. However, it looks like we're going to be spending the night here, and I'd like to find some sort of cover before long." Trillian chewed on the side of his lip, then added, "I guess we didn't think about things like tents or raingear or food. I didn't think it would be like this here. I guess I thought it would be more... Like when we were on the astral—a giant field of mist."

I nodded, wondering if we had made a hasty decision. We had no food. Would we starve? Even though Perri had promised that they would feed us if they noticed us getting hungry, and hydrate us if they noticed that we needed water, it didn't seem to translate over to the way we felt here. I had been thirsty, so I drank. But my thirst hadn't caused the river to appear.

"I'll see if I can pick up Shade's scent again. The cyclops disrupted my focus." I stood back and once again shifted into my panther form. It was a little disorienting. It wasn't that I didn't change shape very often, but more that I usually didn't keep switching back and forth between the two. I realized that the constant morphing was making me feel queasy. I might feel better if I could find something to eat. I moved away from the cyclops's body, down the trail so that I wouldn't keep smelling the scent of his blood. As I began snuffling around, searching the ground for any food that might be familiar, daylight began to fade rapidly as dusk overtook the forest.

As I was hunting, a thought struck me. What if the cyclops had been one of the wandering souls? What if he had been lost here? In destroying his soul, had we just forever destroyed his chance to get back to his body? Overwhelmed by the potential ramifications of what it meant to journey through this realm, I sat down, panting slowly as I stared at the ground.

Nerissa knelt beside me, stroking my head. "Are you all right, Delilah?"

I glanced up at her, staring into her warm topaz eyes. She was an extraordinary woman, and I was grateful that she had fallen in love with my sister. Menolly needed somebody who could be both strong and gentle at the same time. I reached out to lick her hand with a slobbery tongue and stood, returning to the hunt for Shade. A few moments later, I caught hold of his scent again, about twenty yards ahead on the trail. I turned back to the others, letting out a chuff. As I started down the trail again, they caught up to me.

Roz had apparently remembered to tuck a flashlight into his pocket. Even though we weren't into full darkness yet, he flicked it on to direct light on the pathway ahead of me.

He turned it off, saying, "Okay, that works. At least we'll have light when the night drops."

"You thought of just about everything, don't you?" Trillian said with a laugh. "You didn't think to sneak along any more of your armory, I suppose?"

"They wouldn't let me," Roz said.

"I've always meant to ask you about that," Nerissa said. "When did you start playing the Matrix? I always think of some deranged weapons flasher when you open your coat."

Roz usually wore a long duster, with a veritable smorgasbord of weapons on the inside. It can't have been comfortable, but he seemed to enjoy being a walking armory.

"Back in Otherworld, when I was hunting for Dredge, I realized I'd need more than just an itty-bitty stake to take him out. For one thing, he surrounded himself with goons from all walks of life, not just vampires. So I prepared. I gathered every weapon that I could conveniently hook on the inside of my duster, so I'd have whatever I needed at fingertip's reach. It got to be a habit. Now I feel naked without it." He grinned, his eyes sparkling. "Even though Menolly finally took him out, it's remained a force of habit. And as we've learned over the past few years, there are bigger and badder creatures out there than Dredge. Unfortunately, we've encountered a number of them."

Nerissa pressed her lips together, giving him a single nod. I knew she was thinking about Dredge, and what he had done to my sister. No matter how much water had flowed under the bridge, and no matter how much progress she had made, thanks to that monster Menolly would always be a vampire, and always carry the trauma and scars he had inflicted on her.

We fell silent as we worked our way deeper into the woodland. The undergrowth was growing thicker on both sides, and I wondered how broad this forest was. There was no way of telling, but at least we could still hear the river some fifty yards to our right. I could still feel a pull toward it, and realized there had to be some sort of sprites or water Fae over there. Most of them were deadly, unfortunately.

Shade had definitely come this way. His scent was thick in the undergrowth.

All of a sudden, I wondered how long we had been here. The sun had been out when we arrived, but now it was almost set. How long had we been here in the outer world? In fact, when I looked behind us, the trail seemed misty, almost as though it were cloaked in gray fog. For a moment I began to panic as the thought crossed my mind that the forest behind us was disappearing. I realized I had to get out of my head, so I stopped and moved off the path, transforming back into my two-legged self.

"Are you all right?" Trillian hurried over to my side. While he was a caring man, the Svartan wasn't usually quite so attentive.

"Yeah, I was just starting to imagine things. You're unusually considerate today," I said with a smile. We all knew that Trillian wasn't one to stand on niceties. Oh, he did care; it wasn't that he was insensitive. But he definitely wasn't a gentleman either, at least not when it came to calling people on their bullshit.

"Camille told me she'd have my head if anything happened to you. And obviously, I want my wife to be happy. Besides, you know we all care, Kitten."

He seldom called me by my nickname, and it made me smile. He had come a long way from the brash, arrogant, self-centered jerk that he had been the first time I had met him. In fact, when Camille had started dating him back in Otherworld, shortly before Menolly had been turned, it'd taken her a while to introduce him to the family. For one thing, our father was prejudiced. He hated Svartans with a passion. For another, she knew we wouldn't like him.

But that too was a massive amount of water under the bridge.

"Of course she did. I appreciate the concern, though. No, I just noticed the trail behind us was getting misty, and for a moment it felt like it was vanishing."

Trillian glanced over his shoulder, staring at it for a moment. "It does kind of look like that, doesn't it? But I think it's just the way the fog is rolling in."

"I can smell that Shade has been through here. And I don't think it's been too long. It's very heavy, and concentrated off into the undergrowth. I'm hesitant to continue going, though, given how close to nightfall we are. For one thing, it would be easy to miss something—like if he's hurt." Even as I spoke I realized that it sounded odd, because his body was back in the lab. But from what we'd seen, so far, there were a million ways to get hurt here.

"Do you want to break for the evening?" Roz

asked, glancing around. "If so, I suggest we make camp near the river. We're going to need water, and there should be some open ground that we can actually stretch out on. The undergrowth here may not be as thick as it is at home, but it's still a tangle and I think it would hurt sleeping on a pile of brambles." He eyed the verdant foliage suspiciously. "I know you ate a few berries earlier, but it seems to me that it might be a fool's game to try many of the plants here. We might be able to catch fish. I'd trust that more than eating the vegetation."

"What do you think?" I turned to Nerissa and Trillian. I really didn't want to camp by the river, but I wasn't sure if I trusted my own instincts at this point. I'd go with the majority.

Trillian and Nerissa agreed with Roz, so we made our way through the undergrowth over to the riverside. Just as Roz had predicted, there was an open space where we could stretch out on the ground. I thought about trying to light a fire. It was growing cooler by the moment.

"What do you think about a fire?"

"It will give away our position, but then again, it might keep some of the wild creatures at bay. And if Shade's around, he might see it and come over to find out what's going on." Trillian pointed at some of the round smooth rocks that the river had worn down. They were about the size of my fist. "We can use river rocks to surround the fire so it doesn't get out of hand."

"Nope," Roz said. "River rocks have a way of exploding when heated. I suggest that we find a few good-size rocks from inside the forest instead. Don't pick ones that look like they were weathered by the water."

"If we're going to make a fire," I said, "we're going to need kindling and wood. And somebody's going to have to start the fire. I'm not handy with rubbing two sticks together."

"If worse comes to worse, I have a couple more firebombs in my pocket. I hid them from the healers. And you don't need a match to set them off." Roz grinned. "I didn't tell them I was bringing bombs along with me. Somehow, I didn't think they would appreciate it very much. But I had to have something to make me feel secure."

"Well, I for one am extremely glad you had the bomb you hit the cyclops with. Let's gather everything before it really gets dark. It's already dusk and it's going to be hard to see soon, and we just have the one flashlight you brought."

While Trillian and Roz hunted for rocks in the forest, Nerissa and I gathered dry pieces of downed wood. We lucked out and found a rotting log that had pitch on it, which would make extremely good kindling.

By the time we arrived back at the campsite, it was already hard to see in the deepening twilight. Leaving the men to handle the fire, Nerissa and I wandered down to the water's edge. There were fish darting around the river, that much I could see, but catching them would be another matter. Adding that I was phobic of being in water and couldn't bring myself to get any closer than a few feet away from it, I doubted that I'd do us any good at all.

But Nerissa sat down and took off her shoes.

"What are you doing?"

She gave me a crooked smile. "When I was a little girl, I used to go fishing the old-fashioned way. I was pretty good at it, too. Get ready to catch what I send your way."

She pulled the bandana off of her head, stretching it out between her hands as she eased her way down into the rolling white caps of the river, staying close to the shore. As she balanced, staring at the water, I watched, mesmerized. She was frozen, still as a statue, and then, lightning fast, she swept the bandana into the water, then used it to sling her catch on to the shore. The flipping fish landed by my feet.

Instincts took over. I grabbed the fish by its tail and whacked it a good one against the ground to kill it. Three more times, Nerissa used her makeshift net, and each time, she landed another large silvery fish by my feet. By the time she waded back out of the water, I had gathered up all four of the fish. Each one was at least eighteen inches long, and they looked very much like trout from our world.

"Where on earth did you learn to do that?" I was impressed to say the least.

"I told you, I learned when I was a little girl. I've got a number of skills that I've never had the chance to show anyone. But muscle memory remembers, and it's all a matter of focus and concentration."

She motioned for me to lay the fish on a nearby

rock, which had a flat top much like a table. We sat on the ground beside it as she pulled out a knife and began gutting one of the fish. Meanwhile, I used Lysanthra to whittle down the ends of several sticks, and we skewered the cleaned fish on them. By the time we carried them back to the campsite, the guys had built the fire. I wasn't entirely sure how they had managed it, but the crackling flames were welcome and we arranged the skewers over them to roast the fish in the quickly chilling evening.

As the twilight gloom settled into darkness, overhead the clouds thinned out, showing a layer of stars. It had been a long time since I had seen such a vast array. The light pollution over Earthside was pretty bad. The fish sizzled, the aroma making me aware of how hungry I was.

"You should have seen Nerissa," I said. "I'll never go camping without her again." I still didn't feel any better about the water. I still felt incredibly drawn toward it, and for someone who was afraid of water, that wasn't a good thing—or natural. "By the way, watch out for the water Fae. There's a lot of strong energy here, and I don't trust it."

"Not to question your instincts, but are you sure it's not just your phobia of water speaking?"

While I appreciated Roz's thought, I shook my head. "No. If it was that, I'd feel more panic. There is an uneasiness to this area, to the river, that makes me feel uncomfortable. I don't feel like it's coming directly from the water, like an elemental, but from around the water." I huddled closer to the flames, eyeing the fish. "How long will it take to cook those?"

Nerissa poked one with a stick. "Probably another fifteen minutes and they'll be done enough to eat. I wish we had some salt, but they should be good."

"I've never seen anybody catch fish that way before." The panther in me, along with Tabby, was pretty damned impressed. I loved fish, in all three of my forms, and for once I wished I didn't have the insane fear of water that I did. If I could bring myself to step into a river, I would be down there, begging Nerissa to teach me how she did it. Then I realized something. She was a werepuma, and yet she didn't show the same fear that I had.

"Why aren't you afraid of water like I am?"

She shrugged. "I don't know. I don't think I've ever been afraid of it. I can swim, and I enjoy going out on boats. Did something happen to you when you were little that made you afraid? Or do you think maybe it's the fact that one of your forms is a domesticated cat? Most housecats don't care for water."

"That could be it," I said, thinking back. Could she be right? Had something from childhood spurred my fear of water? I closed my eyes, running through every trauma that I could remember from childhood.

The neighborhood boys used to tease me by trying to throw me in the water when I was in tabby form, that certainly hadn't helped, but I vaguely remembered being afraid before then. I leaned forward, wrapping my arms around my knees as I watched the flames lick at the wood. And then, a vague image sprang to mind. I opened my eyes.

I had been two…maybe three, I couldn't remember which, but I knew that I was extremely young. We had been out on a camping trip and something had happened. Mother was still alive, and Menolly hadn't been born yet.

I closed my eyes again, seeing the wide field spreading out around us. There had been flowers—beautiful flowers that had beckoned me to come pick them. I had been running through the field, laughing, and then I heard something call my name. I ran over to the nearby river, laughing…and then all of a sudden…

I let out a gasp.

"I remember something. We were on a camping trip, and I was very little. Mother was still alive. I was picking flowers, and I saw one that was so beautiful. It was a bright blue, in a sea of yellow and green alongside the river. It called me by name, and I ran over to it. The next thing I remember, I was being pulled into the water. Something had hold of me and was dragging me under. The flower vanished." As I spoke, the entire memory opened itself out in my mind.

"What happened? Do you remember?"

I nodded. "I don't think I've ever thought about this before. It felt like seaweed wrapping around my legs and I heard a laugh. I was screaming, and water got in my mouth. Something bit my ankle. The next thing I knew, Camille was yanking on my arms, screaming for help. Mother came running up and she was beating something in the water and hit me on the leg. She hit my leg with a sharp stick.

The next thing I remember, I was on the ground, and Mother was pushing water out of my lungs. There was a smell that I remember, like decaying cabbage."

Trillian stared at me. "A bollywog. A bollywog attacked you. Had to have been."

"What?" I'd never heard of bollywogs before.

"They're uncommon, but they live out in the wild in Otherworld, mostly near streams or rivers that run through gladed woodlands. They're bound to the water, although they can travel a short distance from it. They're known to take the shape of flowers, or pretty plants, and they lure people in. Once they get you in the water, they use their tendrils and roots to drown you, and then they absorb your nutrients. Bollywogs are deadly, but they're small and so they usually target small animals and children."

Something shifted in my stomach as I let out a slow breath. "I can't believe that I never remembered that. I don't even know if Camille remembers it. But yes, after that I was terrified of the water. I must have connected the bollywog trying to drown me with the water itself." I glanced over at the edge of the river, wondering if I could manage to get rid of my phobia now that I knew its origin.

"I don't know if I would have ever remembered that if we hadn't come here. And now that I think about it, the nervousness that I'm feeling is directed toward the shore of the river, not the water itself."

"Then let's go on the assumption that there's something here that doesn't have our best interests in mind. Whether it's a bollywog or something different doesn't matter. We just need to stay alert. I suggest we keep watch in pairs. But the fish is done, so let's eat first."

Trillian helped Nerissa remove the fish from the fire. Roz found four large maple leaves, big enough to serve as plates, and we each took one of the fish. The meat was succulent and juicy. While it could have used a little salt, the flavor was so fresh that it burst on my tongue, dribbling down my throat, making me feel warm and full. As we finished off our dinner, leaving only the bones that we threw back into the water, I realized that I could have gone for a second fish, but at least my stomach wasn't yammering at me now.

Trillian and I took the first watch. Roz and Nerissa settled down on the ground, padding the hard dirt with downed tree branches that the men had brought back when they had found the rocks for the fire. They huddled, back to back for warmth near the fire. Trillian and I moved to the other side so we wouldn't disturb them with our talk.

"Thank you for coming with me today," I said, keeping my voice soft. "I'm scared, Trillian. I'm afraid we won't be able to find Shade, or that we'll find him and he won't recognize us. Maybe he won't want to come back."

Trillian wrapped his arm around my shoulders in a brotherly way. I rested my head on his shoulder, settling against the log that we had braced our backs against.

"We can't ever know the future, but somehow I can't imagine Shade refusing to return to his body.

He loves you too much, Delilah. He's far too loyal to run off and leave you alone."

His reassurance meant the world to me. I wasn't sure he was right, but the fact that he was trying to convince me that I had nothing to worry about made me feel better.

"Thanks, I appreciate it. I told you lately what a great brother-in-law you are?"

Trillian laughed. "You didn't think that way a few years back when I came back into Camille's life."

"Don't remind me. I'm sorry. Menolly and I were pretty rough on you."

"Camille wasn't all that easy, when it comes down to it. I just wish…" He trailed off, staring into the darkness.

"Wish what?"

"I wish she could have trusted me all those years before. I wish we hadn't wasted the years apart. I could never forget her, and she could never forget me. Like it or not, we bound ourselves together with the Ritual of Eleshinar, and nothing can ever undo that. We're still bound by the tattoos under our skin, you know."

"She was just afraid that you would marry somebody else and consign her to only being your mistress. After all, your family didn't like her either."

"You don't see my family anywhere around, do you? I would never have done that to her. My race may be known for its promiscuous ways, but let's face it, Camille's the one with three husbands. I can handle it, because I'm born to it. Smoky accepts it because he loves her so much. And Morio—

Morio is a breed into himself. I've never told her this, although I think she already knows, but those years I spent without her? I never once looked at another woman. There was nobody else for me after I met her."

"You know, telling her that may be the best anniversary gift you could ever give her. After all, your anniversary is coming up next month." Camille and Trillian had married on October 22. She had married Smoky and Morio near the spring equinox.

"I'll think about it. So, you found your wedding dress?" Trillian was one of those rare men who actually enjoyed talking about fashion.

"Yeah, it's beautiful." A catch in my throat made me stumble over my words. "I just hope I get the chance to wear it."

"You will, Kitten. You will." Suddenly, he stiffened, removing his arm as he straightened up. "Do you hear that?"

I froze as a crackle of branches sounded from the forest behind us.

Trillian motioned for me to stay behind him as he slowly rose and reached for his dagger. I eased myself up, drawing Lysanthra. We waited, poised as the breaking of branches continued. And then, before we could wake Nerissa and Roz, the branches parted and a figure staggered out toward us. It was Shade, but his eyes were glowing, and he had his sword out, and he was coming directly at us.

Chapter 9

"DUCK!" TRILLIAN SHOVED me out of the way as Shade staggered toward us, his sword drawn. The crazed look in his eyes told me that he didn't recognize us, or if he did, something was dreadfully wrong.

"Don't hurt him!" I yelled as Trillian darted in, his short sword meeting Shade's.

"I'll try but I can't let him hurt me," Trillian shot back as he deflected the blow. Shade was bigger than Trillian, and far more powerful, and with his next swing he managed to knock Trillian's blade out of his hand.

"Shade!" I screamed out his name at the top of my lungs, startling all of us, including me.

Roz and Nerissa were scrambling up off the ground, looking confused.

Shade froze, turning to me with a bewildered look on his face. He kept his sword pointed toward

Trillian, keeping him at bay.

"Who are you? What do you want?" He sounded genuinely perplexed, but panic was written all over his face and I was afraid he might break again.

"Shade, don't you recognize me? I'm Delilah, your fiancée." I started to move toward him, just a step, but when he tensed again, I froze. "We've come to take you home. Do you know where you are?"

"They're after me. I— I—" The bewilderment was turning to panic again. He looked like he was ready to run for it, or run straight toward us with that damn blade. I didn't recognize the sword; it looked totally unfamiliar to me.

"I don't know who *they* are, but please trust us. Give us a chance." I spoke softly, trying to modulate my voice so that it didn't set him off. I held up my hands after slowly sheathing Lysanthra. "You see? We won't hurt you. I put my weapon away."

"What about him?" Shade pointed to Trillian. "He still has his blade out."

"We just want to make sure that you don't attack us. We aren't here to hurt you. We aren't here to hurt anybody." I kept my hands raised so he could see them, wondering what the hell had happened to send him off the deep end like this.

Roz and Nerissa stood near the fire, uncertain of what to do.

"I know what that blade is that he's carrying," Trillian said softly.

"What is it?" I asked.

"What are you talking about? You're talking about me! You think that I can't fight you. I know it, you think that because I lost my powers, I can't take care of myself." The pain in his voice hit me in the gut as the meaning of his words became clear.

Out here, in the Land of Wandering Souls, our worst fears could take on a reality, we had been told. And Shade was afraid that, because he had lost his Stradolan powers, he was only half a man. I had thought he had been weathering it pretty well, but now it was obvious that he had been hiding his fears from me, and probably hiding his fears from himself.

"What's the blade?" I tried to keep my words very soft, almost monotone so that perhaps he wouldn't pay attention to what I was actually asking.

Trillian took my clue and spoke lightly. "That's the blade he was hit with. The soul-stealer blade."

I worried my lip, wondering just what kind of an effect it would have out here. He was carrying the weapon that had disarmed him and sent him spiraling out here.

"Do you remember what happened?" I asked, speaking to Shade directly. "Do you remember fighting the demons at our home?"

Another look of confusion washed over his face, then there was something—a glimmer of understanding—that vanished as quickly as it appeared.

"I don't know what you're talking about! Where am I? I've been trying to find my way..." His voice drifted off, and for a moment he froze, looking as though he had wandered into a fugue. I thought about trying to disarm him, but I wasn't sure how long his disorientation would last.

Trillian, however, didn't seem to have any such reluctance. Even as I was standing there trying to figure out what to do, he dropped his sword and lunged toward Shade, grabbing the blade out of his hand and tossing it over to Roz, who scrambled to pick it up. He handed it to Nerissa, who quickly backed away from the fracas.

Shade started coming out of the fugue and realized he didn't have his sword. He let out a roar and I was afraid he might change into his dragon shape, and *that* could be the end of everything. I did the only thing I could think of that might bring him out of it. I transformed into Tabby, and leapt into his arms. The shift was so quick that it racketed through my body, and I ached in every joint, including my tail, but I threw my paws up around his neck and began licking his face, purring as loudly as I could.

Shade closed his mouth and shook his head first once, then again. Then he laughed, like a child who had been given an unexpected treat. Once again, the bewildered look returned, but he wrapped his arms around me, and buried his face in my fur.

He began to cry, tears racing down his cheeks as he nuzzled me. Trillian and Roz slowly approached and guided him over to one of the logs where he sat down, still holding me, still crying. I was purring so loudly that my vocal box hurt, but I kept it up, because it seemed to calm him down and I had the feeling that the tactile nature of my fur under his fingers was spurring on some form of recognition. I licked his face again, lapping away the tears, and then pressed my head against his nose so that

I was staring into his eyes.

With Roz and Trillian on guard, and Nerissa keeping the sword away from Shade, we stayed that way for at least another ten minutes.

I slowly reached up with one paw, lightly tapping his face. "Mrow?"

"Kitten?" Shade still sounded confused, but the word felt tentative, as though he were reaching for a memory. I wanted to transform back, but I had the feeling that he would remember me best in this shape. That there was something disarming about my tabby self that made him feel secure.

After another moment, Roz gently cleared his throat. "Do you remember us? You remember Kitten."

Shade let out a long, shuddering breath. "I seem to feel that I should know you. You feel like a friend."

"We are friends. We're all friends. And Delilah—Kitten—is your fiancée. She loves you."

"Delilah…" And then Shade blinked again, and looked down at me with recognition filling his face. "Delilah? Sweetheart? Are you really here? Or is this just another dream?"

That was my cue. I jumped off of his lap and changed back as quickly as I could, even though it hurt. As I slowly leveraged myself off the ground, wincing at the ache in my joints, Shade let out a joyful cry and jumped up, pulling me into his arms.

"Delilah, it's really you?" He sounded joyful and yet still half afraid that I was an illusion.

"It's me. We came to find you. We're really here,

sweetie. We're here to take you back to your body. Do you know where you are?"

Shade shook his head. "No, I can't remember much. What do you mean, take me back to my body?"

"You were sent into the Land of Wandering Souls when Yerghan the Blade stabbed you." I glanced over at Nerissa. The sword she was holding suddenly vanished.

"I think I remember now. Someone was at the door and I opened it and… The next thing I knew my side was burning and then—and then it all goes gray." Shade blinked, looking around. "So this is the Land of Wandering Souls?"

I nodded. "The Autumn Lord sent us here, with help from Camille's healers. We need to go home, though. It's too easy for us to get lost here. I brought our tickets back."

I pulled out the talismans from my pocket—mine and Shade's. Roz and Nerissa and Trillian closed in around us, holding their own talismans. I handed Shade his.

"Hold it tight and whisper 'Take me home,' and we'll be able to leave." I thought for a moment, and then said, "You go first. So we make sure that we've got you."

Shade held tight to the talisman, closing his eyes. He looked tired, as though he had run a great race and stumbled in last. "Take me home," he said, and then with a whistle of wind, he vanished.

I looked at the others. "Let's hope he made it. I suppose there's no other way to find out. Let's get out of here."

Holding tight to the talisman, I whispered the magic words, and everything faded from sight.

"DELILAH? DELILAH? WAKE up now. It's time to wake up."

The voice echoed through my thoughts, annoying me until I opened my eyes. I blinked as Perri stood over me, tapping me on the face.

"Stop that. It's annoying."

She laughed. "I'm really glad to hear you say that. It's time to get up. And before you ask, Shade's awake, and so are the others. You're all safe."

A wave of relief washed through me as I allowed her to help me sit up. My body felt stiff, and I wondered how long we had been out. I glanced over at the other beds, grateful to see everyone was awake, including Shade, who was propped up on some pillows. But his eyes were open, and he was smiling at me.

"Oh thank gods, you're awake." With a deep breath, I threw back my covers and started to stand. But as my feet hit the floor, everything vanished and I began to fall, toppling head over heels, in a freefall toward a quickly approaching river. As I landed in the water, I realized I was sinking, unable to breathe. I floundered, flailing wildly as I managed to come to the surface.

I struggled over to the shore, kicking and splashing as I managed to make my way through the white caps. Dragging myself up on the embankment, I rolled over, gasping for breath. What the hell? I had just been in my bed, and everything had been all right.

As I slowly sat up, looking around, I realized I was alone. Shade, Nerissa, Roz, and Trillian were all gone. And I was here, back on the banks of the river, by myself.

"Hello? Hello? Is anybody there?" I stumbled to my feet, a lump of fear growing in my stomach. I was wet, and cold. "Hello? Anybody! Answer me! What are you?"

The forest echoed with noises around me, but there were no voices, no one answering me. Growing more afraid with every moment, I crossed back over to the logs where we had sat. The fire was still crackling brightly.

Everything was there just as we had left it. But the others were gone, and I was alone. I reached in my pocket, looking for the talisman. Something must have happened and they had transferred over, but I hadn't. But my pocket was empty.

"What? Where is it? What happened?" My voice echoed through the glade, but nobody answered.

Had I really returned to the hospital? I *knew* I had been there. Shade and Trillian and Nerissa and Roz were all awake, but then… Trying to stave off panic, I huddled by the fire to dry out. I was soaking wet, and it felt like there was still water in my lungs.

I decided to try logic. *One:* we had found Shade. We had been sent to the Land of Wandering Souls, we had fought a cyclops, and we found Shade.

Two: Shade had been confused. We had helped snap him out of it. *Three:* I had given him his talisman. And we had all used ours. He went first, and then the rest of us. I vaguely remembered seeing Nerissa shimmer out of view, and then Roz and Trillian, and then I had woken up in the bed back in the laboratory. *Four:* Perri had been there. She had woken me up, she kept tapping my face. And then I saw Shade and I started to get out of bed and... I had fallen into the river.

The fire was starting to die down. Trembling, I grabbed another piece of wood and some more pitch kindling, and stoked the flames. I was still hungry, but the fish were gone and it was far too dark for me to try to catch one like Nerissa had.

Part of me wanted to get up and hunt around to see if anybody else had returned with me. But the light of the fire was too bright, and too welcoming to leave. The forest around me was pitch black now, and noises loomed on every side.

I scooted closer, holding my hands out to warm them. What could have happened? How had I ended up back here? It wasn't like someone hit me with the soul-stealer sword. And it wasn't like I hadn't used my talisman. I remembered taking it out of my pocket along with Shade's. I remembered holding onto it, and whispering—wait.

Had I really whispered those words? Had I actually formed the words to take me home?

Maybe I hadn't! Maybe I thought I had, but something happened and I had dropped the talisman in the dirt and I fainted. Maybe I had started to shift over and something had stopped me and thrown me in the river?

I jumped up and headed over to the spot where we had stood, falling to my knees as I sifted through the grass, looking for my talisman. The ground was hard, so it wouldn't have been buried. It *had* to be here. It just had to.

Another few minutes and my stomach clenched as I realized the talisman was really and truly gone. Could I have dropped it somewhere? Had something interrupted us, shortly before I went home, and the talisman had been knocked out of my hand? I needed to widen my search but I didn't have a flashlight. I didn't have anything where I could see in the dark.

"I just have to wait till morning. Once morning comes, I can figure this out. Dawn can't be that far off," I said out loud. Reassuring myself that I would be all right, I returned to the fire, but every noise and every movement in the bush around me made me nervous. Finally, I decided I'd be less frightened if I were in my panther form, and so I shifted shape.

Immediately, my perception changed. I scanned the area, able to see smaller animals in the bush. The fire frightened me, yet it was warm and so I snuggled down nearby, keeping enough distance so the sparks couldn't pop out at me. The heat felt wonderful, radiating across my fur. As I lay there, alert and yet resting, I wondered if there was some way I could contact Greta. Maybe she would be able to help me. But if Hi'ran couldn't come into the Land of Wandering Souls, could the Death Maidens?

That was a silly question. *I* had come into the Land of Wandering Souls. But I was still alive. Maybe that made a difference. Greta was dead, so maybe she wouldn't be able to enter here. That brought up another question: if someone were sent here, and their body died, would their soul vanish elsewhere, or would they stay here forever?

My mind wouldn't shut up, even in panther form, and I kept racing over possibilities, feeling as though I had had far too much caffeine. Camille could handle caffeine, but for me, it sent my mind into loop after loop, until it felt like my thoughts would drive me nuts.

I needed to focus on something pleasant.

Jerry Springer.

Shade had bought me Jerry Springer tickets. We were going to go see the show in person. I focused on that, focused on anything I could that felt like normality. I had my wedding dress. It was beautiful, and it made me feel like a princess. The house made me sad, given what Yerghan had done to it, but Smoky would fix it. Smoky seem to be able to fix just about anything that was wrong. Camille had promised to send workmen to help him, and maybe we could expand the kitchen, or upgrade it. Marble countertops would be nice, or quartz. And I'd love to have a new refrigerator.

I kept running over the small stuff, the little things that were tangible, that grounded me into the reality back home. Now that Camille was living out at Talamh Lonrach Oll, I was planning on painting her study and enclosing the balcony so that I could sit out there without the mosquitoes bothering me. Shade and I would take what had been her bedroom, and I would turn the entire third story into a nursery and kitty playroom. That led me to wonder something else. When I did have the Autumn Lord's child, would she be a Were at all? I secretly hoped that she would have the ability to transform into a cat. It would be so much fun to teach her about my private world that nobody else entered.

A noise from the forest startled me, and I turned to look. Gasping, I shifted back into my human form without thinking. There, walking out from between the trees, was my mother.

"Delilah? Delilah, *what* are you doing here?" My mother had golden hair like I did, and she was petite. But I remembered her with a smiling face, always laughing with us. Now, she looked angry.

"What are you doing here, Mother? You're..."

"*Dead*? Well, that's bright. Of course I'm dead. You didn't think that I had magically come back to life, did you?" She not only looked angry, she sounded angry.

"I don't understand what's going on. You aren't supposed to be here. I didn't think anybody could be here who was dead. I'm not supposed to be here, either. I'm supposed to be back in Camille's laboratory."

"Excuses, always excuses. You never were too swift on the uptake, were you? I excused it when you were little, but I hoped you'd grow into your intelligence as you grew up. Apparently I was hoping in vain. I knew Arial was smarter than you were. I wish...it would have been better if you were the one taken and she was left." She didn't move to hug me, or even greet me. Instead, she sneered, turning toward the fire. "So, tell me what you've done with yourself. Have you at least made good use of your time?"

"I like to think so," I said, hesitating a moment, my heart stinging from her words. She looked like my mother, her voice was the same as I remembered, but my heart screamed no, it couldn't be her. She wasn't ever this cruel. "I didn't know that you were disappointed with me. I never knew that you wanted Arial to live instead of me."

"She never had a chance, did she? And it was *your* fault, you know that, don't you? She died at birth. She came out second, with her umbilical cord wrapped around her neck. Because *you* took so long to be born, she choked to death. Your father warned me never to tell you, but every day, every time I saw you, I remembered that *you* were the reason that she died."

I pressed my lips together, horrified. Arial had never told me this.

"I've talked to Arial. She told me that *Father* made the choice. That he asked the Autumn Lord to help because you were dying in childbirth." I was feeling confused. Who was telling me the truth? Had Arial spared my feelings out of pity? Had our father told me a lie so that I wouldn't feel bad? The knot in my stomach grew larger, making it hard to breathe.

My mother let out a snort. "Well, it just goes to show. Arial thought about you, even though she's the one who paid the price. I doubt if you would ever have spared *her* feelings that way. You always wanted things your own way, everything had to be just so because Delilah was *so sensitive*. You know Camille resented you. After all, she had to take care of you after I died. And you *needed* taking care of. Menolly was able to fend for herself. But Camille always had to stick up for you, because you refused to grow a backbone."

"Stop! Please stop." Ragged tears welled up in my throat, but I shut them down, feeling both humiliated and angry.

"*Stop! Please stop.*" Maria mimicked me, laughing. "I remember hearing you use those words so very often. The neighbor kids wanted to play and they would tease you, and you would whine and whine. *Stop! Please stop.* If you had stood up for yourself even once, they would never have pulled that crap. But no, as usual, you were the crybaby."

Feeling like one big ball of raging shame, I clenched my fists. I wanted to hit her. I lashed out in the only way I knew how.

"*You're* the one who abandoned us. *You* wouldn't drink the nectar of life, so you died. Father was a broken man after you fell off that horse. You knew how much he loved you, but you wouldn't even consider extending your life for him. Or for *us*. Camille may have had to take care of me, but she wouldn't have had to if you hadn't died. You didn't love us enough to take a chance on living a longer life. You didn't love us enough to *stay with us*."

My words streamed out, hot and furious. Even in a haze of anger, I realized that they were truly how I felt. I blamed my mother for dying. I blamed her for falling off the horse.

She stared at me, her gaze hard and cold. "Do you *really* believe that?"

I wasn't sure what to say. I didn't know what to think by now. I felt lost within myself, unable to form an answer. Panicking, I began to back away, and then I turned into Panther and loped off into the forest, leaving the warmth of the fire behind, and leaving my mother and past behind me.

I DON'T KNOW how long I ran, or how far I went, but finally I slowed to a walk. Everything around me looked unfamiliar. I could probably turn around and try to retrace my steps, except that I had no clue about which way I had come.

The encounter with my mother had left me shaken to the core. Had she really hated me so much? Had she really thought I was such a failure, even at such a young age?

Exhausted, I curled up on a soft bed of moss. I stayed in my panther form, because it felt safest, as I glanced up at the sky. Dawn was finally approaching, and I hoped that with the sunlight would come some sort of clarity.

My stomach rumbled and I realized I was hungry again. But I stayed where I was, trying to understand what had transpired. My mother shouldn't be here. That much I knew. The dead could not walk in the Land of Wandering Souls.

Therefore, if I followed that train of logic, it wasn't my mother I had been talking to. And if not Maria, then who?

A little voice inside whispered, *Maybe you were talking to yourself.* I started to brush it away, then paused. What had Hi'ran said about the Land of Wandering Souls? About our worst fears being embodied out here? If so, maybe that was the case with my mother. Was I really so terrified that she would be disappointed in me? Did I think she considered me a burden, a failure even as a child? Was *I* afraid that I was a failure?

And following that train of logic, did I blame myself for my sister's death?

The thought had never entered my mind before, and the discussion with my father and Arial some time ago had put me at ease. But perhaps…just perhaps…hidden deep inside was the fear that I had been to blame. Because it came down to that Arial had died and I had lived.

I couldn't imagine what my mother had been through, losing one of us. She and Father had kept Arial's presence hidden. Neither my sisters nor I had known about her until a few years back. And if *I* blamed myself for Arial's death, did she, perhaps, somewhere in the depths of her subconscious, blame *me*?

Feeling like my entire foundation had been rocked, I laid my head down on my paws, closed my eyes, and fell into a deep sleep.

"DELILAH?" THE VOICE was soft in my ears.

I blinked, squinting to see Camille kneeling beside me. I let out a soft chuff, but I didn't change back. Remembering what had happened, I couldn't help but wonder if this was really Camille, or maybe another fear come to haunt me. I shifted, raising my head, waiting.

"I've been searching for you. This is a frightening place, I'll tell you that much." She glanced around, shivering. "They didn't want to let me come, but I told them if anybody could find you, it would be me. Come home with me. We need you, sweetie. Shade needs you. He's so afraid now. He thinks it's his fault that you're trapped here. Come on, Delilah, come home with me, please."

I realized that she was doing the same thing with me that I had with Shade. But was she *truly* Camille? Finally, I stepped away from her and shifted back to my human form, slowly this time so it wouldn't hurt. As my body lengthened and stretched, rising upright on two feet, I let out a long sigh and realize that it felt like I had slept for days. Maybe I had. It was impossible to fathom how time ran here in the Land of Wandering Souls. At least I knew where I was, though.

"How do I know it's you? How do I know you're *really* Camille?"

"You can ask me anything." She looked worried now, her brow furrowed. The crown on her head looked heavy.

"But anything I ask you, I already know the answer to. Unless..." I paused. If I asked her something she didn't know, but that I knew...she shouldn't be able to tell me if she was truly Camille. "Before Menolly was born, do you remember a camping trip that we went on with Mother and Father? Where I was lured into the water?"

She frowned, looking confused. "Not offhand. I don't know..." She bit her lip, staring at the ground.

"So you *don't* remember it?" If she was a figment of my imagination, she would probably recall it right away.

"I'm sorry." She shook her head. "I don't think I remember anything like that. Unless... No, I don't know what you're talking about. I'm sorry."

Relieved, I smiled at her. "Don't be. *I* didn't even remember it until this trip. If you had told me that you remembered, I'd think you were a figment of my imagination. So how do we get out of here? And...did I come back the first time?" Now I was confused again. "I remember waking up, then stepping out of bed and then somehow falling back into the river here."

"Oh, Kitten, no. That didn't happen. Shade woke up, and then Nerissa, Roz, and Trillian. But we couldn't bring you back. Here—the Autumn Lord gave me this." She held out a talisman like the one he had given me before. She was carrying one herself. "You go first this time."

I clutched the talisman in my palm, holding it tightly as I whispered, "Take me home." And then, everything felt misty, as the world around me vanished from sight again.

Chapter 10

ONCE AGAIN, I blinked and opened my eyes. This time, Perri wasn't slapping my face trying to wake me up. I was in bed. Turning my head, I tried to figure out if this was real. Camille was in the bed next to mine, but the others were nowhere in sight. I tried to sit up, and Perri ran over, letting out a cry of relief. As she helped me to roll into a sitting position, Camille let out a soft moan, and she too, woke up.

"Is this real? Is this time for real?" I was just a little bit paranoid.

"You're here. Everything's all right."

"I want to stand up. That's the only way I can tell if this is real." Frantically, I was shoving back the covers.

Perri stopped me. "Don't jog the needle in your arm. Here, let me take it out first." I stopped struggling, extending my arm for her to take out the IV.

She pressed a cotton ball over the injection site, and then strapped a piece of tape over it. Next, she stood back and offered me her hand. "You may be a little woozy, so be careful. I don't want you fainting. It's been several days since you stood, or even sat up, for that matter."

Several days? I hadn't realized it had been so long. I eased my feet over the edge of the bed. The floor was cool against my toes, and my stomach lurched as I slowly stood, terrified that everything would vanish again and I found myself back in the Land of Wandering Souls once more. But this time, my feet stayed firm on the floor, and even though they tingled from not having been used for a few days, I actually began to believe I was home. I let out a sigh of relief.

"I'm really here. I really came back?"

"Thanks to your sister, yes, you're here." With a look of relief on her face, Perri motioned for me to sit back on the bed. "Take things easy. One step at a time. Let me go tend to your sister." As she moved over to Camille's bed, I sat back down.

Everything was all right. Everything was going to be okay. I was awake, Shade was home, back in his body, and everything would be just fine. Breathing easier than I had in a while, I turned around and watched as Perri attended to Camille.

A COUPLE OF hours later I managed to make it over to the main chamber where we had eaten breakfast a few mornings before. My muscles ached, but Perri released me, stressing for me to take it easy for a few days until all the drugs were out of my system. She also informed me that I had been gone a total of five days. Three of those were with Roz, Trillian, and Nerissa. The fourth and fifth days, I had been out there alone. I also found out that I really *hadn't* returned to my body when I thought I had the first time. That had been part of the hallucination.

Camille joined me, though Menolly was asleep for the day.

"Where are the others?"

I looked around. "Shade? He's okay?" Perri had told me that Shade had come through all right, but I had a sudden irrational need to see him.

Camille placed a hand on my arm. "Calm down. He's fine. They're just running some tests and checking his wound. It's almost healed now." She paused, then looked at me. "When I found you out there, you seemed terribly confused and afraid. You asked me something. About a trip when we were young—a camping trip. What was that all about?"

I stared at the table as I slid into the chair. Finally, biting my lip, I looked at her. "You know how they said that we might face our worst fears out there? They were right. Apparently, I've been hiding some deep-seated fears that I didn't know I have. I also discovered what's at the bottom of my fear of water."

I hesitated, mulling over everything I remembered, trying to sort out the fears from the facts.

Camille didn't rush me. She just drank her coffee and let me take my time.

"First, I remembered a camping trip. We were out—you, Mother, Father, and me. I don't think Menolly was born yet. I wandered too close to a stream and what I now think was probably a bollywog dragged me under. I almost drowned. Mother saved me, and Father, too, I guess. Anyway, I think I can trace my phobia of water to that point. Does that ring any bells?"

Camille frowned, leaning her elbows on the table. After a moment she let out a little gasp. "*Yes*. Actually, I think I *do* remember it. You were screaming, and I saw you. Mother and Father were going crazy."

She paused, closing her eyes, then opened them wide.

"Oh." She paused. "I know why I blocked it out! I was supposed to watch you, and I didn't want to. I let you wander off and the next thing, I heard you screaming. I ran over in time to see something had hold of you. After they saved you, Father laid into me for shirking my duty. He gave me a horrible spanking—well, it *seemed* horrible at the time. I doubt if it was much more than a few slaps on the butt. He shook me and told me that it was my responsibility to watch over you because I was your older sister. He said that you could have died because of me. In fact, he said that if you had died, it would have been my fault." She paused, shaking her head. "You know, I think that's when I started intervening when the bullies came after you. I think I truly believed that if I didn't watch out for you, you'd end up dead."

"Boy, that trip got to both of us, didn't it? Turns out, camping maybe not so much fun after all." What Camille said sparked off the memory of what I had heard from Mother. At least, from my fears that had taken the form of our mother. "There's more. While I was out there alone, I had another experience."

I spilled it all out. I told her about seeing Mother, and what she had said to me. "Do you think she was right? Or rather, do you think my fears are right? Was I really so much trouble? Did I cause Arial's death? Even if I didn't mean to?"

Camille's eyes narrowed.

"Delilah, none of that's your fault. All three of you would have died if Father hadn't made that pact with the Autumn Lord. Don't you get it? Father chose to save two of you. He couldn't save all of you, so he opted to save Mother and one of you. It was the Autumn Lord who made the final choice between you and Arial."

I nodded. "That's what I keep telling myself."

"That's the truth. And as far as our mother goes, well, I remember her better than you do. Mother loved you so much. She called you her *ray of golden sunshine*. And for me? You've never been a burden. Oh, our father screwed me over by putting the household on my shoulders when Mother died, but I *never* blamed you and Menolly for that. Somebody had to watch after you, and he sure wasn't emotionally capable of it."

I began to cry, softly. "So Mother loved me? She wouldn't be disappointed in me?"

"Mother loved you. She loved all of us. And for what it's worth, I think if she hadn't fallen off that horse, she would have come around and drunk the Nectar of Life. She never had the chance to really think it over."

"I always wondered why she wouldn't."

"She was probably afraid she couldn't handle that much time. Delilah, you're deeply loved. Mother? She adored you. You're our *Kitten*. And Menolly and I love everything about you. Except when you don't clean your litter box." She laughed then, making me laugh, too.

"It's amazing, the shit that gets into our minds. I was so alone out there. I felt more alone than any time in my life. I felt like an outsider in a way that I haven't since childhood. Remember when they used to call us Windwalkers?"

She nodded. "I began wearing it as a badge of honor, but it always stung with you. I could tell, even when you didn't say anything. I know it hurt you dreadfully."

"I suppose. I just wanted to be liked. I wanted to feel like part of something bigger than myself. And I've always felt on the outside. At least, until now. I may not want to be part of this war, but it does make me feel like I have a destiny. I think that's where all of this comes into play. I feel like a fraud, like I'm supposed to be this heroic warrior against a demonic invasion, this woman destined to bear the Autumn Lord's child, and yet inside I still felt like that frightened little girl who was being sucked down by the bollywog and who was constantly taunted for being a Windwalker."

Camille threw her arms around me, giving me a big kiss on the forehead. "Never forget: We make our own rules. When we were little, we swore we would always be there for each other. And I promise you, even though we are on separate paths, even though we have our own lives and destinies to fulfill, we will *always* be here for each other. Aeval and Titania had a fit when I told them to fuck off, that you were my sister and I wasn't leaving you out there. But I didn't trust anybody else to find you, because I *know* you. I knew I could find you."

I shifted, straightening my shoulders. "You actually told Aeval and Titania to fuck off? For me?" I couldn't help but giggle. It tickled me that she had stood up against them for me.

"Yes, and it's going to take a while for me to get back in their good graces. But hell, they knew who I was when they helped me ascend to the throne. With your life at stake, there was no way I was going to let you stay out there. Or trust you to anybody else."

At that point, the door opened. I looked up to see Shade enter the room.

He looked a little worse for wear, but overall, he was alive, and had a smile on his face. I jumped up, groaning as my muscles tweaked. But I ignored the pain as I ran over to his side and threw my arms around him.

I wasn't the only one with aches. "Careful," he said. "I've still got stitches in me. Apparently the soul-stealer blade was pretty damned sharp. And whatever juju it has slowed my healing process."

He eased me to his left side, leaning down to kiss

me. His lips were warm against mine, and I slid my fingers along his face, relaxing as I realized he was going to be okay.

"I was so afraid we were going to lose you," I said, still clinging to his side.

"I think I lost myself for a while when I was out there. You brought me back, Kitten. And I do mean that. If you hadn't changed into your tabby self, I don't know if I would have recognized you. Sometimes a gentle force is stronger than all the brute strength in the world. I think that was a lesson I needed to learn."

There was still a haunted look in his eyes, and I wondered if he still felt like half a man. I wasn't sure whether or not I should ask him. It seemed like such a private fear and I didn't want to embarrass him, but neither did I want him to go through life feeling incomplete. And perhaps thinking that I saw him as incomplete.

When I thought back to my own fears, it occurred to me that we all hid shadow selves. We all felt like we weren't good enough, we weren't pretty enough, we weren't strong enough. That we just weren't *enough*. Human, Fae, or Dragon, we all had our inner demons and they could be just as deadly as the demons we faced from the SubRealms. Oh, our fears might not attack us directly, but they were sneaky. We sabotaged ourselves, letting them eat away at our self-esteem, preventing us from growing and evolving.

"Do you remember much about what happened?" I decided the best way to handle this was to feel him out, to see how much he was willing to tell me.

"I remember *too* much. Everything has come back to me. When I first woke up, a lot of the memories were hazy but over the past couple of days I began to remember everything I encountered, and everything I said."

He gave me a long look. "You know, when I woke up, and Roz and Trillian and Nerissa woke up, but you didn't...that was probably the worst moment of my life."

From the table, Camille cleared her throat. "I know there's a lot you two want to talk about, but the others will be here in a few moments. While you were all out of your bodies, we did everything we could to locate the whereabouts of Yerghan the Blade. Today, we need to talk about what we found."

I wrapped my arm through Shade's and led him over to the table.

"She's right. We do have a lot to talk over. But for now, we're both here, and we're both safe. And I am so hungry I could eat a horse. Or a mouse. But I'd rather have a bag of Cheetos and a burger, and a milkshake. Any chance of that?"

Camille laughed. "We should be able to rustle up something like that. I can't guarantee we have any Cheetos in the house, but I'll see." She motioned to one of the serving men. He'd been standing close enough to hear the entire exchange, but now he looked at her, clicking his heels and bowing, as though he hadn't heard a thing.

"Your Majesty?"

"Please have one of the maids bring my sister

something to eat. If possible, a cheeseburger, some Cheetos, and a strawberry milkshake."

"Very good, Your Majesty. Should I have refreshments brought for your entire party?"

"That would be a good idea. I'm sure we could all use something to eat. But make it the usual fare. I don't want a dozen bags of Cheetos sitting around." She laughed as he gave her another bow and walked away.

"Is it really very strange? Having servants like this?" I asked. "He was close enough to hear everything we were saying, but he acted like he hadn't heard a word."

"That's their job. That's why we choose our guards and servants so carefully. There's no way to avoid sensitive material being overheard, so we have to be able to trust them. And it's their job not to listen unless it sounds like there's a threat being made. Trally overheard every single word, and he could have easily just taken care of matters without me. But it's *my* place to instruct him." She shrugged. "It's a complicated situation. And it does feel strange at times. But I'm getting used to it, and I'm not sure whether that's a good thing."

Shade leaned his elbow on the table, and with his other hand pushed back his hair. For once, his shoulder-length hair was hanging free. He usually kept it in a ponytail, but today the amber strands were loose around his face, giving him a softer look. The scar down his cheek was half hidden by his hair, and his eyes were luminous. He was truly a beautiful man.

"In dragon culture, this would be casual. Camille

knows—she's seen it from up close and personal. The hierarchy there is fiercely enforced."

"Now, how do shadow dragons play into it again? You've never really talked about it much," I said. Even though Shade was half–shadow dragon, he seemed almost as distant from his heritage as he was from humankind.

"Unlike the other dragons who all live in the Dragon Reaches, shadow dragons inhabit the Netherworld. We are third in the hierarchy ranking. Silvers are always at the top. And then the gold dragons. Shadow dragons come next. Blue dragons are at the bottom. But as Smoky has told you, you can marry up. Which is why Hyto held the power he did."

Camille winced, and a cloud raced across her face. She seldom talked about Smoky's father and what he had done to her, but no matter how much time passed, I suspected there would always be a certain amount of PTSD. As Menolly had said long ago, you can drop the baggage and leave it behind, but you always carry the claim tickets.

"I think we should leave talk of Hyto out of this." I flashed a look at him.

He grimaced. "I'm sorry, I didn't think."

"It doesn't matter," Camille said. "What happened, happened. I've come to terms with it for the most part. But Shade's right. Heritage is *everything* in the Dragon Reaches. If you don't have a lineage, you might as well not exist. Orphans aren't considered part of society. *Everything* is based on your ancestors, and while you *can* marry up, that offers no guarantee of lifelong success or respect."

"What about us? How do they see the Fae and humankind?"

"Normally, the dragons wouldn't blink twice in my direction. It's only because of what happened with Hyto that they felt they owed me a debt—they do live by honor. I think when I took the throne here, in Talamh Lonrach Oll, it may have helped matters. But when you get down to the nitty-gritty, dragons are an elitist, classist, and bigoted society." She glanced over at Shade. "How does the fact you are half dragon play into matters?"

"That again depends on heritage. Smoky holds prominence because his mother is a silver. In cases of half-breeds, the higher blood wins out. As far as shadow dragons go, we're accorded a separate status. Because we inhabit the Netherworld, and because the Stradolan race is the only one that can interbreed with us, we stand outside of the class structure. You'll never find a half-shadow, half-silver dragon, for example."

"So shadow dragons can only breed with their own kind, or with Stradolans?"

"Yes, and because of the realm we inhabit, both full and half-breeds are accorded great respect. Shadow dragons tend to be given a wide berth by the others, precisely because they don't quite understand how we work. It isn't like we're a great authority, not like the silvers, but because we truly represent the dead in a way. We're what you would call the shamans of our race. And those of us who are part Stradolan...well...we seem mysterious and deadly to the other dragons."

At that moment, the door opened. In trooped

Smoky, Morio, and Trillian. Behind them were Roz, Menolly, and Nerissa. Vanzir and Trytian followed. I didn't see Iris, Bruce, or Hanna.

I leaned close to Camille. "Where are Iris and Hanna? And Maggie?"

"I told them to stay with the twins." She paused for a moment, then added, "Yerghan the Blade is one of the most dangerous warriors who ever lived. He's carrying a soul-stealer sword. I refuse to allow Iris or Hanna to come near this. Especially Iris. I know she's faced a lot of foes with us, but she has children. I won't risk losing her. I would never do that to Bruce, or the twins."

I nodded. And Hanna had to take care of Maggie, and Hanna wasn't a warrior, either. "Good call."

A couple of serving women entered the room, pushing carts filled with food. One of them set a tray in front of me, and on it was a small bag of Cheetos, a triple-stack cheeseburger, and what had to be a twenty-ounce strawberry milkshake. I licked my lips.

Menolly let out a snort. "Never change, Kitten. Never change."

"Hey, I'm hungry. I haven't eaten in days. Hell, I didn't even realize that it was evening until you showed up. I had no clue how long I was out there."

She sobered. "Well, I can tell you this. You gave us quite a scare." And in those few words, I knew how relieved she was.

After everybody had eaten, we settled down to business.

"All right, here's the rundown. When you four went after Shade, Trytian and Vanzir began searching for information on Yerghan. I'll leave it to them to tell you what they found." Camille motioned to Vanzir.

"Our first thought was to talk to Carter, and it was a good choice. He was a great help. Apparently, Trytian's father was right. Shadow Wing has been absorbing the power from his sorcerers down in the Sub-Realms." Vanzir let out a sigh.

"What do you mean, 'absorbing their power'?" I tore open the bag of Cheetos, absently popping one in my mouth.

"What I mean is that he has been feeding on their life essence. Sucking them dry. And when he does that, he absorbs their magical abilities. Now, he's never been able to do this before, so something has either shifted in his makeup, or he has discovered a new alchemical process. Either way, it's trouble. Remember when we talked about him being called the 'Unraveller'?"

It had been some time, but I nodded. At one point, Shadow Wing's focus had shifted from simply taking over Earthside and Otherworld to razing both to the ground. Speculation ran that he had been gathering the spirit seals in order to reunite them and obliterate all three of the worlds—Otherworld, Earthside, and the Sub-Realms—with the resulting implosion. As long as the seals didn't *touch* one another and weren't magically bound together again to reform the one seal, the three realms would stay separate.

The Great Divide had resulted in an unnatural

balance, and it wasn't holding up quite as well as the Great Fae Lords had thought it would. But to reunite the spirit seals together? The disasters that would unfold would shake all three realms.

"At least he doesn't have any of the spirit seals anymore."

"Yeah, well, we think *that's* what has triggered this current mania. Basically, when Menolly went down to rescue Nerissa and managed to win back all of the spirit seals, it pushed Shadow Wing over the edge. We're not sure what he intends on doing now, except for the fact that he's totally focused on destroying the three of you and anybody surrounding you. Basically, Shadow Wing's lost it, but he's far too powerful to catch and throw in the loony bin."

"So whatever it takes, his goal is to take us out."

"Pretty much," Trytian said. "He's still got enough deranged followers to help him. Although I'm pretty sure that Yerghan the Blade agreed to this simply to win his freedom. I doubt if he wants to stay Earthside. My guess? His goal is to work his way back to Otherworld and disappear into the mountains somewhere."

"That sounds about right. There isn't much over here for a barbarian warlord," I said.

"Anyway," Trytian continued, "Vanzir and I asked some of our contacts to snoop around. The Demon Underground is pretty rife with knowledge, especially since a number of the minor demons escaped over here to get away from Shadow Wing. They're as afraid of him as we are and the last thing they want is for him to manage to get over here. It appears that Shadow Wing *did* put a geas on Yerghan. He can't go free until he returns with your heads to Shadow Wing."

I gulped, fingering my neck. "Then he can't back off until he's dead."

"Pretty much. Carter said there's been some unusual activity down in the industrial district. Several transients were found murdered, and a small tent city abruptly up and moved to a different area of the city a few days ago." Vanzir shrugged. "The transients who were murdered were stabbed. And it wasn't for their money, because they didn't have any."

"What makes Carter think it was Yerghan?" Any number of loonies could run around through a homeless tent city, stabbing people.

"As you know, Carter monitors the police reports. Actually, he monitors just about everything. The police found a couple of witnesses willing to talk. They mentioned a huge, burly Viking-type going off on the homeless. Now, we know Yerghan isn't a Viking, but he could be mistaken for one. They also said he was carrying a very large sword that looked, according to one bystander, 'Brutal as hell.' Since most citizens in Seattle don't carry swords, I think we have our man. To cap it off, the witness also said that the sword was glowing. *Glowing sword*? Try *magical sword*." Trytian shrugged. "I'd bet good money that it's Yerghan."

"I have to admit," Menolly said, "that sounds about right. So Carter thinks he's hanging down in the industrial district? He couldn't have just passed through?"

"Think about it," Vanzir said. "There are a lot of abandoned buildings down there, as well as several magical bars and dives. Just the type of scum Yerghan would hang out with."

"There's more," Trillian said. "After we got back—while you were still lost in the Land of Wandering Souls, Delilah—Roz and I did some reconnaissance work. We tapped Morio's computer skills, and he brought up a list of abandoned buildings, so we paid a cursory visit to all of them. We didn't go in just in case he was in there, but we noticed that one of the buildings seems to have lights on at night, even though it's supposed to be empty. Since Yerghan came over here with four demons, it's likely that he prefers to have companions to back him up. And since he lost all four of those demons, chances are good he'll be looking for some new muscle. I doubt if Shadow Wing sent him over with no resources, so he's probably got money on him."

"It's the best lead we've got so far." Vanzir leaned back in his chair. "The sooner we act, the better. We can't give him a chance to build up a private little army. I don't know if he knows about the Demon Underground, but the demons down there wouldn't give him the time of day anyway. So he'll probably be looking for humans or Fae to fill out his roster."

"What about vampires?" I asked. "Do you think he'd work with them?"

Menolly shook her head. "Roman and I have spies out watching the community. We've passed along the word that anybody found working with anybody questionable will be staked upon contact. Most of the vampires around here have accepted Roman's rule, and they know he doesn't mess around when he puts out a decree like that."

"Shifters?" I asked. "There's a large Were community, and I wouldn't put it past a number of them to sign up for something like that. Tensions have been running high lately. Maybe it's because Chase suddenly quit his job to join the Keraastar Knights. And Yugi has yet to win the full respect and trust that Chase managed to incur. All I know is at the last Supe Community Action Council meeting, there were several arguments that almost turned into brawls."

Camille pressed her lips together, shaking her head. "Unfortunately, I wasn't able to make that meeting. As you know, I did send a representative, and he told me about it. There's just so much flux going on within the internal politics of the Supe community right now that I think everybody's a little on edge. I don't think that Chase changing jobs has a great deal to do with it. I think we're just undergoing one of those times when the power structure shifts. Also, remember, with the vampire rights bill sure to pass, there's a lot of stress among the human community from that."

"Whatever the case, I think there's a better chance than usual that Yerghan could recruit followers from the Supe community. I think he'd scare off most humans."

"Point taken," she said, nodding. "So, what are our next steps?"

"We check out the building. I suppose we *could*

do a stakeout first, but if we see Yerghan, we're going to want to make our move as soon as possible. I suggest we move in tonight." Even though I was feeling a little rocky, I was itching to get back to normal—or at least as normal as I could.

"All right, so what's our plan? It's 7:30 now, so whatever we do, we'd better get started." Camille leaned back in her chair, looking at the laptop.

"Once again, *you* don't go," Morio said. He leaned forward, staring hard at her. "Unless we're actually facing Shadow Wing, you don't get to play anymore. Your duties are here, in this Barrow, to the people who live here." He said it so bluntly that I almost gasped.

Camille glowered back at him. "Yerghan the Blade was sent by Shadow Wing. I feel like I *should* be there."

"We need a strong contingent, yes. But we don't need *everybody* there to take him on. Just like you decided that Iris doesn't get to go this time, Aeval and Titania will have your hide if you decide that you need to be part of this. You're already in the doghouse for going after Delilah. The day you accepted that crown, you signed away your freedom." Morio held her gaze.

"Menolly gets to go, and *she's* a princess." But even as she said it, Camille's voice fell and I knew she had accepted the inevitable.

"I may be a princess, but I don't rule the kingdom." Menolly flashed her a sympathetic smile. "At least not right now. I'm not betting it will always be that way, and in fact, I have a feeling the day will be coming when Blood Wyne imposes limitations on my activities as well. And since I've given my promise and my oath to her and to her son, I'm going to have to accept it when she does. Morio's right. As much as we love you, the fact is, your place is here."

Vanzir cleared his throat. "To that end, Aeval doesn't want me going in either. Though if this were a war that all of the Fae were involved in, I think she'd want Camille and me to be at the head of the pack. And she'd be there with us. But Yerghan the Blade coming after the three of you? I think she's pretty much only concerned about Camille's life."

That stung a little, but it didn't surprise me.

"I don't think we should be surprised at all by that. Let's face it, the two of you are benched for this battle. Nobody blames you. But the rest of us can take him on." I straightened. "So, who does that leave to go?"

"I told Nerissa to stay here, too," Menolly began, but I cut her off.

"Don't underestimate her. You should have seen her take on the cyclops." I flashed a grin at Nerissa, who smiled back.

"*Thank you*. I appreciate someone finally standing up for my skills. I worked hard to get where I'm at, and I can fight just as well as anyone of you. Well, maybe not *as* good, but I'm no slouch." She snorted, then gave Menolly a long look. "You are not going to sideline me anymore. It's not that I enjoy fighting, but I want to do my part."

"Touché. I'll stop being so protective. At least, until the next time." Menolly reached out a finger, tucking it under Nerissa's chin, and pulled her forward to give her a long kiss.

"So who all is going? I am, and I assume Shade? Or are your wounds still too severe?" It suddenly occurred to me that Shade might not want to face down Yerghan again, given he still had that damn sword.

"Oh, trust me, I'm coming along. My stitches are almost all healed, and I want a crack at him. I plan on giving him a little taste of what he gave me. And what he did to our house." Apparently Shade's self-doubt didn't impair his desire for revenge.

Roz raised his hand. "I'm going."

"Of course I will go, and Trillian and Morio," Smoky said.

"I'm going, too," Trytian said. "I think we should try to capture him alive, so we can question him."

"You really think we can manage that?" I stared at Trytian, wondering what the daemon had been smoking.

"I intend on trying. Think about it: if we can capture Yerghan the Blade, he can tell us a hell of a lot of useful information about Shadow Wing." Trytian's eyes gleamed, and I had the feeling he was actually looking forward to the prospect.

"What makes you think he's going to talk?"

Trytian stared straight at me, holding my gaze. "I have ways to make him talk. And I don't have the same moral compass as you."

My stomach lurched. I wanted to protest. The thought of torture made my stomach queasy, even if it was Yerghan. But the idea of having an arsenal of information about our enemy was so tempting that I couldn't just blindly say no. I glanced around at the others, wondering what they were thinking.

"Opinions on the subject, please?"

Smoky gave a little shrug. "I think it behooves us to consider the option. After all, we're planning to kill Yerghan. We know that. We're not going in there just to catch him and put them away behind bars. That didn't work so well the first time, did it? Even if the bars were the Sub-Realms."

"I know, but the concept of torturing someone is hard for me. I've come a long ways from my rose-colored glasses days, but there are lines that are hard for me to cross." I thought for a moment. "Is there some magical potion that can force them to tell the truth?" And then I realized what else was bothering me. "It's more than the concept of torture that bothers me. Trytian, I don't want to see you resort to that. I think you're better than that."

He blinked, then let out a sigh. "Delilah. I'm a *daemon*. I know you don't like to think that some people have it in them to torture someone without recrimination, but *I do*. Whether I choose to do so depends on the situation. But we're in a battle against an insane Demon Lord who would love nothing better than to destroy your world—well, both your worlds—and you and your sisters. If Shadow Wing had his way, Earthside and Otherworld would be overrun with demons. Billions of people would be enslaved, and *he would revel in every moment*. So if torturing Yerghan the Blade helps lead to Shadow Wing's downfall? I'll jump in with joy and take the responsibility."

I swallowed my protest. Trytian meant business,

and he was here to help us. And no matter what I said or did, he made a valid point. I was squeamish, and I didn't think I could ever do what he was thinking of, but I had to put my feelings aside in the situation.

"Never mind. I won't fight you on it. But I won't help you, either. I'll help you capture him, and oddly enough, I can help kill him, but I can't inflict torture."

"I won't ask you to be there. If we're lucky, we might be able to get the information out of him by lying, although he's probably smart enough to see through the ruse. We can always tell him we'll let him go if he tells us everything he knows." Trytian paused, then gave me a sly grin. "Would you do *that*? Would you lie to someone to get information?"

I felt like he had put me on the hot seat. Because I knew that I would do exactly as he had said. And I knew that wasn't much better than what he was suggesting.

"Leave the philosophical arguments on morality out of this." Camille sounded irritated. "Whatever it takes, we need to destroy Yerghan. Beyond that, any information we can find about Shadow Wing will help. I'm not going to ask how you get it, because in the long run, Shadow Wing needs to die. We'll never be free of danger, but if he stays in power, everybody connected with us will also be in danger. So Vanzir and I are staying here, and the rest of you are going. Morio, can you show them a map of where the building is? I wish I could stay, but Aeval has requested my presence. I think I'm about to get dressed down for what I did to rescue Delilah."

She stood, looking like she'd rather do anything else in the world except what she was about to. "Vanzir, why don't you stay and help them make plans? I'll tell Aeval you'll be back in a bit." And with that, she left the room, shutting the door behind her and her guards.

Chapter 11

AS SOON AS she left, we got down to business. Morio brought up a map of the industrial district, pointing out the building, which was on the other side of the railroad tracks. It was in a row with a bunch of other abandoned buildings, but this one had two stories. Looking at the satellite view, we could tell it was a metal building, looking as though it was made out of aluminum.

"Both buildings on either side are empty. This entire complex used to be owned by TruFly Airlines until they went out of business. And before you ask, it was a small airline, local to the Northwest, catering to the eco-community. I think they even had composting toilets on their planes. But the other airlines put them out of business with cheaper fares. Of course, with cheap fares comes cheap service, but in this economic recession, those who want and can afford first-class aren't looking to use a composting toilet."

I tried not to laugh. This was serious business, but all I could think about was an in-flight outhouse.

"Did Carter suggest anything?" Nerissa asked.

Vanzir nodded. "He suggested talking to Hercules. And again, before you ask, Hercules happens to be a giant, like your bouncer, Pieder, Menolly, except he's half-blood, not full. Hercules owns the bar across the street from the Sega building. It's called the Rockface. Apparently, if you need to know anything about that particular neighborhood, Hercules is *the* man to ask. Especially if there's a twenty involved."

"So we know that Yerghan has a soul-stealer blade. Trytian, do you know if he's got any other dangerous weapons? Any artifacts? After all, Shadow Wing sent him over and he probably has a massive stash of stuff." My eyes lit up as I spoke. The thought of plundering Shadow Wing's treasure trove and seeing just what he had stashed away made for a good fantasy. I wasn't mercenary, and I didn't focus on belongings, but it was always fun to see what kind of goodies somebody had.

"There are so many possibilities that I couldn't begin to answer that question. Whatever it was, it would have to be something he could carry on him, so he may have an amulet, or a talisman, or some sort of dagger, or even a wand. But bear in mind, Yerghan the Blade is a *soldier*. He left the magic to Telazhar. Which is probably why Shadow Wing sent him over here. If he *had* been a sorcerer, Shadow Wing would have drained him dry. So I doubt if he's got too much magic hidden up his sleeve, other than whatever's inherent to the items he carries."

The daemon leaned forward, resting his elbows on the table. "To be honest, we don't know what we're getting into. You guys were the only ones who've seen him since he gated over, at least among the people we know. Whatever you remember is what we have to go on."

"I have a question," Menolly said. "You said that several transients were found murdered, stabbed to death. Didn't the soul-stealer blade just send them out to the Land of Wandering Souls? Why aren't they alive, like Shade was?"

Shade shook his head. "I'm part dragon. That is the only thing that saved me. I still have stitches, and I heal up far faster than any human ever could. I can't imagine being on the other end of that blade if I was an FBH."

"Yeah, you're right. I hadn't thought about that. Does that mean their souls are forever lost?" A shadow crossed her face, and I realized what she was thinking.

Any human killed by that sword would lose their soul *and* their chance to move on, forever. It was a sobering thought.

"I'm pretty sure that's a big fat yes," Trytian said. "The sooner we can prevent anybody else being hurt by him, the better."

As I stared at the daemon, I realized he *did* have a compassionate side. He might not want to admit it, but I doubted that Trytian would ever harm an innocent person who hadn't attacked him first.

There was a lot he was capable of, but he wasn't really the bad guy he let on to being.

"Is there a back way into the building?" I asked.

Morio minimized the map, then brought up another screen and opened up in the file. "In anticipation of that question, I contacted Tim Winthrop about it. He was able to hack into the blueprints office of the city. I didn't think we'd have the time to go about it the regular way. Anyway, he found this schematic. Here it is." He enlarged the window as large as could.

Tim Winthrop was our go-to guy when it came to computer needs. He had been a female impersonator while he finished college to get his degree in computer science, and we had attended his wedding to the love of his life—Jason Binds, our go-to mechanic. Tim had a little girl from his first marriage. While he and his ex-wife weren't on good terms—she had been taken off guard when he came out—she made certain he had plenty of time with his child.

I suddenly realized that Morio had to be using the laptop on battery. "The battery's not running low, is it?"

"No, and you can thank the techno-mages," he said without missing a beat. "It's running on captured lightning. See that little USB plug?" He pointed to what I had thought was a jump drive. I nodded. "That's actually a power pack, created by the techno-mages. It will run a laptop for about twelve hours on a single charge. Anyway, we have plenty of juice left. And I've got more of these if we need. Now, take a look at the layout of this building."

The building was two stories aboveground, with a basement level. There were three entrances. One, the main front door, was open to the street. The other two entrances were around back, in the alley. One was a large set of hangar doors, allowing deliveries to easily be transferred into the building. The other was a normal-size door, to one side of the hangar.

"Windows?"

"You notice there are two on the upper floor looking over the street, and none in back. There's a front window on the main floor, but it's been barred off. Iron bars. And from what I could tell, they're still firmly in place. No secret entrances, either. Remember, this was a human-made building, designed for business, so it didn't need any secret passages. And Yerghan hasn't had time to create any. Of course, that doesn't mean somebody *else* wasn't using it before, but I seriously doubt that we're going to find anything like trapdoors or entrances through the sewers."

In other words, it hadn't been abandoned long enough for anybody to turn it into a secret lair. We crowded around the blueprints, looking for anything that might help or hinder us.

"Vanzir, you said that Carter suggested we talked to Hercules at the Rockface. Have you guys done so yet?" It occurred to me that we'd been out in the Land of Wandering Souls long enough that maybe they had already taken care of that.

Vanzir shook his head. "I went in the other night, but the bar was so busy that it was hard enough to find a waiter. And then it turned out that Hercules had the night off. We should drop in there tonight before we go over to the hangar."

"All right, here's what we know. Yerghan the Blade has a soul-stealer sword. He may have had time to hire some thugs. For all we know he could have some sort of magical device on him as well. Do we know how he started the fire in the house?" Everything had gone too fast for us to talk to the fire marshal.

"Yugi's team detected some sort of magical firebomb. Which doesn't surprise me," Nerissa said.

"Well, we have our own dealer for those." I glanced over at Roz and laughed. "You've got a steady supply of ice and firebombs, it seems. Bring as many as you've got. Also, bring along your magical stun gun. That thing can take down a horse, so it should be able to take down Yerghan."

We had managed to pick up a magical stun gun in one of our raids, which had also been down in the industrial district. There were a lot of seedy characters that flocked to the area.

"Good idea. And with all of us going in together, we know what to expect out of him, so we can hopefully keep him from attacking anybody else with that damned sword. Also, Trytian's idea of capturing him would be a whole lot easier if we can stun him." Morio leaned back in his chair, shutting his computer. "I suggest we get a move on. Do we need to stop at the house for weapons?"

"I do," Roz said. "I left everything in the studio, but I locked it up and hopefully everything's still in one piece."

Now that Vanzir lived out at Talamh Lonrach Oll, Roz was the only one living in the studio on our land. Once again I felt an overwhelming sweep of nostalgia.

Shade led me back to the bedroom we were using. I turned to him, wanting him, but also hesitant. So many things had gone on that I wasn't sure where we stood. And knowing what personal fears he was fighting only made me more uncertain of how to act.

"We need to talk when we have a chance. I need to talk to you about what you said over in the Land of Wandering Souls. About your fear..."

He let out a sigh. "I know. We really do have to talk. I suppose it's time to get everything out in the open, but let's leave it until after we take care of Yerghan. Then we'll lay all our cards on the table. I guess I've been hiding a lot of things from myself, not just you. I truly didn't realize that losing my Stradolan powers affected me so much. I'm embarrassed." He ducked his head, staring at the floor.

"Don't be, please. We all have our fears. I had no clue that I was still harboring some of the things I discovered while I was over there. And I'll tell you everything, so that you'll know my deepest secrets as well." I leaned down, pressing my lips against his. They were warm and flush against my own, and he pulled me onto his lap, kissing me deeply as his hands stroked my back. After a long moment, he pulled back and stared into my eyes.

"I suppose the best way to start a marriage is with complete honesty. Perhaps Yerghan the Blade has done us a favor without realizing it."

"I wouldn't go that far," I said. "But you're right, sometimes blessings come disguised as curses. Come on, let's get changed and go take care of Yerghan."

As we changed clothes, I glanced over at Shade. He was gorgeous. He had his share of scars and so did I, and so did anybody who had lived a full life. Sometimes those scars were on the surface, and sometimes they were buried deep inside. But scar tissue hurt, no matter which form it took.

WE STOPPED AT the house, and I was surprised to see so many armed guards from Talamh Lonrach Oll there. Camille had been busy, all right. They escorted us onto the land, reporting that no one had been seen at the house since we left. A stray bloatworgle had been found prowling around and quickly dispatched, and the neighbor's dog—Speedo—kept wandering onto the property, but otherwise it had mostly been local wildlife come to visit.

While Roz went to the studio to gather his weaponry, the rest of us walked over to the house. I stared at the charred remains of the back porch and the kitchen. My stomach sank as the scent of soot filled my nostrils. But I noticed that a lot of the stray debris had been cleared away, and a dumpster sat nearby, full of charred timbers. Apparently, work had already begun on repairing the house. I also noticed that stakes had been pounded into the ground, and from those I guessed the kitchen and the back porch were going to be en-larged. We had already enlarged the kitchen once, and I wondered just how many children Camille thought I was going to have. But I wasn't about to complain. The bigger the kitchen, the better.

I dithered about going inside. Part of me didn't want to return home until it was back together again, until it felt whole. Shade seemed to pick up on my feelings, because he draped his arm around my waist and pulled me to him.

"Think of it this way. Our house was wounded. You don't turn away when someone you love—or some*thing* you love—is hurt. You take care of it, and you nurture it, and you nurse it back to health."

I flashed him a smile. "Thank you. I needed to hear that. Hold on, I'll be right back."

I dashed inside the house, one of the guards following right on my heels. I realized I wasn't going to shake him, so I let him come along. I didn't really care what he thought.

As I stood inside the living room, staring at the familiar surroundings that made me feel so grounded, I realized just how much I loved this house, and how much it meant to me. Even though I loved my home in Otherworld, I realized I never wanted to go back. Not to live, at least. This house had become my foundation, my anchor, a part of my very core. Camille and Menolly might not live here anymore, but their memories were deep within the walls, and they would always be a part of this home.

"Hey house, listen up. You need to get better! Get well for me, for Shade, for Maggie and Hanna. You're *our* house, and you mean the world to me. I love you, I love everything about you. We're going to build you back strong and safe, I promise you that."

I glanced at the guard. He smiled at me with a soft glow in his eyes, and I realized he understood what I was doing. I might not work magic like Camille, but I believed with every fiber of my being that everybody had a little magic in their heart, and love only spurred it on.

"Delilah? We're ready!" Shade's voice echoed from the door.

Blowing a kiss toward the walls, I turned and headed back outside.

WE TOOK TWO cars. I drove my Jeep, and Shade, Trytian, and Menolly rode with me. Morio drove his Subaru, and Smoky, Trillian, and Nerissa rode with him. As Camille had predicted, Aeval had put the brakes on Vanzir coming with us. And she had also laid down the law regarding Camille.

It was 10:30 by the time we reached the industrial district. Traffic was light, and because it was the middle of the week, there didn't seem to be much foot traffic on the streets. But the parking lot by the Rockface was jumping. We parked in the last two open spots, and headed toward the door.

As we entered the bar, we were assaulted by the

smells of hard liquor, spilled beer, and fried food. My nose was on hyperdrive, and I could tell that whatever they were serving had been fried in rancid oil that had been around a little too long.

The bar was laid out like a lot of dives—a long counter, jammed with barstools, packed with patrons, and then a series of booths near the windows. The booths were full, although I saw one that was open and sent Morio over to claim it. It was one of those corner booths, shaped in a semi circle, and I thought we might all just barely fit.

Menolly motioned for us to join Morio as she headed up to the bar. A few moments later, she returned, followed by a very large man—he stood ten feet tall—who had a buzz cut, and who was wearing a Nirvana T-shirt. For some reason I hadn't expected the giant to be a grunge fan.

Behind him, a waiter expertly maneuvered a tray with seven beers and a bottle of blood on it. I noticed the beers were microbrews, which meant expensive. I had to hand it to Menolly for knowing how to subtly bribe as well. She motioned for me to scoot over and sat down beside me.

"Hey guys, meet Hercules. He's the owner." She gave him a fangy smile and he returned it with a lopsided grin.

"I never thought I'd have the owner of the Wayfarer as a customer," he said and I heard a muted awe in his voice. It made sense, given Menolly was a minor celebrity among bar owners.

"Hey, we've heard good things about this place. I'm just sorry that I haven't had the time to drop in before now." She motioned to the end of the table.

"Why don't you pull up a chair and join us for a few minutes?" She waited until he had done so, before resting her head on my shoulder. "It's been a long day, I can tell you that."

I wasn't quite sure what angle she was playing, so I kept my mouth shut and gave Hercules a friendly nod.

"I see you have one of your sisters with you! Where's the other one? I heard she's a *queen* now," he said, his voice dropping as though he were speaking about a goddess.

I realized right then that Hercules had a nose for gossip and anything we said would be fair game for the rumor mill. He was a celebrity horn dog and, probably, a name dropper. That could work to our benefit, I thought.

"So, a really nice joint you've got here. What's the foot traffic like?" I asked.

"Pretty good. There's been an uptick in sales over the past week, which suits me just fine. So, your sister…" He glanced around, expectantly. "Will she be in?"

Menolly cleared her throat. "Unfortunately, she's busy with *royal business* right now. I suppose I should be home too, taking care of issues with the Vampire Nation, but you know, sometimes a *princess* just has to have a night out." She pointed out Nerissa. "Let me introduce my wife, Princess Nerissa."

Nerissa gave her a look that would have withered a blackberry bush. But Menolly just smiled at her, blinking.

"How do you do, Mr. Hercules? What a lovely

establishment." Nerissa was laying it on thick, but Hercules seemed to eat it up. He had perked up at the word *princess*. Yep, celeb stalker, all right.

"Wow, I've got two princesses in my establishment. I'd love to take a picture with you both, if you don't mind."

Menolly looked like she was about to lose it, but she managed to suppress her laughter. "Uh, Hercules, I hate to remind you, but I don't show up on camera. Remember, I'm a vampire? And vampires aren't exactly photogenic."

I was doing *my* best to stifle a laugh. Nerissa and Menolly were playing him like a violin. I wondered how often they had done this, especially while out clubbing.

"You can take a picture of me, though," Nerissa said. "I'd be happy to pose with you, if you'd like." She leaned forward, dazzling him with her best Barbie-smile.

Hercules nearly knocked over his chair as he scooted out of the way. Morio, Smoky, and Trillian stood so that Nerissa could squeeze out of the booth. None of the guys looked amused, but they didn't interfere. *I* wouldn't interfere with Menolly's plans, either. Or with her wife. Not when they were on a hunting trip like this.

Nerissa wound her way over to Hercules, draping her arm around his shoulder. He slid his hand around her waist, holding her firmly, and I winced, glancing away, thinking that the ick-factor would be a whole lot less if we just paid him for information. But he was much more likely to give us whatever we wanted if he felt special.

Menolly used his phone to take a picture of them. Then, handing it back, she gave Nerissa a look that I noticed, but I didn't think Hercules caught. Nerissa quickly disentangled herself from his embrace, and slid back in the booth, motioning for the men to sit down quickly so that Hercules didn't try to squeeze in beside her.

Menolly handed his phone back to him. "So, Hercules. What's the area down here like? I've got a friend who's thinking of opening a tattoo shop. There are a few abandoned buildings across the street. Do you think that would be a good location?"

I had to hand it to my sister. She was smooth.

"I'm a little leery about the people over across the street. Those buildings look abandoned, but I've noticed some strange things going on there the past week. I think somebody may have rented the big one, but I haven't seen any renovation going on. I get a bad feeling every time I walk past there." The question seemed to have taken Hercules's mind off the fact that he was hanging with local celebrities.

"What do you mean? What kind of a bad feeling?" I decided to play along too.

He puffed up a little. "I like to think I'm a good judge of energy. I'm not sure what it is, but there's something lurking in that center building that scares the hell out of me, and I don't scare easy. It could be a ghost, maybe. I didn't notice it before last week. And then, the lights are on. That building has been abandoned for a couple years. I *know* there haven't been any squatters there, because I was looking after it for a while. I made sure everything was locked tight. The company went bankrupt and stopped paying me about two months ago, but I still take a walk over there now and then. So I know the feel of it. You know, buildings do have feelings at times."

When you yanked him off "Star-Central Lane," Hercules actually had some substance to him.

"You said you think it might be a ghost. Could it be something else?" Morio asked.

Hercules gave him a shrug. He had barely noticed the men. But now he leaned forward, resting his elbows on the table. "My first thought was a demon of some sort. But there aren't any demons around here, are there?"

I was sitting next to Trytian, and I felt him tense up. I gave him a quick look, but he was staring at the ceiling.

"Well," I said, "you never know. But you're probably right. It's probably a spirit of some sort. Would you like us to take a look for you?" This seemed the perfect opportunity to avoid any questions as to why we were over there prowling around.

He looked all excited again. "You'd do that? I figured you guys must have a really busy schedule."

I wanted to mutter that he didn't know just *how* busy our schedule was, but decided I didn't need to muddy the waters. "I think we could do that. We have a little free time." I glanced around at the others, and they quickly nodded.

"That would be great. I like to keep this neighborhood safe if possible. I have a good clientele, and frankly," he leaned closer and lowered his voice, "some of these guys don't have homes. They come in here for a drink, and then go back to wherever they're staying—an alley, underneath the bridge. I like to keep a watch out for them. I give them a free meal when I know they're on the skids, too."

My feelings for Hercules had shifted in the past few minutes. At first I thought he was a blustery idiot, but now I decided that he really did care about people. After all, if I managed to meet Jerry Springer at the show, I'd probably be about as fangirl as they came. I resolved to try not to embarrass myself, or Shade.

"That's a good thing," Smoky said. "If we'd all look out for our neighbors, life would be a lot nicer. How much do we owe you for the drinks? We'll get a move on and check things out now, while we have the chance." He paused, then added, "We'd appreciate it if you didn't talk about this to anybody, though. Sometimes they can get a little..."

"Jealous? Oh, don't worry, I won't tell anybody that you're doing a favor for me. Then everybody would be after you. I understand," Hercules said, standing up and pushing back his chair. "The drinks are on me. Please, come back anytime. I'm here most evenings except for Tuesdays."

As he backed away, we slid out of the booth and headed for the door. Nerissa paused beside Hercules, leaned up on her tiptoes, and gave him a quick peck on the cheek.

"For luck, for your bar. Thank you." And before he could answer, we were out the door and across the street.

THE ABANDONED BUILDING was covered in aluminum siding, and even the roof looked to be aluminum. When it rained, it had to sound like thunder on the inside, I thought. We skirted the front door, heading around back. Even though Hercules knew what we were doing, we didn't want to attract any other unwanted attention.

"Well, he didn't say he saw a large group of people coming in and out, which gives me hope." Menolly glanced up at the building. "Maybe Yerghan hasn't had time to gather new followers. It wouldn't be nearly as easy over here as it would be in Otherworld, either."

"That's for certain. Just the sight of him would frighten away a lot of people." I bit my lip for a moment, trying to figure out how to phrase what I wanted to say. "I know we want to catch him alive, to question him. But I'm just gonna say this right now. If he comes at me with that sword, I'm going to do whatever I can to kill him. I never want to be sent back into the Land of Wandering Souls. That experience was more than I needed for one lifetime."

"Trust me, if it looks like he's going to hit anybody with that sword, we'll do whatever we can to take him down. We won't put anybody in danger just to trap him." Smoky glanced over at Trytian. "Right, Trytian?"

The daemon gave a shrug. "Whatever you say. I'm just saying that it would do us a lot of good if we could probe him for information."

As we headed toward the back door, I glanced over at the hangar bay. A lot of these old buildings had large storage doors that opened up so that they could be used for loading and unloading. While I figured that no airplane parts had ever been stored here, I couldn't help but wonder what they had used the warehouse for. I had never heard of the airline before, and it didn't surprise me that they had gone out of business.

"I have a question, and I don't really want to bring it up, but I figure somebody should." Nerissa motioned for us to pause as we approached the stairs going up to the door. "If Shadow Wing has a geas attached to Yerghan, does that mean that Shadow Wing can see through his eyes? Will he know that we're attacking? And if we managed to capture him, and question him, will Shadow Wing know what we're asking? Won't that give away our hand?"

"Damn it, I didn't think about that." Trytian flashed her a nasty look.

"Don't blame *me* for your lack of foresight," Nerissa tossed back. "I just figured that somebody ought to ask the question."

I let out a long sigh. "Well, does that change matters? Or we could hustle him into the safe room at the Wayfarer and question him there. There's no way Shadow Wing could see through his eyes then, could he?"

Menolly gave me a nod. "That's a good idea.

If we catch him, we can blindfold him and stick earplugs in his ears. That way Shadow Wing won't be able to see through his eyes, or hear anything going on. We just keep our own mouths shut until we get there, and then Trytian and whoever else wants to question him can go inside. Even demons can't get out of that room."

"That's a good plan," I said. "So we take him down with as little chatter as possible, slap a blindfold on him, and hustle him down to the Wayfarer pronto. At least Shadow Wing can't gate in to help him."

"No, but can Shadow Wing gate him back to the Sub-Realms? There's another question we haven't considered," Menolly said. "He won't be able to if Yerghan's in the safe room, but until we get there..."

"Hell. I hadn't thought about that." It occurred to me that we did our best thinking after the fact. It would have helped if we had come up with all these questions while we were making plans back at the Barrow, but apparently our minds didn't work that way. "There's no way to know. We have to go on hope and a prayer."

"All right, we wing it. And hopefully not *Shadow Wing* it." Morio grinned as we all groaned.

"Oh, so very clever," Menolly said. "After the war, we can start our own improv group."

The concrete walkway in front of the hangar was about six feet wide. I saw paint markings on the concrete and they confused me until I realized that they were guidelines for trucks as they backed up to the bay to unload.

The hangar doors themselves were barricaded, and it looked like they hadn't been touched since they had first been barred. But when we looked at the other door, the wooden slats had been pried off and tossed to the side.

I eyed the doorknob, wondering whether just to open it and barge through, or have Morio check it for any traps. Morio decided for me. He motioned for me to get out of the way, then handed me a flashlight and had me hold it so that the beam illuminated the lock while he inspected it. A moment later, he shook his head.

"Looks clear to me. No traps, at least. I wonder if the door is locked."

"Only one way to find out," I said as I reached for the knob.

Chapter 12

AS I OPENED the door, a breath of stale air rushed out. There was a hush that seemed to come with it, as with all abandoned buildings left to fester on their own. But I couldn't feel any ghosts inside. Not from here.

We entered into one large, open room. From where we stood, I could see the hangar bay doors to our right. Toward the back of the room, a spiral staircase led to the second level. On the other side of the room, a door against the right wall had the words STAIRS stenciled on it, and probably led to the basement. Another door, flush against the opposite wall, most likely led to the front of the building. The room was lit with a series of fluorescent lights that hung from the ceiling, bare-bulbed and flickering with age. Dilapidated pallets were scattered around the room, which was about as large as a good-size high school gymnasium.

There was no sign of movement, except for a stray rat that I spotted across the room. I restrained myself from chasing after it, which was my natural inclination. Roz shut the door quietly behind us and we gathered near the wall, trying to figure out what to do next. I had half expected Yerghan the Blade to be waiting for us, but he wasn't, which meant we had to decide our next step.

I glanced over at Shade. "Up or down?" I asked softly.

He cocked his head, listening, as did Menolly. After a moment, Shade shook his head but Menolly pointed up toward the ceiling.

"You hear something?" Shade whispered.

She nodded. "Scuffling, and it's not mice." A hard look entered her eyes, and her fangs descended. Her predator was awake, which meant she sensed something.

I straightened my shoulders, slowly withdrawing my blade. I could feel it now, the sense that we weren't alone in the building. Yerghan the Blade had spent thousands of years growing into his power, and life in the Sub-Realms had to have groomed him. He was evil when he was sent there to begin with, but I couldn't imagine what he was like now, or how ruthless he had become.

"If we go up that spiral staircase, we'll be sitting ducks, and he'll be able to pick us off one at a time. Is there another way in? Through the roof, perhaps?" While the room we were in was at least fifteen feet high, it didn't show us the state of the roof, given there was an upstairs.

Shade motioned for us to head back out the door. Once we were standing out on the hangar bay, he leaned against the door to keep it shut.

"Delilah's right, If we go upstairs, he'll have a clean shot at us, one at a time. And we have no clue whether he has any distance weapons." He glanced over at Smoky. "You can't go through the Ionyc Seas, can you?"

Smoky shook his head. "I have no clue where I'm going, so it wouldn't be safe."

Now would be the perfect time, I thought, for Shade to have his Stradolan powers back. They would allow him to go through as a shadow, filtering up the staircase without really being seen. But I wasn't about to say anything, because I didn't want to trigger off his insecurities again. And it would do no good, anyway. If Vanzir had been able to come with us, he could probably travel through on the astral realm. As it was, we had to make up our minds soon. We couldn't just sit out here until Yerghan decided to go get himself a hamburger.

"Is there any way to head up to the roof?" I asked.

"Yes, and I will be the one to do it." Menolly stepped to the side. "I can fly up there and take a look around. Meanwhile, I suggest that at least two of you go around front to make certain that our burly soldier doesn't decide to take off through the front door." And with that, she turned into a bat, and began to fly toward the roof.

Smoky motioned to Trytian. "Come on, we'll watch the front."

Trytian looked as though that was the last thing

he wanted to do, given Smoky had threatened him numerous times about harassing Camille, but he followed the dragon without saying a word. The rest of us kept an eye on the back.

About ten minutes later, Menolly returned, quickly shifting back into herself. She had gotten really good with transforming into her bat shape, and with flying, thanks to Roman's coaching.

She shook her head, her eyes gleaming. "There's no way you're getting through the roof. I looked everywhere there and couldn't find any holes or trapdoors or anything of the sort. Whoever runs this building is going to have solid protection from the rain, I'll tell you that."

"Then I guess it's the staircase." I pulled out my phone and texted Smoky, telling him and Trytian to come back around to the alley.

WE'RE HEADED IN, I texted.

WE'LL COME IN THE FRONT DOOR SO THAT HE DOESN'T HAVE THE CHANCE TO ESCAPE AT ALL.

I pocketed my phone and pulled up my dagger. "Smoky and Trytian will meet us in there just in case Yerghan decides to head out in the next couple of minutes." And with that, I yanked open the door and headed in. "It occurs to me if we make enough noise he'll come down."

"It's a calculated risk, but go ahead." Shade looked around, then picked up a broken piece of a wooden pallet and slammed it against the metal staircase. The reverberation echoed through the room. We heard a cursing from upstairs, and spread out around the staircase just as Smoky and Trytian joined us from the front.

Menolly quickly turned back into a bat, and I wondered what she was doing. But as she flew toward the spiral staircase, I realized that she was getting into position, a surprise of sorts.

"What the hell is that racket down there? You'd better have my dinner, you scumbag." The man's voice bellowed through the room as footsteps echoed from the metal staircase. A few seconds later, we saw Yerghan there, pausing halfway down the staircase, his jaw hanging open.

Within a blink, Menolly turned back into herself, leaping directly down on the staircase where she blocked Yerghan from heading back up the steps.

"Oh, we have your dinner, all right," Menolly said, giving him a massive shove so that he fell over the edge of the railing, hitting on the floor in front of us. She leapt over the side, landing beside him, in a crouch.

Yerghan rolled to his feet, surprisingly unhurt. But then again, a couple thousand years in the Sub-Realms had to have toughened him up.

I glanced at his side. No sword, but he did have at least one dagger that I could see. But instead of reaching for his blade, he reached inside his coat, and before we could do anything, he threw something on the ground in front of us.

"I suggest you take a moment to think about what you're doing." Even as he spoke, I knew something was wrong.

As the smoke billowed out from whatever charm

he had used, I tried to move but found myself frozen. It was like playing statues as a child. I tried to speak and found I couldn't move my mouth either. Terrified, I wondered if my lungs were working, but then I felt myself draw a very slow, shallow breath of air. I was at least getting enough oxygen to keep from suffocating.

I tried to look around, but I couldn't even move my eyes from side to side. From what little I could see, nobody else was moving, either. Except Trytian.

Trytian closed in on Yerghan. They were directly in front of me, so I could see them. The daemon had a long blade out, a gleaming, wicked-sharp blade that looked to be made of obsidian, glassy and shining with a black sheen.

"You're not getting away that easy," Trytian said, cautiously approaching the warrior.

"Don't bet on it," Yerghan said. He pulled out his dagger, and looked straight at me.

Panicking, I realized that if he managed to reach my side—or Menolly's—he could finish two-thirds of his task right here. And there was nothing we could do. I couldn't see Menolly, so I couldn't tell whether she had been affected by the paralysis spell as well.

Trytian must have noticed Yerghan's focus, because he darted to the side, standing in front of me, between me and the brute.

"You have to go through me first," he said, swinging with his blade. The obsidian landed against Yerghan's arm, slicing deep. I could almost hear the sound of flesh rending.

Yerghan let out a loud curse as blood began to spill from his arm, spurting out so fast that it looked like Trytian had cut into a major artery. The gash looked deep and ugly.

Yerghan growled and once again reached in his pocket. This time, I wasn't able to see what he withdrew, but he slapped it against the bloody gash and instantly, the wound stopped bleeding. It didn't heal, from what I could tell, but the blood flow had stopped.

Meanwhile, Trytian darted in, slashing at him again. This time his sword met Yerghan's leather armor, cleaving through it, and sending another fountain of blood spraying out of Yerghan's side.

I felt my nose itch, and wriggled it, suddenly aware that I was starting to pull out of the paralysis. I tried to move my fingers, but they weren't free yet. However, the next moment, Menolly darted past my line of vision, slamming herself against Yerghan and knocking him down. He managed to throw her off, and she went sailing across the floor, a look of astonishment in her eyes.

At that moment, Smoky broke free, but there was a sound behind us, and Smoky turned, his eyes growing wide. I could move my arms now, and then my head, so I glanced over my shoulder just in time to see several demons enter the room.

Holy crap. Yerghan had managed call for backup somehow.

As Trytian took on Yerghan again, Menolly went racing past toward the demons, followed by Smoky. I was finally able to move, and I followed them, Lysanthra out and ready, as the demons descended on us. They were the same type we had met at the house, so I knew just how tough they were.

By then, everyone was free of the paralysis. Shade was helping Trytian, while Nerissa, Trillian, and Morio joined Smoky and Menolly and me.

As we engaged, Nerissa and I took on one of the demons, while Trillian, Morio, and Smoky each took on another, and the sounds of combat filled the room. Nerissa and I looked at each other and nodded, thinking the same thing. We both sheathed our weapons and shifted form, she into her puma self and me into Panther. We were much more effective in combat this way, and we both leapt on the demon, knocking him down with our weight.

As she stood on his chest, her claws digging deep into his stomach, I pounced on his head, holding him down with one paw, as with the other I began slashing through his throat. I grabbed hold of one of his horns, shaking my head this way and that, using my strength to try to break his neck. Nerissa held him fast, digging in deep, while I lunged for his throat, bit deep, and then began to hack away.

The sound of rending flesh filled my ears and the smell of blood rose thickly as his skull broke away from his spine and the edges of his skin began to rip from his shoulders. And then I was standing there, the demon's head hanging from my mouth. Disgusted, I shook my head again, letting go of the head, sending it rolling across the floor.

Nerissa and I turned to see that Smoky had eviscerated his demon, the entrails splashing across the floor. Morio was in his youkai form, eight feet tall and engaged in a wrestling match. Trillian was having trouble, however.

Before I could move, Nerissa had joined the fray, launching herself onto Trillian's demon from the side. She managed to knock him down. Trillian plunged his blade through the demon's head, cursing as the tip of his sword broke against the concrete floor. But it had done its job. The demon thrashed, then lay still.

Panting, Nerissa pulled back, as Trillian tossed her a quick *Thank-you*.

I turned, intent on helping Trytian, just in time to see Yerghan plunge his blade through Trytian's heart. The daemon let out a cry as Yerghan twisted the dagger, and then Trytian fell to the floor. Yerghan yanked his blade out of Trytian's body and looked over at us, a smug smile on his face.

A dark fury filled my soul, and I felt the power of Hi'ran rise up in me as I bounded across the floor, launching myself onto Yerghan, knocking him down. I focused my attention into his eyes, forcing myself into his soul.

Ten thousand deaths weighed heavy on his conscience. Ten thousand screams of pain, and more—there were so many victims lined up, throughout his memory, to the point where they became legion, and then, a blur, and then, they faded into a whisper and a joke for him to laugh at.

The images flashed past.

Yerghan, a young and idealistic soldier, wanting only for a better world. And then came Telazhar, who promised him a new order, in which magic and might would rule hand in hand. Images of a bright future loomed large, filled with flame and drive and passion. But the brilliance promised turned into darkness. An ocean of blood descended as Telazhar and Yerghan drove the purifying flames ahead of them, purging the land of all that was fruitful and growing.

And Yerghan the idealist became Yerghan the Blade, became Yerghan the executioner, became Yerghan whose only hunger was for power and strength. It was at the tip of their fingers, right within their grasp until the opposition struck, driving them down.

And then he became Yerghan the enslaved when he and Telazhar were cast into the Sub-Realms, where Shadow Wing the Unraveller loomed like a hope and scourge in the night, and his will became their will.

The screams of ten thousand more voices blended into one cry in my ears, surrounding me like ghosts in the night, and I could feel their pain and Yerghan's joy as he destroyed them.

A little girl stared up at me, or rather Yerghan, as I looked through his eyes. Her mother lay on the ground beside her, dead. The girl couldn't have been more than five years old. And then Yerghan raised his blade, and as her eyes widened, he swung, cleaving her head from her shoulders.

No more, I whispered.

No more deaths. No more anger. No more terror. No more victims. No more existence.

I rose in front of him in my Death Maiden persona, cloaked in a flowing gown the color of the night sky. The crescent blazed on my forehead, brilliant against my skin. I caught hold of his soul and dragged him into the stars, into the space between worlds where his fate would be decided.

He stared at me, finally looking frightened for the first time. A swirl of mist rolled around us, and we were in that land that hangs between the balance, the land where I was at my full power, where I could easily destroy his soul forever and wipe him out of existence, sending him spiraling into the primal pool of energy, to erase his presence forever. Where I could consign him into an existence as mere energy to be used again, clean and clear, with no trace left of the corroded soul he had been. It was cold here, bone chilling cold, and it seeped through every cell in my body, every fiber of my being. I could see he felt it, too.

He was shivering as he fell to his knees.

"Who are you? What do you want?" His voice echoed through my mind, and I knew he wasn't really speaking, but I could catch his thoughts as easily as I could catch my own.

"I am your end. I am handmaiden to the Autumn Lord, a servant of the Harvestmen. I claim your soul for the sins you have perpetuated against the innocent. I come to destroy you, Yerghan the Blade, to un-make you. I come to forever obliterate you from this world, or any world. I consign you to the emptiness, I consign you to the depths of the universe, I consign you to oblivion. It is the *only fitting punishment* for the crimes you have committed."

I was towering over him now, so tall that I could barely see him from where he groveled below me. Around me, the stars wheeled in a spiraling gyre. I could feel Greta near, but she did not interfere.

Yerghan the Blade stared up at me defiantly, holding his arms out at his sides.

"Then be done with it. Be done with it and have it over."

I caught another wisp of his thoughts.

He was tired. He was so tired of the never-ending blood and gore and battle, but he didn't realize it. He didn't know that he was done. He had been going through the motions like an automaton, a puppet on a string, so numb to the world around him that he was numb to even himself. Nothing mattered anymore to him, not freedom, not glory, not even life itself.

"A change is as good as a rest," I said softly.

I didn't feel sorry for him, but a part of me understood his weariness, and I was grateful for it. It made my job easier. As I was about to send him into oblivion, I paused, realizing that I could look into his mind and find out what I needed to know about Shadow Wing. We wouldn't have to question him. I could find out everything I needed to know right here.

I reached out, plunging my mind into his, ignoring his shriek of pain as I intruded into his thoughts. I didn't care. He had inflicted so much anguish over the millennia that he could handle a little himself. I tore through his thoughts, sifting through his memory as I searched for any mention or vision of Shadow Wing. And there it was. Or

rather, there *he* was.
Shadow Wing. In all his vile glory.

THE DEMON LORD rose up in front of me, complete with wings and horns that spiraled into the sky. Shadow Wing the Unraveller, Shadow Wing the Corrupter.

He was massive, terrifying in his size, and yet his eyes were more fearsome than his muscles or talons or magic. Because his eyes held nothing but madness, a spiral of insanity.

How he hated, hated *everything* that he could not touch or corrupt. There was no reasoning with this creature, for he was just that—a creature, not a being with whom we could reason or use logic. His hunger was a wound so deep that there was no filling it up. He was the pit and the void, a black hole embodied, sucking in everything that was good or caring, then spitting it out as a tainted version of itself.

Shadow Wing the Unraveller stood there, laughing at Yerghan as the warrior groveled on the ground before him. He lashed out with whip and flame, scarring Yerghan's back, sneering as he kicked the soldier in the ribs so hard that they were permanently deformed.

I forced myself to watch as Shadow Wing used Yerghan as a toy, for his pleasure, whispering in his ear that if he behaved, if he willingly gave Shadow Wing whatever he wanted, Shadow Wing would make him his right hand when he broke through the portals. That together, they would rule. And Yerghan believed, because he had no other option. I began to understand Shadow Wing's followers and their devotion.

If they had not given into Shadow Wing, thrown themselves in with his lot, it would have meant unending torture, with no hope for escape. And all beings needed hope to survive. So the hope that he offered them, even as he mocked them, was that of power and fame and fortune, and their choice of the spoils. And even though they knew it would never happen, they chose to believe in order to survive.

As much as I hated both Telazhar and Yerghan, a very small part of myself felt an empathy for them. They had met their match and failed.

I watched, steeling myself as I searched for any vulnerability.

Shadow Wing was definitely mad, so full of his own ego that he didn't believe he could fail. And he hated us, I could hear it in his voice when he ordered Yerghan to destroy us to win his freedom. He hated us with every fiber of his being, because we had disrupted his plans.

I didn't reach out to touch Shadow Wing himself because I couldn't bring myself to, but I knew that, in this space, the Demon Lord couldn't follow us. It was better than the best safe room we ever could offer, this space between worlds.

As the Demon Lord ranted away, Hi'ran suddenly stood by my side. I looked up at him, my heart racing as he slid his arm around my waist.

"Please don't stop me," I said. "I want to end Yerghan's life. I want to end him forever—I don't ever want his spirit to break free and return in any form or fashion."

"Oh Delilah, my dearest, I'm not here to stop you."

"You aren't?" I was surprised.

"No. Although you've taken this on yourself, and in doing so, you fulfill my hope. You are worthy of being my mate. You withstand this brutality spreading out before you, while you search for answers that will help you to save others. Your actions are those of a queen. Your courage is that of a warrior. You have become everything I hoped and believed that you would be. I leave you to your task, but I would say this. Look for the source of Shadow Wing's power. It may not be what you think it is. Find the source, and you can find a way to destroy him."

He vanished, and I returned my attention to the Demon Lord.

I watched him through Yerghan's eyes, and then as I tried to watch with a keen eye, I saw it. Or rather, I saw *them*.

Two jewels, embedded one to each side by the base of Shadow Wing's horns. They glimmered. There was something about them that kept my attention. As I focused, I realized they reminded me of the spirit seals. And yet, they weren't the same.

But they *were* magical, radiating a powerful force. And right then, I knew exactly where Shadow Wing sourced his power. Those jewels gave him the strength to command his armies. I forced

Yerghan to look at them closely, and through his eyes I saw that they were a deep jet with a sparkling white center.

Yerghan tried to pull away. He didn't want to look at Shadow Wing, just as he didn't want to look at his own memories. But I forced him to concentrate as I reached out, trying to suss out just what the gems were. Yerghan screamed at that moment, and I felt him losing grasp of reality. He couldn't look upon the Demon Lord for long without going mad.

Realizing that I had learned all I could, I loosened my grip and stood back. Yerghan cowered in front of me, his hands over his face.

"It's time. We're done. It's over."

I cut the cord, sending Yerghan's soul into the depths of oblivion forever as I eliminated him from the wheel of life. He screamed once, and then disappeared, vanishing into the mist, vanishing into that primal pool that sources all life within the universe.

Yerghan the Blade would never again walk any world, in any form.

I let out a deep breath, and turned to leave. Hi'ran was there, and he pulled me into his arms. He kissed me deeply, and this time he didn't suck my life out of me, but simply kissed me, sending every cell in my body into an orgasm. As he let go, holding my hand, he smiled.

"It's nearly over. And our new life is about to begin. Yours, and mine, and Shade's. Kiss him when you open your eyes. I'm sending him a gift through you."

And then he was gone, and I left the realm of the dead.

SHADE WAS THERE by my side as I opened my eyes. Yerghan was dead on the floor, and I was in my two-legged form. "Are you all right? What did you do to him?"

Before I spoke, before I said a word, I pulled Shade into my arms and kissed him deeply. I could feel the transfer of energy through me, into Shade. I kissed him long and hard, a wave rushing through me into my love. Finally, whatever the Autumn Lord had sent to Shade was through and done. And as I stood back, Shade's eyes widened, and he clutched my shoulders.

"What have you done to me?" The next moment, he vanished into a puff of smoke, into a wisp of shadow, and was gone.

Chapter 13

FRANTIC, I STUMBLED back, terrified. Something had gone wrong. Maybe the energy I had used to destroy Yerghan the Blade had transferred itself into Shade? Maybe I had sent his soul along with Yerghan's into oblivion? Maybe Hi'ran had used me to punish Shade for something? I let out a cry and turned, wanting to run anywhere but here.

"Delilah, stop," Smoky shouted. He reached out and grabbed hold of my wrist. "It's all right, calm down."

"How can it be all right? I just killed the man I love!" I struggled against him, but dragons almost always win out in a battle against the Fae.

He grabbed hold of my other wrist, holding me firmly. He gave me a little shake, staring down into my eyes. "Stop. Listen to me, Delilah. It's okay. You didn't kill Shade."

I looked around, unable to see Shade anywhere.

"If I didn't kill him, then where is he? I don't see him, Smoky!"

As I spoke, a wisp of smoke and shadow surrounded me, circling me, gently touching my skin. And then, it formed itself into a tendril, and stroked my nose. I suddenly calmed, looking up at Smoky, who nodded.

"But... How did he..." And then I knew. Hi'ran had given Shade a gift that no one else could. A gift I had prayed for, for months.

The shadow moved away from me. Then, slowly coalescing into a shape out of the shadows surrounding him, stepped Shade. His face was filled with wonder, and a joy that I hadn't seen in a long, long time.

"I can't believe it. How did you do that?" He shook his head, looking overwhelmed.

"The Autumn Lord did it. He told me to kiss you when I got back. He said he had a gift for you. I had no clue."

And then I realized Trytian was still on the floor.

"Trytian? Is he all right?" I hurried to his side, sliding onto my knees beside him.

The daemon stared glassy eyed at the ceiling, his chest unmoving. Trytian was dead, and there would be no bringing him back. All of the conflicting emotions of the past week or so snowballed into one giant mire, sucking me down. I began to cry, not realizing until now how deeply I had valued Trytian's help. He had been an asshole at times, but he was our ally, and he had given his life protecting me. I reached out, closing his eyes, and then looked up at the others.

"He's dead."

"We know." Menolly crossed to my side, kneeling beside me. She took my hand, holding tight. As she cleared her throat, I tried to find my voice.

"What was life has crumbled. What was form now falls away. Mortal chains unbind and the soul is lifted free. May you find your way to the ancestors. May you find your path to the gods. May your bravery and courage be remembered in song and story. May your parents be proud, and may your children carry your birthright. Sleep, and wander no more."

Even as our words faded away, I slumped down on the floor, leaning against Menolly, who rocked me gently. The damage in this war had grown old, and yet every time we lost someone it was a new wound, cleaving deep into our hearts. Trytian may not have been our favorite person, but he had been on our side and he had helped us time and again. And he had paid the final and highest price.

WE REGROUPED AT the Barrow. Camille took one look at us, scanning our faces, and she knew.

"We lost Trytian, didn't we? How do we get word to his father?"

Vanzir's expression was bleak. "I can send word through the Demon Underground. It will get there. I don't know how long it will take, but it will reach his father's ears."

"Tell him that Trytian fulfilled his mission. He

prevented Yerghan from killing us. Tell him... Tell him that we will avenge his son's death." It was the only thing I could think of to say.

"And what of Yerghan? Does he still live?"

I shook my head. "I took him out. For good. Forever. He will never cross the wheel again." But I felt no joy in the victory. So much had happened. I was just tired. I wanted to rest and sleep and forget about all the damage and death that we had been through. As joyful as I felt over Shade recovering his powers, right now life felt a lot like an albatross around my neck and I just wanted this fucking war done. And afterward, I wanted to retire from the OIA. I wanted to kick back, and raise a garden, and live a quiet life.

Camille must have sensed my weariness, because she motioned for her servants to help us. "Go, bathe, eat, and rest. We can talk tomorrow morning. If Yerghan is dead, then we have a little breathing room."

But the thought hung heavy in the room between us, unspoken, but as vocal as if someone had given voice to it, that we were one step away from the end. One step away from finally putting a stop to all the pain and anguish that this demonic war had cost us. I knew how to kill Shadow Wing, but that didn't mean that it would be easy. But I knew where his powers were hidden, and that was half the battle right there.

Wearily, we all trooped to our private chambers.

Shade sat on the bed, slowly removing his clothes. He looked up at me, his eyes warm and luminous.

"Did you have to promise *him* anything for this? Please tell me you didn't make a deal for this?"

And right then, I realized that he was terrified that I compromised myself for his comfort. I crawled on the bed beside him, folding my legs cross-legged, and rested my head against his shoulder.

"It was a gift, as I said. Hi'ran didn't make me promise anything. I didn't offer him my life. Or anything else. He already has everything that I own. Sweetie, he gave this freely and I was just the go-between. Welcome back. But I need you to know something."

"What?"

"Even if you *never* got your Stradolan powers back, it wouldn't matter to me. I have never seen you as impotent, or as *half a man* or anything like that. You're the man I love, powers or not. Even if you somehow ended up human, with nothing but your heart, I would love you until the day you die. Until the day *I* die. You are my heart and soul, Shade. You are my mate. Hi'ran may have brought you to me, but it was fate. We're meant to be together."

He was crying now, the tears streaking down his cheeks. "When we were out in the Land of Wandering Souls, when you found me and I was so confused... I was afraid that one day you'd get tired of me. That one day, you'd be angry that I was chosen for you. That you didn't have a choice in the matter. That's *really* what my fear was. I could live without any powers as long as I have you."

"Shut up, you beautiful man. Kiss me, kiss me,

and make me feel whole again."

And so he did, laying me back in the bed, kissing me all over. We were too tired to make love, but we lay long into the night, holding each other, saying nothing, letting our love buoy us up, and heal us.

IN THE MORNING, we gathered back in the Council chamber after sleeping late. Breakfast was spread across the sideboard, and smelled fantastic. I didn't realize I was so hungry, and I piled my plate high. Menolly was missing, of course, she was deep into her sleep, but the rest of us were here. Except Trytian.

As we settled around the table, Camille lifted her glass.

"I want to toast to Trytian. He and I butted heads a lot, but in the end he came through for us. And he gave his life helping us. Here's to the only daemon that I can probably ever call my friend." She paused, glancing at Vanzir, and then smiled. "And that does not include demons."

We all cheered, toasting Trytian's memory.

I was still smarting from his death. I hated losing any member of our team, and the fact that he had died helping to protect me didn't make it any easier. But we had lost a lot of people over the years in our war against Shadow Wing. Perhaps we could put an end to the collateral damage once and for all.

"I have some news," I said, pushing myself to my

feet. "I didn't tell you last night because we were too tired, and there was no need given Yerghan's death. But I need to tell you something. I've found a turning point in the war. When I destroyed Yerghan's soul last night, before I did, I tore through his memories. I observed Shadow Wing through his eyes. I know what Shadow Wing's weakness is."

There was a sudden hush, and they all stared at me. I glanced around the room.

"Is it safe to talk here?"

Camille nodded. "Yes. Tell us what you found out. Anything that can help us is a great gift."

I told them what I had seen. I edited out some of the torture scenes, not wanting to even speak the words. But I told them about the gems below Shadow Wing's horns, and how I knew he sourced his power through there. I described them as best as I could.

"I'm not sure what they are, but they are the source of his power, and if we can destroy them or even remove them, we can kill him without much trouble."

"You say they were like the spirit seals?" Trillian asked.

I shook my head. "In a way they reminded me of the spirit seals, in terms of the fact that they possess energy. But they *aren't* spirit seals. I don't know what they are. We need to do some research as soon as possible. Shadow Wing is going to figure out that Yerghan is gone sooner than later. I think we should follow through with our plan to gate him over here and destroy him as soon as he arrives. We have Yerghan's possessions, including the soul-stealer sword. Shadow Wing touched it, that much I know. We can use that as an anchor to link to him. We just need a sorcerer powerful enough to cast a demon gate."

"To that end, we have one," Camille said softly.

I gazed into her eyes. "Shamas?"

She nodded. "I've been talking to him. He's still very fuzzy on a lot of things, but he's become very powerful since his death, and I think... I believe the Moon Mother has sent him back for this very reason."

My stomach churned. "What do you think will happen to the Keraastar Knights once we've defeated Shadow Wing?"

She stared at the table, not answering. I broke into a cold sweat, thinking about Chase and his daughter. About Luke, and Venus the Moon Child, and all of the Knights.

"You can't mean..." I couldn't even finish the sentence.

"I don't know," she said. "The truth is, I *don't know* what will happen to them. I don't know how they play into this, but they do. And the outcome? At least for them? Remains a mystery, hidden from my sight. I don't think I'm supposed to see the outcome because my seeing it might affect it." She sounded defensive, and I backed off.

I let out a deep breath, trying to sort out everything in my mind. "So Shamas can cast a demon gate powerful enough to bring Shadow Wing over?"

"I believe he can, if he has the right anchor. And

if you are correct, we have the anchors he needs. The question is, when do we do this?" She looked about as bleak as I felt at the moment.

"We need to find out what those jewels are before we bring him over here. And how to destroy them, if that's what it's going to take." Smoky leaned forward, his hands pressed against the table. His hair moved as though it was agitated. "So we have research to do. I don't think we have to move immediately, but we can't let this linger. Meanwhile, we'll be able to finish fixing the house for Delilah and Shade. And since Shade has his full powers back, we have more ammunition."

"I'll get right on the research," Morio said. "I'll start in as soon as breakfast is over and we're done here. There has to be some mention of those gems, somewhere."

"If worse comes to worse, we can visit Grandmother Coyote. She might be able to tell us," Camille said.

That was a bucket of cold water in the face. I was already nervous, but the thought of visiting Grandmother Coyote to ask for her help in such an important matter was enough to nauseate me. Who knew what her price would be for that sort of aid?

"I know it seems frivolous to go forward with our wedding, given what we're facing, but the Autumn Lord was clear. Shade and I have to get married as soon as possible, and since the equinox is coming up in just a few days…" I felt odd talking about wedding plans and Shadow Wing in the same conversation, but at this point, it was just another part of our new normal.

"Of course," Camille said. "And it's not like Shadow Wing can gate over here right now on his own. Your wedding will be beautiful, and we'll enjoy the day, and we will make it as special as we can possibly make it. Do you still want to hold it down at Birchwater Pond?"

I nodded, glancing at Shade, who gave me a smile. "It's only fitting. Do you mind?"

"Mind what?" Camille asked.

"If we have it there instead of here. I mean, we wanted to have it at the pond, but we've been staying out here so…" I wasn't sure *what* I was saying anymore. I just felt so tired and in a tizzy that the words were babbling out like I was some sort of out-of-control brook.

"Of course not. That's where we were always planning to hold it. We may have to wait on your honeymoon for a bit, but I hope you don't mind." She glanced around at everybody else, who was sitting there silently, listening to us. "And we're all going to make it a wonderful wedding, aren't we?"

"Of course we will," Trillian said, perking up. I wasn't sure if he felt as cheerful as he sounded, but I was grateful to him nonetheless.

"Thank you," I said, reaching for Shade's hand. "I never expected to be getting married in the middle of a demonic war, but I guess that seems to be the MO of the D'Artigo sisters." And at that, everybody laughed and the tension finally broke.

Chapter 14

***FOUR** DAYS LATER...*

Even though the equinox was the next day, somehow I wasn't feeling any jitters. When we had arrived home, we were greeted by an almost fully renovated house. Or rather, kitchen and back porch. The kitchen was rebuilt, bigger and better than ever, as was the porch, the new counters and cupboards were in, and all new appliances. All that was left was to move in the furniture. The workmen had painted the walls a soft yellow, one of my favorite colors, so the kitchen reminded me of morning sunshine. When we first arrived home, I stood in the center of the room and whirled around, absolutely in love with the way it looked.

Now, on the evening before the equinox, it was well past sunset.

Menolly was sitting in the kitchen with me, in

the rocking chair. She was playing with Maggie, who was holding her Yobie doll, as outside twilight gently faded into night. Over the past couple of days, I'd had time to shake out, to let go of some of the tension. For whatever reason—maybe it was that we had a plan, or maybe it was that, finally, the war felt like it was coming to a close—I was actually relaxed and happy. I was fixing dinner for myself, while Menolly drank a bottle of flavored blood. I was making a grilled cheese sandwich, and tomato soup.

"I wish Camille could be here tonight," I said.

"Me too, but at least she'll be here tomorrow." Menolly paused, staring down at Maggie as she stroked the gargoyle's silky fur. "Blood Wyne is returning to Europe. She's leaving Roman and me in charge of the North American Vampire Nation. It's going to mean a lot of pomp and circumstance, and time for me spent by Roman's side. Nerissa will be there too. I hate to say it, but we've had to ask her to quit her job."

"What? She loves that job!"

"Yes, but it's too dangerous for her now, with as many vampire-phobes as there are. Even though she's not a vamp, she's married to two, and that puts her in danger. So I guess our lives are changing, too."

I carried my plate over to the table and sat down, sighing.

"I wondered how long it would be before the two of you got caught up in the politics. Do you really want to do this? Is there a way you can get out of it?" Even as I asked the question, I knew the answer. I could see it in her face.

"I can make a difference, Kitten. Roman and I have been talking a lot about the vampire rights bill that just passed. There's a great deal of backlash, but we can help put a stop to it. With Wade's help, and Vampires Anonymous going nationwide, maybe we can turn things around for the vampires in this world. This is a chance to create a new bond with others, a new way of life for my kind. If we can remove some of the stigma and fear that surrounds our existence, the world would be a safer place for all of us."

I listened, nodding, as I ate my dinner.

She paused, and gave me a lopsided smile. "When Dredge turned me, I thought everything was over. The only thing I could think about was blood and stakes, and how much I had lost. I was so bitter and hateful. And it's true, I had lost so much. But now, things are different."

"You have Nerissa, and you love her." I knew my sister and Nerissa had had their share of problems, but they had worked them out. They seemed deliriously happy together, even with the weight of the tiaras on their heads.

"I have Nerissa, and I can't imagine life without her. But it's more than that."

She stared at Maggie, kissing her again. "I actually do love Roman, in a way. We have chemistry, and I can be as rough as I want to with him. Nerissa's safe from that side of me as long as I have an outlet. And he's very fond of her, too."

"Go on," I said. I had thought that Nerissa barely tolerated him, and vice versa.

"No, really. They've discovered that they actually have more in common than he and I do. They play chess for hours, and they discuss books. Well, we all love to read, but they love the classics. In some ways, she's actually a better match for him than I am. But beyond all the relationship stuff, I have the chance to make a difference in ways I never thought I could. Erin's accepted Wade's invitation to join him on the road. I'm going to miss her, but they're going to make it possible for us to do our work better."

There was a glow in her eyes that told me just how happy she was. I realized that sometimes responsibility was more than a yoke. I had begun to realize that about Camille, as well. As tired as she seemed at times, she appeared at home out at Talamh Lonrach Oll. She seemed to fit in a way that I'd never expected to see. She was settling into her cloak of authority, and every time we talked, it became more apparent that my sister truly was growing into her title.

"So, tomorrow's the big day. Are you excited? Or do I even have to ask?" Menolly laughed as Maggie reached up and tickled her nose. She kissed Maggie's finger. "The one thing I truly miss, more than anything else, is hearing Maggie laugh."

"I know, and when Aeval suggested that Maggie move out to Talamh Lonrach Oll, it just about tore me up. But I think we're going to let her go. Camille can protect her better, and now that I realize the Triple Threat isn't going to send her back to Otherworld, it just seems safer. Besides, pretty soon..." I glanced over at Maggie, biting my lip.

"I feel so horrible for what I'm about to say, but I don't think that I can take care of Maggie and the child of an Elemental Lord at the same time. I don't know whether I'd be more afraid of Maggie hurting her, or *her* hurting Maggie."

"So you know it's going to be a girl?"

I nodded. "The Autumn Lord has made it clear. I'll have a little girl. That makes me happy, but at the same time, I'm scared. What is she going to be like? Part Fae, part human, part Elemental Lord? I suppose Shade can help keep her in line if she gets a little too rowdy, especially now that his powers are back. I wonder what it's going to be like, being pregnant? I mean, it's not like I've ever had the experience before. And neither have you or Camille, so I can't call on you for help."

Menolly snickered. "Maybe you and Aeval can compare notes?"

I gave her a long look, glaring. "Don't even go there. Besides, she's going to give birth long before I will. I still have to go through the secondary ritual before I can get pregnant. But that's not all that far away."

After I finished off my grilled cheese and tomato soup, Menolly and I carried Maggie upstairs to my bedroom, where we went through my wedding ensemble. Shade was sleeping down at the studio with Roz, in the old tradition of the groom not seeing the bride the night before the wedding day. Menolly was staying overnight, sleeping in her old lair to keep me company.

After we had organized everything, we retreated to the living room and turned on the TV. We sat up half the night, laughing and talking and playing with Maggie, watching black-and-white science fiction movies, and for a brief moment, it felt like old times.

THE NEXT NIGHT, we gathered at Birchwater Pond.

Shade and I had chosen a simple ceremony. No marching up the aisle, no dramatic entrance. We gathered with family and friends in the clearing where we had held so many celebrations.

Camille was there, dressed in full regalia including her crown. Menolly stood by my left side as my matron of honor, and Nerissa and Iris stood to my right, my bridesmaids. They were dressed in pale green chiffon, and I was wearing my hunter green wedding dress with a gold cape that trailed behind me. I wore a wreath of lily of the valley, the fragrance calming me.

Shade stood to the other side of the altar, wearing a flowing brown satin robe over black trousers, bound by a golden sash the same color as my cape. To his side stood Smoky, his best man, dressed in all white as usual.

Come to bear witness were our friends and family. Bruce and the twins, of course. Hanna, holding Maggie. Morio and Trillian, Vanzir and Roz, Roman and Erin. And our friends Tim and Jason were there, and Chase as well, holding Astrid. Lash sat beside them, and Seratha, Shade's mother, had also joined us.

A gentle breeze flowed through the forest, but the sky held no clouds, and the stars were beginning to twinkle. It was cool, but not cold, and the distant smell of smoke wafted through the air, from a dozen chimneys of a dozen houses along our road.

The breeze rippled over the surface of Birchwater Pond, concentric rings of water echoing out, lapping gently at the edges of the pond. The leaves of the trees were just barely starting to turn, but I could feel autumn in the wind, even as I could feel it in my blood. We were entering the harvest, my season, my time of year. The longer I was pledged to the Autumn Lord, the stronger I could feel this burnished orange time echoing in my soul.

I looked over at Shade, who stood proudly, smiling as if this were the best day of his life, and my heart welled up. I had never thought I would see this day. When I thought back to the frightened young woman I had been when we first came over Earthside, to the naïve girl who couldn't see past her rosy view of the world, it felt like a different lifetime. I had grown so much during the past years, some of the growth from heartache, some of it from joy, and some of it from just accepting that life changes as we go along.

I finally understood the change was necessary, that evolving was a good thing. Stagnation was our true enemy, ignoring the signs that prompted us to grow.

Camille motioned for us to approach the altar. I could see her wings gently waving in the dusk.

She was letting us see them more now, letting her differences shine forth. I realized that I, too, was starting to embrace my own differences.

We weren't Windwalkers anymore. We might straddle worlds, but we no longer did so out of *not belonging*. When I thought about it, the three of us were too complex to live in simply one world.

"We are here to witness a union of hearts and souls. We are here to witness a commitment between lovers. We stand here in the presence of two people ready to join their lives together. Delilah Maria te Maria D'Artigo, do you approach the altar voluntarily, to engage in the union of matrimony?"

"I approach voluntarily, of my own volition and will." As the words flowed out of my mouth, I realized that all my fears and worries over getting married, over whether I was responsible enough, had faded away.

"Shade, shadow dragon of the Netherworld, do you approach this altar voluntarily, to engage in the union of matrimony?"

Shade's voice was soft, but it still resonated through the clearing. "I approach voluntarily, of my own volition and will."

"You have written your own vows. State them now in the presence of your friends and family, knowing that what you pledge here binds you to your future. This pledge is sacred, not to be broken." She turned to me, her wings fluttering gently in the wind. They were gossamer, and I had to resist the momentary urge to spring after them and play with them. "Delilah, state your vows to Shade."

I turned to my love. "I, Delilah D'Artigo, pledge to you, Shade, my undying love and devotion. I pledge my support in good times and in bad times. I pledge my heart and my soul, as long as love shall last. I promise my loyalty, my honesty, my passion, and my devotion to the Autumn Lord and what he has planned for us. All of this I give to you, as your wife and mate."

She turned to Shade, motioning for him to go ahead.

"I, Shade, shadow dragon of the Netherworld, pledge to you, Delilah, my undying love and devotion. I pledge my loyalty, my honesty, my passion, and my protection. I will stand by you in good times, and I will stand by you in bad times, I pledge my devotion to the Autumn Lord and what he has planned for us, and all of this I give to you, as your husband and mate, as long as love shall last."

She motioned for us to hold out our hands. I held out my right hand, and Shade held out his left. Camille took a heavily braided cord and wrapped it around our wrists, binding us together.

"As this cord so binds your wrists, it binds your vows together. You have made these vows under the watchful eyes of the gods. You have made them in front of family and friends. You have made them to me, High Priestess of the Moon Mother. Be aware, should you break your oath, you do so at your own risk, dishonoring your name forever. Answer me now, and your answers will hold. Delilah D'Artigo, do you take Shade to be your wedded husband, to have and to hold, as long as love shall last?"

I sucked in a deep breath, letting it out slowly, and then feeling my choice settle on my shoulders, I turned to Shade and, looking into his eyes, said, "I do thee promise."

"Shade, shadow dragon of the Netherworld, do you take Delilah to be your wedded wife, to have and to hold, as long as love shall last?"

Without hesitation, Shade looked at me and said, "I do thee promise."

Camille placed her hand atop the cord that bound our wrists together. "Then in the sight of the gods, and under the pledge of the Immortals, and in the presence of your friends and family, I now pronounce you husband and wife, bound by oath, bound by love, for as long as your love shall last." She unwound the cord, then motioned to Shade. "You may kiss the bride."

Shade pulled me into his arms, kissing me deeply. Then he whispered, "I will never let you down. I will never hurt you. I love you, Delilah, and I always will."

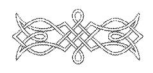

CAMILLE AND MENOLLY and I walked along the side of the pond. The guys were manning the grills, and the smell of food filled the air. The crickets were chirping, echoing through the clearing, and everything felt exactly as it was supposed to be.

"How many times have we taken this walk

together?" I stopped, cautiously sitting on a log, trying not to tear my wedding dress. Camille and Menolly sat beside me as we stared at the pond.

"I have no idea," Camille said. "Too many times, and never enough. How does it feel to be an old married lady now?" She smiled at me, then laughed and gave me a big hug. "I'm so happy for you and Shade. And I'm so happy he's got his powers back. I know we're facing the greatest test yet, but right now I couldn't be happier."

I felt like crying and laughing at the same time. So many emotions were racing through me, and yet the words *I'm married, I'm Shade's wife*, kept running through my head like an earworm.

"I can't believe I'm actually married now. We actually made it to our wedding in one piece, and now..." I let the words drift, thinking ahead to Samhain, and the next ritual that we would face. "I think I'm scared. I'm happy, I couldn't be more happy, but I'm scared. What if I'm not going to be a good mother? What if I don't know how to be a mother? What if—"

"What if you quit worrying, and let life happen?" Menolly said. "We all have our inner demons, and they can haunt us night and day. But if the Land of Wandering Souls has taught you anything, maybe it's that sometimes we have to leap on fate. We have to take that leap and trust that we're going to land on our feet. We have to quiet those demons, shut them down, and stamp them out because they only hold us back. They stop us from doing the important things in life, they're roadblocks and obstacles and landmines."

Camille nodded. "I was terrified when I took the throne out at Talamh Lonrach Oll. I didn't know if I could be queen over a kingdom. I mean hell, look at me—I'm about as refined as a lumberjack." She paused, holding up her hand when we started to protest. "No, don't stop me. The thing is, I'm learning. Yeah, I'm learning on the job, but I've got this. And you can do this too. You're going to be a wonderful mother, whether it's to the child of the Autumn Lord or a litter of your own kits. You've got the heart for it, Delilah. You've got that instinct. And that's a wonderful thing."

"I wish Father could have been here to see. And Mother. I wish Arial could be here. But I guess they are in spirit." Even as I spoke I looked up toward the woods, and saw the faint image of a big leopard, watching. I realized Arial had been at my wedding after all. I started to cry, overcome by emotion.

Camille and Menolly let me cry, handing me tissues, not asking what was wrong because they knew very well that nothing was wrong. Sometimes joy carried its own form of heartache. Sometimes our emotions welled up so strong and so thick that the only way to express them was through tears. They were cathartic, allowing us to release into the world the emotions that ran so deep there were no words.

As my tears slowed, I stared out the pond, realizing that this wasn't the end. And even after we took care of Shadow Wing, our lives would go on. For the first time, I felt hope that we would destroy him and then go on to live the rest of our lives in...

if not peace, hopefully joy.

There would be more tears, and more laughter, and probably more weddings. There would be pomp and circumstance, protests and fighting for what was right, magic and mayhem. There would be a child in my future, and maybe more than one if I was lucky.

But right now, at this very moment, the only thing I wanted was to sit here with my sisters as my husband grilled our wedding feast, and our friends and family mingled and chatted and laughed. All I wanted was to celebrate the fact that we were together, and regardless of all the pain and loss that we had gone through, our love still stood as the pillar of our foundation, keeping us strong, keeping us whole.

I hope you enjoyed this book. The last Otherworld Book, BLOOD BONDS, will be out in 2019.

Meanwhile, I invite you to try my new Wild Hunt Series, which began with THE SILVER STAG. The second, OAK & THORNS, will be out in a few months.

I also invite you to visit Fury's world. Bound to Hecate, Fury is a minor goddess, taking care of the Abominations who come off the World Tree. The first story arc of the Fury Unbound Series is complete with: FURY RISING, FURY'S MAGIC, FURY AWAKENED, and FURY CALLING.

If you prefer a lighter-hearted paranormal romance, meet the wild and magical residents of Bedlam in my Bewitching Bedlam Series. Fun-loving witch Maddy Gallowglass, her smoking-hot vampire lover Aegis, and their crazed cjinn Bubba (part djinn, all cat) rock it out in Bedlam, a magical town on a magical island. BLOOD MUSIC, BEWITCHING BEDLAM, MAUDLIN'S MAYHEM, SIREN'S SONG, WITCHES WILD, BLOOD VENGEANCE and TIGER TAILS are available. And more are on the way!

If you like cozies with an edge, try my Chintz 'n China paranormal mysteries. The series is complete with: GHOST OF A CHANCE, LEGEND OF THE JADE DRAGON, MURDER UNDER A MYSTIC MOON, A HARVEST OF BONES, ONE HEX OF A WEDDING, and a wrap-up novella: HOLIDAY SPIRITS.

For all of my work, both published and upcoming releases, see the Bibliography at the end of this book, or check out my website at Galenorn.com and be sure and sign up for my newsletter to receive news about all my new releases.

Playlist

I often write to music, and HARVEST SONG was no exception. Here's the playlist I used for this book:

Android Lust: Here and Now
The Bravery: Believe
Broken Bells: The Ghost Inside
Buffalo Springfield: For What It's Worth
Chumbawumba: Tubthumping
Corvus Corax: In Taberna, Ballade de Mercy, Bucca
The Cure: The Hanging Garden, Cold, From The Edge of the Deep Green Sea
Damh the Bard: Silent Moon, Tomb of the King, Obsession, Cloak of Feathers, Grimspound, The Wicker Man, The Cutty Wren, Matty Groves, Twa Corbies
David and Steve Gordon: Shaman's Drum Dance
Dire Straits: Down to the Waterline
Don Henley: Sunset Grill
Eagles: Life in the Fast Lane
Eastern Sun: Beautiful Being
Eels: Souljacker Part 1: Love of the Loveless
Faun: Lupercalia, Iduna, The Market Song,

Golden Apples, Adam Lay Ybounden, Rad, Sieben, Tinta, Tanz mit mir

Foo Fighters: The Pretender, All My Life

Foster the People: Pumped Up Kicks

Gabrielle Roth: Raven, Red Wind, Cloud Mountain

Gerry Rafferty: Baker Street

Gorillaz: Hongkongaton, Rockit, Kids with Guns, Dirty Harry, Last Living Souls, Feel Good Inc., Dare; Fire Coming Out of the Monkey's Head, Demon Days, Stylo

Harry Nilsson: Coconut

Eric Burdon & War: Spill the Wine

Hedningarna: Tulli, Chicago, Ukkonen, Grodan/Widergrenen (Toadeater), Raven (Fox Woman), Juopolle Joutunut, Drafur & Gildur

The Herbaliser: You're Not All That

In Strict Confidence: Wintermoon, Tiefer, Snow White, Silver Bullets, Silver Tongues

Ladytron: I'm Not Scared, Burning Up, Ghosts

Mark Lanegan: The Gravedigger's Song, Bleeding Muddy Water, Riot in My House, Wedding Dress, Phantasmagoria Blues, Methamphetamine Blues, Creeping Coastline of Lights, Little Sadie

Ohio Players: Fire

Oingo Boingo: Dead Man's Party, Elevator Man

The Police: Don't Stand so Close to Me, King of Pain

Queen: We Will Rock You

REM: Drive

Screaming Trees: Where the Twain Shall

Meet, Dime Western, Gospel Plow
  Sister Sledge: We Are Family
  Spiral Dance: The Goddess and the Weaver, Boys of Bedlam, Asgard's Chase, Tarry Trousers, Rise Up
  Stealers Wheel: Stuck in the Middle with You
  Steppenwolf: Born To Be Wild, Magic Carpet Ride, Twisted
  Tempest: Queen of Argyll, Nottamun Town, Buffalo Jump, Black Jack Davey
  Three Dog Night: Mama Told Me
  Tom Petty and the Heartbreakers: Mary Jane's Last Dance
  Wendy Rule: The Circle Song, The Wolf Sky, Evolution, Elemental Chant
  Woodland: Silent Dance, Blood of the Moon, Golden Raven's Eye, First Melt, Conjure, Bacchus and the Maenads, Secrets Told
  Zero 7: In the Waiting Line

Cast of Major Characters

The D'Artigo Family:

Arial Lianan te Maria: Delilah's twin who died at birth. Half Fae, half human.

Camille Sepharial te Maria, aka Camille D'Artigo: The oldest sister; a Moon Witch and Priestess. Half Fae, half human.

Daniel George Fredericks: The D'Artigo sisters' half cousin; FBH.

Delilah Maria te Maria, aka Delilah D'Artigo: The middle sister; a werecat.

Hester Lou Fredericks: The D'Artigo sisters' half cousin; FBH.

Maria D'Artigo: The D'Artigo Sisters' mother. Human. Deceased.

Menolly Rosabelle te Maria, aka Menolly D'Artigo: The youngest sister; a vampire and *jian-tu:* extraordinary acrobat. Half Fae, half human.

Sephreh ob Tanu: The D'Artigo Sisters' father. Full Fae. Deceased.

Shamas ob Olanda: The D'Artigo girls' cousin. Full Fae. Deceased, but returned to life as one of the Keraastar Knights.

The D'Artigo Sisters' Lovers &

Close Friends:

Astrid (Johnson): Chase and Sharah's baby daughter.

Bruce O'Shea: Iris's husband. Leprechaun.

Carter: Leader of the Demonica Vacana Society, a group that watches and records the interactions of Demonkin and human through the ages. Carter is half demon and half Titan—his father was Hyperion, one of the Greek Titans.

Chase Garden Johnson: Detective, director of the Faerie-Human Crime Scene Investigation (FH-CSI) team. Human who has taken the Nectar of Life, which extends his life span beyond any ordinary mortal and has opened up his psychic abilities.

Chrysandra: Waitress at the Wayfarer Bar & Grill. Human. Deceased.

Derrick Means: Bartender at the Wayfarer Bar & Grill. Werebadger.

Erin Mathews: Former president of the Faerie Watchers Club and former owner of the Scarlet Harlot Boutique. Turned into a vampire by Menolly, her sire, moments before her death. Human.

Greta: Leader of the Death Maidens; Delilah's tutor.

Iris (Kuusi) O'Shea: Friend and companion of the girls. Priestess of Undutar. Talon-haltija (Finnish house sprite).

Lindsey Katharine Cartridge: Director of the Green Goddess Women's Shelter. Pagan and witch. Human.

Maria O'Shea: Iris and Bruce's baby daughter.

Marion Vespa: Coyote shifter; owner of the Supe-Urban Café.

Morio Kuroyama: One of Camille's lovers and husbands. Essentially the grandson of Grandmother Coyote. Youkai-kitsune (roughly translated: Japanese fox demon).

Nerissa Shale: Menolly's wife. Worked for DSHS. Now working for Chase Johnson as a victims-rights counselor for the FH-CSI. Werepuma and member of the Rainier Puma Pride.

Roman: Ancient vampire; son of Blood Wyne, Queen of the Crimson Veil. Menolly's official consort in the Vampire Nation and her new sire.

Queen Asteria: The former Elfin Queen. Deceased.

Queen Sharah: Was an elfin medic, now the new Elfin Queen; Chase's girlfriend.

Rozurial, aka Roz: Mercenary. Menolly's secondary lover. Incubus who used to be Fae before Zeus and Hera destroyed his marriage.

Shade: Delilah's fiancé. Part Stradolan, part black (shadow) dragon.

Siobhan Morgan: One of the girls' friends. Selkie (wereseal); member of the Puget Sound Harbor Seal Pod.

Smoky: One of Camille's lovers and husbands. Half-white, half-silver dragon.

Tanne Baum: One of the Black Forest woodland Fae. A member of the Hunter's Glen Clan.

Tavah: Guardian of the portal at the Wayfarer Bar & Grill. Vampire (full Fae).

Tim Winthrop, aka Cleo Blanco: Computer

student/genius, female impersonator. FBH. Now owns the Scarlet Harlot.

Trillian: Mercenary. Camille's alpha lover and one of her three husbands. Svartan (one of the Charming Fae).

Ukkonen O'Shea: Iris and Bruce's baby son.

Vanzir: Was indentured slave to the Sisters, by his own choice. Dream-chaser demon who lost his powers and now is regaining new ones.

Venus the Moon Child: Former shaman of the Rainier Puma Pride. Werepuma. One of the Keraastar Knights.

Wade Stevens: President of Vampires Anonymous. Vampire (human).

Zachary Lyonnesse: Former member of the Rainier Puma Pride Council of Elders. Werepuma living in Otherworld.

Glossary

Black Unicorn/Black Beast: Father of the Dahns unicorns, a magical unicorn that is reborn like the phoenix and lives in Darkynwyrd and Thistlewyd Deep. Raven Mother is his consort, and he is more a force of nature than a unicorn.

Calouk: The rough, common dialect used by a number of Otherworld inhabitants.

Court and Crown: "Crown" refers to the Queen of Y'Elestrial. "Court" refers to the nobility and military personnel that surround the Queen. "Court and Crown" together refer to the entire government of Y'Elestrial.

Court of the Three Queens: The newly risen Court of the three Earthside Fae Queens: Titania, the Fae Queen of Light and Morning; Morgaine, the half-Fae Queen of Dusk and Twilight; and Aeval, the Fae Queen of Shadow and Night.

Crypto: One of the Cryptozoid races. Cryptos include creatures out of legend that are not technically of the Fae races: gargoyles, unicorns, gryphons, chimeras, and so on. Most primarily inhabit Otherworld, but some have Earthside cousins.

Demon Gate: A gate through which demons may be summoned by a powerful sorcerer or necromancer.

Demonica Vacana Society: A society run by a number of ancient entities, including Carter, who study and record the history of demonic activity over Earthside. The archives of the society are found in the Demonica Catacombs, deep within an uninhabited island of the Cyclades, a group of Grecian islands in the Aegean Sea.

Dreyerie: A dragon lair.

Earthside: Everything that exists on the Earth side of the portals.

Elqaneve: The Elfin city in Otherworld, located in Kelvashan—the Elfin lands.

Elemental Lords: The elemental beings—both male and female—who, along with the Hags of Fate and the Harvestmen, are the only true Immortals. They are avatars of various elements and energies, and they inhabit all realms. They do as they will and seldom concern themselves with humankind or Fae unless summoned. If asked for help, they often exact steep prices in return. The Elemental Lords are not concerned with balance like the Hags of Fate.

FBH: Full-Blooded Human (usually refers to Earthside humans).

FH-CSI: The Faerie–Human Crime Scene Investigation team. The brainchild of Detective Chase Johnson, it was first formed as a collaboration between the OIA and the Seattle police department. Other FH-CSI units have been created around the country, based on the Seattle prototype. The FH-CSI takes care of both medical and criminal emergencies involving visitors from Otherworld.

Great Divide: A time of immense turmoil when the Elemental Lords and some of the High

Court of Fae decided to rip apart the worlds. Until then, the Fae existed primarily on Earth, their lives and worlds mingling with those of humans. The Great Divide tore everything asunder, splitting off another dimension, which became Otherworld. At that time, the Twin Courts of Fae were disbanded and their queens and the Merlin were stripped of power. This was the time during which the Spirit Seal was formed and broken in order to seal off the realms from each other. Some Fae chose to stay Earthside, others moved to the realm of Otherworld, and the demons were—for the most part—sealed in the Subterranean Realms.

Guard Des'Estar: The military of Y'Elestrial.

Hags of Fates: The women of destiny who keep the balance righted. Neither good nor evil, they observe the flow of destiny. When events get too far out of balance, they step in and take action, usually using humans, Fae, Supes, and other creatures as pawns to bring the path of destiny back into line.

Harvestmen: The lords of death—a few cross over and are also Elemental Lords. The Harvestmen, along with their followers (the Valkyries and the Death Maidens, for example), reap the souls of the dead.

Haseofon: The abode of the Death Maidens—where they stay and where they train.

Ionyc Lands: The astral, etheric, and spirit realms, along with several other lesser-known noncorporeal dimensions, form the Ionyc Lands. These realms are separated by the Ionyc Seas, a current of energy that prevents the Ionyc Lands from colliding, thereby sparking off an explosion of universal proportions.

Ionyc Seas: The currents of energy that separate the Ionyc Lands. Certain creatures, especially those connected with the elemental energies of ice, snow, and wind, can travel through the Ionyc Seas without protection.

Kelvashan: The lands of the elves.

Koyanni: The coyote shifters who took an evil path away from the Great Coyote; followers of Nukpana.

Melosealfôr: A rare Crypto dialect learned by powerful Cryptos and all Moon Witches.

The Nectar of Life: An elixir that can extend the life span of humans to nearly the length of a Fae's years. Highly prized and cautiously used. Can drive someone insane if he or she doesn't have the emotional capacity to handle the changes incurred.

Oblition: The act of a Death Maiden sucking the soul out of one of their targets.

OIA: The Otherworld Intelligence Agency; the "brains" behind the Guard Des'Estar. Earthside Division now run by Camille, Menolly, and Delilah.

Otherworld/OW: The human term for the "United Nations" of Faerie Land. A dimension apart from ours that contains creatures from legend and lore, pathways to the gods, and various other places, such as Olympus. Otherworld's actual name varies among the differing dialects of the many races of Cryptos and Fae.

Portal, Portals: The interdimensional gates that connect the different realms. Some were created during the Great Divide; others open up randomly.

Seelie Court: The Earthside Fae Court of Light and Summer, disbanded during the Great Divide. Titania was the Seelie Queen.

Soul Statues: In Otherworld, small figurines created for the Fae of certain races and magically linked with the baby. These figurines reside in family shrines and when one of the Fae dies, their soul statue shatters. In Menolly's case, when she was reborn as a vampire, her soul statue reformed, although twisted. If a family member disappears, his or her family can always tell if their loved one is alive or dead if they have access to the soul statue.

Spirit Seals: A magical crystal artifact, the Spirit Seal was created during the Great Divide. When the portals were sealed, the Spirit Seal was broken into nine gems and each piece was given to an Elemental Lord or Lady. These gems each have varying powers. Even possessing one of the spirit seals can allow the wielder to weaken the portals that divide Otherworld, Earthside, and the Subterranean Realms. If all of the seals are joined together again, then all of the portals will open.

Stradolan: A being who can walk between worlds, who can walk through the shadows, using them as a method of transportation.

Supe/Supes: Short for Supernaturals. Refers to Earthside supernatural beings who are not of Fae nature. Refers to Weres, especially.

Talamh Lonrach Oll: The name for the Earthside Sovereign Fae Nation.

Triple Threat: Camille's nickname for the

newly risen three Earthside Queens of Fae.

Unseelie Court: The Earthside Fae Court of Shadow and Winter, disbanded during the Great Divide. Aeval was the Unseelie Queen.

VA/Vampires Anonymous: The Earthside group started by Wade Stevens, a vampire who was a psychiatrist during life. The group is focused on helping newly born vampires adjust to their new state of existence, and to encourage vampires to avoid harming the innocent as much as possible. The VA is vying for control. Their goal is to rule the vampires of the United States and to set up an internal policing agency.

Whispering Mirror: A magical communications device that links Otherworld and Earth. Think magical video phone.

Y'Eírialiastar: The Sidhe/Fae name for Otherworld.

Y'Elestrial: The city-state in Otherworld where the D'Artigo girls were born and raised. A Fae city, recently embroiled in a civil war between the drug-crazed tyrannical Queen Lethesanar and her more level-headed sister Tanaquar, who managed to claim the throne for herself. The civil war has ended and Tanaquar is restoring order to the land.

Youkai: Loosely (very loosely) translated as Japanese demon/nature spirit. For the purposes of this series, the youkai have three shapes: the animal, the human form, and the true demon form. Unlike the demons of the Subterranean Realms, youkai are not necessarily evil by nature.

Biography

New York Times, Publishers Weekly, and *USA Today* bestselling author Yasmine Galenorn writes urban fantasy and paranormal romance, and is the author of over fifty books, including the Wild Hunt Series, the Fury Unbound Series, the Bewitching Bedlam Series, and the Otherworld Series, among others. She's also written nonfiction metaphysical books. She is the 2011 Career Achievement Award Winner in Urban Fantasy, given by RT Magazine. Yasmine has been in the Craft since 1980, is a shamanic witch and High Priestess. She describes her life as a blend of teacups and tattoos. She lives in Kirkland, WA, with her husband Samwise and their cats. Yasmine can be reached via her website at Galenorn.com.

Indie Releases Currently Available:

Wild Hunt Series:
The Silver Stag

Bewitching Bedlam Series:
Bewitching Bedlam
Maudlin's Mayhem
Siren's Song
Witches Wild
Blood Music

Blood Vengeance
Tiger Tails

Fury Unbound Series:
Fury Rising
Fury's Magic
Fury Awakened
Fury Calling

Otherworld Series:
Moon Shimmers
Harvest Song
Earthbound
Knight Magic
Otherworld Tales: Volume One
Tales From Otherworld: Collection One
Men of Otherworld: Collection One
Men of Otherworld: Collection Two
Moon Swept: Otherworld Tales of First Love
For the rest of the Otherworld Series, see Website

Chintz 'n China Series:
Ghost of a Chance
Legend of the Jade Dragon
Murder Under a Mystic Moon
A Harvest of Bones
One Hex of a Wedding
Holiday Spirits

Bath and Body Series (originally under the name India Ink):
Scent to Her Grave

A Blush With Death
Glossed and Found

Misc. Short Stories/Anthologies:
Mist and Shadows: Short Tales From Dark Haunts
Once Upon a Kiss (short story: Princess Charming)
Silver Belles (short story: The Longest Night)
Once Upon a Curse (short story: Bones)
Night Shivers (an Indigo Court novella)

Magickal Nonfiction:
Embracing the Moon
Tarot Journeys

For all other series, as well as upcoming work, see Galenorn.com

Printed in Great Britain
by Amazon